PRAISE FOR
THE FEATHERED MAN

'Jeremy de Quidt has crafted a fine gothic suspense
thriller which at times becomes gruesome as well
as truly creepy. *The Feathered Man* deserves
to be read. 10/10'
Starburst Magazine

'I loved the originality of it all, the classical feel, and
the uncompromising commitment to the main theme
– where does life go when it leaves the body?'
The Bookbag

'A gripping and frightening story with an ending
that will leave the reader wanting more'
The Bookseller

'Dark, thrilling, suspenseful and macabre,
this is not a story for the faint-hearted'
Booktrust

'A helter-skelter ride from the slightly scary
to the terrifying. Not to be read alone'
Serendipity Reviews

www.davidficklingbooks.co.uk

Also by Jeremy de Quidt

The Toymaker

THE FEATHERED MAN

Jeremy de Quidt

David Fickling Books

OXFORD · NEW YORK

31 Beaumont Street
Oxford OX1 2NP, UK

THE FEATHERED MAN
DAVID FICKLING BOOKS 978 1 849 92164 0

First published in Great Britain by David Fickling Books,
a division of Random House Children's Publishers UK
A Random House Group Company

Hardback edition published 2012
Paperback edition published 2013

1 3 5 7 9 10 8 6 4 2

The Random House Group Limited supports the Forest Stewardship Council®
(FSC®), the leading international forest-certification organisation. Our
books carrying the FSC label are printed on FSC®-certified paper. FSC is
the only forest-certification scheme supported by the leading environmental
organisations, including Greenpeace. Our paper procurement policy can be
found at www.randomhouse.co.uk/environment

Set in Goudy

DAVID FICKLING BOOKS
31 Beaumont Street, Oxford, OX1 2NP

www.randomhousechildrens.co.uk
www.totallyrandombooks.co.uk
www.randomhouse.co.uk

Addresses for companies within The Random House Group Limited can be found at:
www.randomhouse.co.uk/offices.htm

THE RANDOM HOUSE GROUP Limited Reg. No. 954009

A CIP catalogue record for this book is available from the British Library.

Printed and bound in Great Britain by CPI Group (UK) Ltd, Croydon, CR0 4YY

for Lizzie, Jack, Alice and Bea,
sailors still in the sieve.

Chapter One

The window of Kusselmann's shop was full of teeth. They were laid out in neat rows along polished ebony shelves, and piled into small mounds in blue and white porcelain bowls the size of your hand.

Teeth.

Hundreds of teeth.

And that was just the window. If you were to go inside, you would find even more laid out on cloth-lined trays along the counter and in glass-fronted cabinets along the walls.

People always need teeth.

When their own were rotten through and the pain of them was unbearable, swollen-jawed, they would go to Kusselmann. He would sit them down in his black leather chair, take his blunt-nosed pliers in his fat, damp hand and, opening their mouths . . .

Well, you can guess the rest.

The boy would stand in the road outside the shop – dust in summer, mud in winter – and, with a big drum hitched to his waist, beat it as hard as he could to drown out the sound of the screams.

His name was Klaus.

He must have been about twelve years old, though it was hard to tell, he was so pale and thin. But he had fine white teeth. That was why Kusselmann had chosen him – for his teeth. Only now, two of them were missing – big ones at the side.

You could choose whichever teeth you wanted in Kusselmann's shop. That was the point of it – he was a tooth-maker as well as a tooth-puller. He would set them out for you to see, measure them with his fine tools and fix them in clay gums like a jeweller arranging diamonds in a ring or a brooch; then, if you liked them, he would make them up for you. There were plenty to choose from, different sizes and colours – the whitest were the most expensive. Ivory was not the same: it stained in the mouth. No. If you wanted new teeth, real teeth, Kusselmann would find them for you, and then fix them on a spike in your jaw.

It was very painful.

Of course, you could just wear them on a plate, and some people did – he made those too – and others that were joined by small springs that opened and shut as you chewed.

They were all very expensive. But people need teeth when their own are rotten and pulled. And a mouthful of Kusselmann teeth were white and perfect. They were very much admired. Fathers even gave their daughters presents of his teeth on their sixteenth birthday. Then they had all their own ones pulled.

And why not? It would have to happen one day. Why not get it over and done with – have new white teeth that would never rot? Ladies of fashion eyed each other's perfect white smiles, and knew to a golden guinea exactly how much they had cost.

But where did Kusselmann find all these perfect white teeth if most people's were worn and rotten and yellow?

I'll tell you.

Dead men.

And women.

And boys.

And girls.

He would pull the teeth from the bodies. And there were always bodies. Sometimes it was the family who sold them. Kusselmann would pay a few pennies for each tooth, and if you are poor that is a very great deal. Besides, the dead have no need of teeth. Sometimes he would find a body in the morgue, or a boatman on the river would tell him of some drowning. But he never took just any teeth of course, only the whitest and the best.

And sometimes not all the mouths he pulled teeth from were dead.

Like Klaus.

It was why he'd chosen him.

He'd found him amongst the street children sleeping rough on a ledge under the town bridge, and brought him back to the shop. He'd be able to use fine white teeth like that. Better that than have them just go to waste in a gutter boy's mouth.

Klaus slept beneath the shop counter now. When he wasn't beating the drum, he was sweeping the floor, or doing the hundred other things that Kusselmann found for him – like washing the blood from the teeth that the tooth-puller had pulled, or holding the tin can while he worked each tooth loose from some corpse and, one by one, dropped them in. Klaus would shut his eyes and try not to hear the sound of the tooth being pulled from the jaw or the little noise it made when Kusselmann opened the pliers and dropped it into the can.

But what was he to do? He knew what it was like to go to sleep hungry, and to have to find a dry ledge under the bridge and lie down amongst the other street children with a stick in his hand to beat off the rats in the night.

In winter it was cold, in summer it was hot.

You see, sometimes there really isn't any choice.

And Kusselmann could turn him back out onto the street if he wanted. One day he would, when all those fine white teeth had been used up. That's what he'd done to his last boy, not that Klaus knew that. All Klaus knew was that he had a dry bed and hot food. Not much food, but it was better than he'd ever had before. Better than begging, better than the ledge beneath the bridge with the rats and the other hungry children.

Even if it had cost him two teeth already.

But there was one particular place where Kusselmann came by the teeth that filled his shop.

And that was how it all started – with a visit to Frau Drecht's house.

Frau Drecht's house stood at the corner of Bergenstrasse. It was not a good part of town. The children who slept on the streets there were pale-faced and hollow-eyed. Klaus had learned a long time ago to be wary of them. The fronts of the houses leaned drunkenly towards each other over the dirty gutter of a street below. Frau Drecht's was a tall house with one dark, narrow, unswept staircase that wound up through it past blank dull doors, right up to the loft. Frau Drecht herself had the rooms at the bottom of the house, facing the street. Those above she let out. The higher you went into that damp dark that smelled of rats, the cheaper the rent, until the cheapest of all was at the very top, where she'd divided the loft into stalls – more like a stable than a house. There were bare rafters and partitions made from blanket and thin wood, and dirty mattresses – one to each stall – stuffed with more lice than straw.

You wouldn't want to stay in that loft.

But sometimes, you see, there really isn't a choice.

So people did.

But they didn't last long.

They tended to be people who had been moved

6

up through the house by Frau Drecht – maybe as their rent fell behind, or their health failed them. Up they would go, floor by floor, until at last they arrived in that dark, damp, foul-smelling loft.

And there they died.

They always died.

Sooner or later.

And then there would be a place for someone else in the house: Frau Drecht would put a card in her window, and everyone would move up, and someone else would be found.

But whoever it was that was found always had good white teeth. Frau Drecht was quite particular about that.

Klaus didn't like going to Frau Drecht's house one bit. The visits were always the same.

At some point in the morning, Kusselmann would receive a note – one of the hollow-eyed children from the doorways in Bergenstrasse would bring it – and then he'd tell Klaus to collect his black leather bag – the one with the tin can and the pliers – and off he would go. He was a very fat man, but he walked remarkably quickly for all that. He would go quickstep down the streets, along the wharves with their ships all fresh from the sea – their paintwork and ropes salt- and weather-stained – his wide black hat on his head and his silver watch chain tight across his fat stomach. The chain held an enormous watch, its tick so loud that in a quiet room Klaus could hear it going *ticker-tick, ticker-tick, ticker-tick* beneath Kusselmann's coat. Klaus would follow behind him with the bag. He had to carry it in both hands and it was hard to keep up. But it didn't matter because he knew exactly where Kusselmann was going.

Bergenstrasse.

He would follow as quickly as he could along the crowded wharves, making his way between the barrels and the ropes, through the catches of blue and silver fish spread underfoot across the splintered boards, ready to be gutted and salted, and all the while the hard horn handles of the big black bag dug into his fingers. He always arrived at the house a little after Kusselmann, and Kusselmann would already be taking coffee with Frau Drecht in her rooms.

But that was always the same too.

Klaus would knock at the door, and a tall girl about his own age – a Bergenstrasse girl, pale-faced and hollow-eyed – would open it. Her name was

Liesel. He knew that because he'd heard Frau Drecht bawl it at her often enough – that and a sewerful of other names as well.

The first time she opened the door to him she stood stock still, staring at him as though she'd seen a ghost, and even now, each time he came she watched him silently from the shadows at the foot of the stairs. She never spoke, and he didn't like it one bit. He could feel her eyes on his back as he stood outside the parlour door with the heavy black bag in his hand.

You see, you could never be too careful in Bergenstrasse, and Klaus knew that.

He'd knock quickly at the parlour door, then go in, leaving the tall girl in the damp dark of the hall. Frau Drecht would have a small table set with her best cups, and she would be holding a small cup carefully with her finger a little bent, and there would be a small glass of schnapps on the table beside the saucer, and a little cake – a pastry – for Kusselmann. And Kusselmann would be wearing a napkin spread across his large front like a flag.

Klaus would sit on the wooden chair by the wall, and wait. Sometimes he'd catch a last glimpse of the girl through the half-open door as she turned and went about her work.

Frau Drecht would listen to Kusselmann's news of the town, and purse her lips and shake her head. She had long, tight ringlets that Klaus didn't believe for one moment were her own. They were raven-black, and when she shook her head they moved very prettily – at least Frau Drecht must have thought they did, as she would turn her head to show them off to their best advantage at every opportunity. Her voice was soft as butter for Kusselmann, but hard and grating if she said any-thing to Klaus or Liesel.

After her coffee she would light a small cigar, and then would come the business of the visit. She would lead Kusselmann up the stairs through the house to the loft, the smoke of her cigar filling the stale air. Klaus would follow with the bag. Usually they went to the loft, but this time they paused at an open door on the landing below it. Through the door Klaus could see into the dirty little room. There was an iron bedstead and a man on it. The man was sunk down into the sheets and the greasy pillow. His mouth was open and he was staring glassy-eyed at the ceiling, his breath coming in long shallow wheezes.

But they only paused by the door, just long enough for Frau Drecht to purse her lips and put her head to one side. 'Poor man,' she said. 'Not long for this world, I fear.'

Then she drew on her cigar and led them up the last of the stairs to the loft. 'You'll find him at the end,' she said and, touching Kusselmann lightly on the arm, added, 'And don't forget to come and see me when you've done your little business.'

Kusselmann bowed and she left them in the half-dark. The loft was empty, except for the last stall. Frau Drecht had given them a small lantern. Kusselmann hung it on a hook, took the black bag from Klaus, opened it and pulled out the blunt-nosed pliers.

In the room on the floor below them, Frau Drecht stood for a short while looking at the wheezing, glassy-eyed man. She was wondering how much she might get for his teeth. They were very white and even.

And Kusselmann was only upstairs . . .

'Shame for him to have to make two visits, dearie,' she said.

And gripping her cigar firmly between her teeth, she pulled the greasy pillow from under the man's head, and pressed it firmly down over his face.

In the loft, Kusselmann grunted as he worked each tooth loose. It wasn't easy, but his wrist was as

11

strong as a steel spring. When each one came free, he held it up to the light of the lantern and, like a connoisseur, carefully inspected it. If it was no good he'd toss it away over his shoulder; if it would do, he'd drop it – *tang* – into the tin that Klaus held.

When he'd done, he carefully counted the teeth and worked out how much he'd have to pay Frau Drecht; then, screwing down the lid, he dropped the tin back into his bag. He took down the lantern and, stepping carefully around the mattresses on the floor, went down the stairs. Klaus followed.

But Frau Drecht wasn't in her rooms at the bottom of the house. She was waiting for them on the landing.

'Eleven,' said Kusselmann. 'At the usual?'

Frau Drecht frowned. 'Are you sure it's not more?' she asked.

Kusselmann shook his head sadly. 'Broken,' he said.

She pursed her lips as though she'd taken the trouble to investigate the matter already and was sure there should be more than that. But Kusselmann pulled his purse from beneath his coat, counted out some coins and held them towards her.

She looked at them for a moment, then took them. 'If you say so,' she said.

He was about to step past her down the stairs when she put her hand on his arm and stopped him. Pulling a sorrowful face, she jerked her head towards the sick man's door – only now it was closed.

She dabbed at her cheek with a small black lace hankie. She always kept it tucked into her sleeve. 'Passed on,' she said. 'Even as I arranged his pillow for him.'

Kusselmann took his hat from his head and held it to his chest in a brief token of respect. Then he looked at Frau Drecht. 'Would you like me to . . .?' he said, leaving the question unfinished.

She pursed her lips again. 'Might as well,' she agreed, and opened the door.

What struck Klaus, as he stepped into the room, was how quiet and still it had become. Even that gasping breath had been more than this silence.

'Just passed on,' said Frau Drecht. She stood for a moment contemplating the composed figure, the pillow now carefully plumped up and replaced beneath its head. 'I'll leave you to it.'

Kusselmann waited for her to go, then he opened the man's mouth.

The teeth were finer than he'd expected. Klaus saw the expression of surprise cross his face. But then Kusselmann frowned and bent closer.

They were too fine. Too even.

He made an irritated clicking noise with his tongue and, opening the bag, reached in for his pliers. He gripped one of the front teeth and roughly worked it to and fro. Just as he thought: the tooth was cheap plasterwork. It looked very fine but it was as false as a lead penny. It broke and crumbled in the jaws of the pliers as he twisted them.

And then he stopped.

He stuck his finger into the man's warm wet mouth and raked out the broken pieces. Then he put the pliers in again and, breaking the next tooth, did the same. Then he straightened up. Breathless and sweating, he turned to Klaus. 'Go and shut the door,' he hissed in an urgent whisper.

Klaus didn't understand what Kusselmann wanted him to do. He stood holding the tin ready for the tooth.

'Shut the door!' Kusselmann hissed again and, seeing Klaus not move, knocked the tin out of his hands. 'The door!' he said, little drops of spittle on his lips. 'Quick!'

Klaus went and closed the door.

Kusselmann already had his pliers back in the man's mouth; he was hurriedly breaking every tooth and raking out the little pieces. Despite himself, Klaus leaned forward over the bed, and as he did so, he saw why.

Beneath their plaster covering, every tooth in the man's head was made of solid gold.

Every tooth, that is, but one.

And that one, pinned deep into the bone of the man's jaw, was made from a single brilliant diamond as big as the top of Kusselmann's fat thumb.

Chapter Two

Kusselmann stood with his mouth open, staring at the dead man in the bed.

Then he suddenly came to his senses. He pushed Klaus towards the door. 'Don't let anyone in,' he hissed.

Klaus couldn't imagine anyone wanting to come and see Kusselmann pull a dead man's teeth, but he stood by the door as he was told. Kusselmann opened the man's mouth and pulled each golden tooth out, wrapping it in the folds of his hand-kerchief. Last of all he removed the diamond. Klaus watched him carefully ease it out of the man's slack jaw. It made a little sucking noise as it came free. Kusselmann held it up to the light. Even in that dim room with its one small, grime-smeared window, it burned like a star. Kusselmann swallowed. He took the diamond and carefully tucked it into the pocket of his waistcoat. Then he dropped the pliers into the black bag, picked up the tin from the floor and, dropping that in as well, snapped the catch shut.

Klaus hadn't moved.

Kusselmann swept towards him, black bag in hand, and pushed him aside, but as he turned the door handle, he stopped and looked sideways at Klaus as though a sudden thought had struck him. He reached out his fat hand and, gripping Klaus's face, squeezed it hard between his fingers. His grip was like a vice. 'Not – a – word,' he hissed. 'Not to anyone. Do you understand?'

Klaus nodded. Small quick nods. He knew better than to argue with Kusselmann. Kusselmann had a thick leather belt that hung in the shop, on the wall behind the counter. It was the first thing Klaus saw each morning when he opened his eyes. Sometimes it was needed to hold people in the chair when Kusselmann pulled their teeth. But he used it on Klaus as well. It had a hard metal buckle, and he didn't stint when he gave a beating.

'Good,' said Kusselmann, and he patted Klaus's cheek.

Back down the dark stairs they went to Frau Drecht's front parlour, where the coffee pot was waiting on the table.

Frau Drecht had already counted the dead man's teeth, and although she couldn't judge the quality of them as well as Kusselmann, she was very good at counting teeth.

'A fine set, I think, Herr Kusselmann?' she said with a small movement of her head that set the little ringlets dancing.

'Indeed so,' he replied.

But Klaus noticed that there was a nervousness to his manner, a small cough as he cleared his throat.

'Indeed so,' he said again.

And if Klaus had noticed it, so had Frau Drecht. She looked up at Kusselmann suspiciously, then filled his cup with coffee. 'How many were there?' she asked.

She thought that Kusselmann might have in mind short-changing her a tooth or two. She still had her suspicions that this is what he'd already done in the loft.

But no.

'A full set,' said Kusselmann, coughing again. 'Pearl-white, and perfect too.'

Frau Drecht hesitated, the spoon resting just above Kusselmann's cup. 'All thirty-two?' she said.

'Indeed. Every single one.'

Klaus was watching her very carefully; he could do this because she never paid any attention to him, and there was an awful fascination in watching Frau Drecht – the way her face was powdered a pale chalky pink, her lips greased rose red and her eyes like little black raisins in a cake. But this time she suddenly shot a cold, sharp look straight at him, as though wanting to see in his face what she already suspected in Kusselmann's. She caught his eye before he had a chance to look away.

And what she saw there was enough for Frau Drecht. 'Every one, you say?' she said, and she stirred Kusselmann's coffee.

Kusselmann's face had become a little damp. There was a sheen to his skin. He started to pull his handkerchief out of his pocket so that he could mop the moisture from his fat chins, but remembered just in time that it was full of the golden teeth. He stopped, and instead passed his hand across his chins, and wiped it on his coat.

'I haven't any more small coins about me now,' he said. 'I will send the boy straight back, if that will be in order.'

He'd done that once or twice before. He knew that Frau Drecht would have no reason to complain this time.

And she didn't.

'Of course, Herr Kusselmann,' she purred. 'I know I can trust you.'

Only she didn't trust Kusselmann, not one bit.

And for good reason – Frau Drecht was very good at counting.

She knew that there'd only been twenty-five teeth in the dead man's head. So why would Kusselmann want to pay her for thirty-two? That wasn't like him, she thought. He wasn't one to part with his money so easily. Which meant that there was something amiss here.

'Send the boy along,' she said, and filled another small glass of schnapps for Kusselmann to drink with his coffee. She picked up her own cup and sipped at it, her little finger crooked just so. 'Such a good boy,' she said, and her voice was like butter, all smooth and oily, but she gave Klaus another of those cold, quick looks as she said it. Whatever it was that

Kusselmann was up to, she'd have it out of that boy.

Kusselmann drank his coffee and his schnapps, then stood up and, taking Frau Drecht's hand, kissed it. She smiled prettily and her ringlets trembled against her pale pink powdered cheek. She sat like that, still smiling, as Liesel showed Kusselmann and Klaus out. It wasn't until she heard the front door slam shut that the smile disappeared and her face became hard and sly.

'Thirty-two teeth, my arse!' she said.

Klaus followed behind Kusselmann as he went puffing and blowing along the street. Kusselmann's pockets held all the gold teeth and the big bright diamond. Maybe that's why he walked even quicker than usual: he wanted to get them safely home. Klaus had to jog to keep up with him.

Kusselmann wasn't an honest man. Klaus had seen him take things before – small things he'd found in a drowned man's coat pocket: the watch and chain. He'd even seen him going through the rags of coats in Frau Drecht's loft, though what he'd thought to find there, apart from lice, heaven only knew. But this was different, and Klaus knew it. People just didn't have solid gold teeth and large diamonds in their mouths for nothing. And if they did, they'd show them off, not hide them away like that.

And that was it.

That was the thought that was unwinding in Klaus's head as he jogged along the street behind Kusselmann. If you hide something, it's because you don't want someone else to know you have it. And if you don't want them to know you have it, there's always a reason. Like, perhaps they're looking for it.

What Kusselmann had done didn't seem like a good idea to Klaus.

And do you know what?

He was right.

There was a little painted card in the window of Kusselmann's shop telling the passing world that it was CLOSED. Kusselmann usually turned it round so that it said OPEN when he came back in, but this time he didn't bother – at least not yet. He dragged Klaus in from the street, shut the door behind him and slid the bolts across. At the back of the shop there was a door, and through the door were Kusselmann's own rooms. Klaus wasn't allowed to go into them. He'd had a beating with the belt once, just for looking in through the doorway.

Kusselmann disappeared into the back of the shop. He wasn't gone for more than a few moments, and when he returned he held a small purse in his hand. He put it down on the counter in front of Klaus. 'There's enough to pay her,' he said.

As Klaus reached forward to pick it up, Kusselmann grabbed hold of his wrist. 'Not – a – word,' he said again, and looked sideways to where the thick leather belt hung on the back wall of the shop. It wasn't a threat to be ignored.

Klaus took the purse, dropped it inside his shirt, then went back out into the street and towards the narrow alleys that led to Bergenstrasse. He wasn't worried that the street children might try to take Kusselmann's purse off him – he had only to say that what was inside belonged to Frau Drecht and that would be enough to make them change their minds pretty quickly – but what did worry him was that look that Frau Drecht had given him. He had an uncomfortable feeling about it. So as he went along, past the forest of ships' masts that lined the wharves, past the weather-tanned men unloading the barrels and crates and the fish-gutters spreading out the catch, he'd already decided what he was going to do.

He'd knock on the door and give the money to the girl. Frau Drecht never opened the door herself, so he wouldn't have to see her. He didn't actually have to go in, so that would be all right. But even so, that uncomfortable feeling gnawed away at him as the alleyways became narrower and darker, until finally it was like a little knot in his stomach as he stood at the bottom of the steps outside Frau Drecht's house.

He took a deep breath. He made sure that the purse was still in his shirt, then went up the steps. There was no knocker. You had to thump hard on the door if you wanted to be heard. He was still rubbing his hand when the door swung sharply open.

Only it wasn't the girl who'd opened it.

It was Frau Drecht.

Before he could even take a step back, she had grabbed Klaus by his hair and, yanking him forward, pulled him inside. She banged his head hard on the doorpost for good measure as she did it, then kicked the door shut behind him with her little buttoned boot and, with her fingers wound tightly in his hair, dragged him into her little parlour.

'What are these?' she growled.

The coffee pot and the cups were all gone.

24

Spread out on the now bare table were all the bits of broken plaster that Kusselmann had raked out of the dead man's mouth. For the most part they made no particular shape, but Frau Drecht had carefully put some of the larger pieces back together so that they looked like teeth again, only they were hollow, as though something had been inside.

'What was in them?' she asked.

She shook Klaus hard by his hair. He tried to hold onto the roots, but she slapped his hands away and shook him again, like a rat.

'Teeth!' he gasped.

'Don't lie to me.' Her voice was hard and grating.

She didn't bother asking him again. She wound her fingers deeper into his hair and, dragging him out into the hall, pulled him past the staircase and down the passage to the small dark hole of a kitchen at the end. Liesel was standing by the table. She turned round in alarm when she heard Frau Drecht coming. She'd only just drawn a bucket of water from the pump in the yard and was about to pour it into the large copper to heat up. Frau Drecht pushed her out of the way with one hand, and in one movement shoved Klaus's head deep down into the bucket with the other.

'I'll give you *teeth*,' she said.

Klaus kicked and struggled, but Frau Drecht was a strong woman. She had her fingers wound tightly in his hair and she held him down with the flat of her other hand on the back of his head. The water was ice-cold. He held his breath until he could hear the blood thumping in his ears, and then he couldn't hold onto it any more. In an instant he'd swallowed one great lungful of water. Frau Drecht pulled him up, gagging and choking, just long enough for him to take half a breath, then shoved his head back into the bucket again. Only this time there was no breath in him to hold onto and he swallowed another lungful of water. But she didn't let him up. She held his head under.

Liesel had pressed herself up against the dirty wall. Her hands clutched at her apron as she watched Frau Drecht shove Klaus's head back into the water and hold him down. 'No,' she said in a frightened gasp. She hadn't meant to say it, but she just couldn't help it. It had slipped out.

Frau Drecht shot a cold look at her. '*No?*' she said dangerously. '*No?* I'll give you *no*.' And she pushed Klaus's head down to the very bottom of the bucket. 'Another sound from you, girl, and you'll be next.'

Liesel bit at her lip as Frau Drecht held Klaus in the bucket for what seemed like an age; then pulled him out coughing and retching, banged his head hard down onto the table top, and leaned over him.

'What was in the teeth?' she hissed.

Klaus couldn't answer. He couldn't even breathe.

'I think you need the bucket again,' said Frau Drecht, and she hauled him upright.

Desperately he shook his head from side to side, water streaming from his nose and mouth. She pulled him over to the bucket and held him there with his face poised just above the cold water.

'What was in the teeth?'

He choked out one word: 'Gold!'

She wasn't sure she'd heard him right. She leaned her head closer, the better to hear. 'What?'

'And a diamond!' gasped Klaus.

She heard that all right.

For a moment Frau Drecht's pink powdered face was a picture. Then it became hard. 'Well, well, Kusselmann,' she said to herself. 'I think we'd better have that back.'

The yard at the back of the house was no more than a cold crevice made by the high walls of the buildings that enclosed it. No light got down there even on the sunniest of days. It was dark and damp. In one corner was a hole where the buckets of filth from the house were tipped, and in the middle the water pump dripped onto the slimy, worn bricks.

Frau Drecht opened the door to the yard and shoved Klaus through. Then she slammed it shut and slid the bolts across, top and bottom. She was going to keep him there, just to make sure, until her business with Kusselmann was done.

'Get my hat and coat, Liesel,' she said.

While Frau Drecht waited for Liesel to come back, she stood at the dirty mirror in the passage, pursing her lips and tidying her ringlets, then she put on the thick coat and hat that Liesel brought her.

As she opened the door to the street, a thought crossed her mind. She looked back down the passage to where Liesel stood in the dark by the stairs. 'He'd better still be out there when I get back, girl,' she said. 'Or it's the hot iron for you.' Then she shut the door with a slam.

For several moments Liesel stood in the quiet of the dark passage watching the door, but it didn't open again. She couldn't hear anyone moving in the rooms above. Turning her head, she looked back down the passage towards the kitchen, towards the boy shut up in that small damp, dark yard. In her mind's eye she could still see the terrified look on his face as Frau Drecht had pushed him down into the bucket that second time.

She'd had a brother of her own once. He would have looked exactly like that tooth-puller's boy if he'd lived. That was why she'd stared at Klaus the first time she saw him. Why she'd watched him from the shadows in the hall every time since. He was the the spitting image of him, right down to the way he turned his head and only half looked at her as he stood by the door.

She'd tried never to think about how it had happened, how he'd died, but she thought about it all the time – because it had been her fault. At least, she told herself it was her fault: he'd been sick and cold, and when he'd needed her most, she hadn't stayed with him; she'd gone with that man instead, the one with the theatre coat and silk hat who'd come looking down the street – the one who'd said he wanted to give her some money and food, and that all she had to do was go with him and he'd show her where he kept it. Only there wasn't any money and there wasn't any food, just a dark doorway and a hard step and no one to see what had happened, and by the time she'd understood, it was too late for her to run away. And when she'd finally got back to where she'd left her brother, that was too late as well.

And now she stood in the dark passage looking at the kitchen door. She couldn't leave him there like that.

Only she knew all too well what Frau Drecht would do to her if she let him out. She put her hand on the sleeve of her blouse. Under the cloth she could feel the row of raised marks that the hot iron had left on her arm. There were lots of them. It was Frau Drecht's favourite punishment, but it was that or go back on the streets again, back to wait beneath the Beggar Boys' window of the convent of the Marienkirche for the nuns to lower a basket of bread on a rope to the cold, starving street children below. Often it had been the only food she got, and even then she'd had to fight for it, even just for a crust.

Sometimes, you see, there really isn't any choice.

But she couldn't leave the boy there. She couldn't do the wrong thing again, and leaving him would be wrong, she knew it.

She bit at her lip and looked at the closed front door.

Making up her mind, she took a deep breath and went back down the passage to the kitchen. Stretching up, first top, then bottom, she slid back the bolts of the door to the yard.

She was just about to lift the latch when someone beat on the heavy front door of the house.

Chapter Three

Liesel stopped quite still, listening, her hand on the latch of the door to the yard. For one moment she thought it was Frau Drecht come back, and her mouth went dry. But then she heard a man's voice, as though he'd stepped back from the door and was calling up at the windows. It was a hard voice, cold as ashes.

'Is anyone there?'

She lifted the latch and, putting her finger to her lips to silence him, beckoned Klaus out of the gloom of the yard. He looked like a drowned rat. His eyes were rimmed red; a little blood vessel had burst in one of them, and the white of the eye was flooded with red too. He was shaking. But for all that, she saw it even more clearly now – saw how like her brother he really was. It made her heart hurt.

'It's all right,' she said. 'I'll get you out, but there's someone at the door.'

He looked at her, wide-eyed. She wasn't sure he'd understood what she'd said. She could hear his teeth chattering.

'It's all right,' she said again. 'Wait here.'

She went back down the dark passageway and, putting her eye to a crack in the door, squinted through it to the street outside. She saw a tall man dressed in a long black coat. He was standing at the bottom of the small flight of steps. It took her a moment to realize that it was a priest: she could see the flare of his coat, the long row of buttons right up to his throat. He was looking up at the front of the house, but as she watched him, he suddenly stared straight at her. She knew he couldn't see her, but all the same he looked at her as though he'd felt that he was being watched.

She stepped quickly back from the crack, hesitated; then, pulling back the latch, opened the door. The priest came slowly up the steps like a long black knife. He wore wire-rimmed spectacles with thick glass. Unhurriedly he took them off and polished them on a cloth from his pocket, then put them on again and looked at her. Behind the thick lenses were the palest eyes she'd ever seen, almost colourless, like water. Their gaze made her feel quite unsafe.

'Sir?' she said.

'This is Bergenstrasse?' he said in a voice that was like dry paper.

She nodded.

He pulled something from another pocket – a letter; she could see the writing on it as he unfolded it. He looked down at it as though reminding himself of some detail. 'Frau Drecht's house?'

She nodded again.

'Then there is someone here I wish to see.'

Without waiting to be asked, he put his hand on the door and, pushing it wider, stepped past Liesel into the dark passageway. His face wrinkled in distaste at the stale, verminous smell of the house. 'Frau Drecht is here?' he said. It wasn't a voice you argued with.

'No, sir,' she answered.

He looked at her again with those pale, cold, water-clear eyes. 'Then you will have to do,' he said. 'I wish to see Herr Siger.'

34

Involuntarily Liesel shot a glance up at the dark staircase. In her mind's eye she could see the iron bedstead in the small room at the top, and the toothless man lying with his head on the greasy pillow. Frau Drecht had been too concerned to find out what Kusselmann had been doing to have that body taken away – or indeed the one in the dark of the loft above it. She was usually very quick with things like that, because if she was quick, the Anatomy School would take them, and that was worth a whole lot more to her than just pennies for the teeth. But not this time. They were both still there. And though Liesel wasn't new to the house, she didn't know which was which – she knew that one of the men, loft or bedstead, was Herr Siger. She'd often heard the name called up the stairs with oaths and curses by Frau Drecht wanting her rent, and she'd heard Frau Drecht that very morning damn the man for dying before he'd paid her. So it had to be one of them.

'He's dead, sir,' she said.

The effect of her words on the priest couldn't have been more startling. He turned round sharply – so sharply that Liesel took a step back, but he caught her by the shoulder and leaned forward so that his face was level with hers. He had a single long

35

black hair growing from the side of his nose. 'Dead?' he said.

She nodded her head quickly. 'This morning, sir.'

'How?'

'Ill, sir.'

He looked up the stairs. 'Show me.'

Liesel led him up the dark, narrow staircase, darker and narrower the higher it went, only she wasn't sure where to take him. But she didn't want to go into the loft – not into the rat-infested stalls up there – so by the time they'd reached the last landing she'd made up her mind what she was going to do. She stopped by the closed door of the room where the man lay on the cold iron bedstead.

'In here, sir,' she said. She'd show him this one. If she was wrong, then he could go and find the other himself.

The priest's long fingers closed around the handle and he opened the door.

In the time that had passed since Frau Drecht had held the pillow over his face, death had begun to work its grey business upon the man in the bed. His skin had taken on the colour of old wax, and one eyelid had partly opened of its own accord, revealing the yellowed white beneath. The empty jaw hung open.

The priest stood for a moment by the bedside and looked down at the dead man, at the toothless mouth. Then he turned and looked at Liesel. 'This is Herr Siger?' he asked.

And suddenly it dawned on her that he didn't know who Herr Siger was either.

But before she could answer, he'd pulled back the bedclothes and, first one, then the other, rolled up the sleeves of the dirty nightshirt and looked at the dead, waxy grey arms beneath. There was nothing on the first one, but even from where she stood by the door Liesel could see that on the second – though she couldn't have said what it was of – were the dark inky blue lines of a thin winding tattoo. The priest let the arm fall. Then he put his finger in the corner of the man's cold, wet mouth and hooked the cheek back.

'Who did this?' he said. 'Who took the teeth?'

'The tooth-puller, sir.'

The priest pulled the cloth from his pocket and wiped his finger dry. Then he stood taking in the small dirty room around him. There wasn't much to see. The man's clothes, such as they were, lay in a pile on the floor next to a plain wooden chair. There was a table and a cracked glass. Nothing else. Liesel waited by the door, and watched as the priest picked up the clothes one by one, felt the pockets and shook them. Then he took the man's boots and, turning them over in his hands, shook them too. But if he was looking for something, he did not find it – not in the boots or the clothes. He dropped them onto the bare floorboards and looked at Liesel again with those pale eyes.

'Did he have nothing else?' he said. 'Leave nothing?'

Liesel shook her head.

'Where does the tooth-puller live?' he asked.

All in that one moment Liesel had an idea.

She'd hadn't had a clue until now how she was going to explain to Frau Drecht how the boy had got out of the bolted yard – she hadn't even wanted to think about what would happen when she did. But here was a golden chance. She could say the priest made her do it. Frau Drecht couldn't expect her to argue with a priest.

'I don't know, sir,' she said – and then, as though it were only an afterthought, added, 'But his boy's downstairs. He came to pay for the teeth. He'll tell you.'

She'd tried to make it sound as though that was

all there was to it, but that wasn't easy under the gaze of those cold, clear eyes. And as they looked at her, Liesel was suddenly sure of something. The priest knew exactly what had been in the man's mouth. And worse than that, he'd guessed that she did as well.

'You'd better show me where he is,' he said.

There was something not right here. Liesel could feel it like a pricking at the back of her neck.

Not at all sure now that this was such a good idea after all, she led the priest back down the dark narrow staircase to the dirty kitchen where, wet and shivering, she'd left the boy waiting.

Only when they got there, the boy wasn't waiting.

He wasn't there at all.

When Frau Drecht slammed the door of the house behind her, she went quickly down Bergenstrasse – *tack-tack, tack-tack* – on her little button boots with the hard wooden heels, but she didn't go straight to Kusselmann's shop. She went somewhere else first, and this promised far worse for Kusselmann.

At the end of Bergenstrasse where the street divided – one way to the town bridge and the other down to the wharves and landing piers by the wide river – there was a dark little alley, and that's where Frau Drecht went. She had use of someone who lived there. Frau Drecht was not beyond putting a hot iron to a girl's arm or a pillow to the face of a dying man or a boy's head into a bucket – and if truth be told, there were a thousand things worse than those – but when someone really needed to be taught a lesson, she had another way of going about her business, and he was called Mutzi.

Everybody knew Mutzi. At least, everyone who'd ever watched the bare-knuckle fighters square up to each other in the stable yards of The Angel or The Greyhound. Mutzi was quite a pet of the crowd there – that's where his name came from. If he'd ever had another one, no one bothered to use that any more. He was a broad-shouldered, big man with a fat beer gut and breath that smelled of stale pork and onion. His hair was cropped short. There was always a lot of money bet on Mutzi when he stripped off his shirt and, bare to the waist, stepped up to the mark, because it didn't matter how big and strong or young and fast his opponent was – they could hit him as hard as ever they could, he just kept coming. Finally, when they had no strength left to hit him any more, Mutzi would catch up with them and, with hands the size of two loaves of bread, beat their faces to a pulp. If you wanted to see a lot of blood, Mutzi was the man to watch.

But what the crowd liked most about him wasn't just that he won his fights or that they were always so messy, it was what he did at the end – 'Mutzi's Salute', they called it. They'd wait for it, clapping and shouting him on. He'd loosen the belt of his britches, settle himself above the man he'd left blind and half dead on the straw-strewn cobbles and, teeth clenched with the effort of it, fart in his face.

Yes, everyone knew Mutzi.

But not everyone knew that he was Frau Drecht's son.

When Frau Drecht had really dirty work she wanted done, it was Mutzi she would get to do it for her. So it wasn't on her own that she finally made her way towards Kusselmann's neat little shop with its hundreds of teeth lined up in rows along the polished ebony shelves. If there was one thing you didn't do to Frau Drecht, it was try to cross her. Kusselmann hadn't learned that yet. But he was about to find out.

He was in his rooms at the back of the shop, just beginning to wonder where Klaus had got to – the boy had been an inordinately long time – when he heard the bell above the shop door ring as it opened, and then again as it closed. He dabbed the crumbs from his face – he liked to have a small pastry at that time of the afternoon – and dropping the napkin on the table, he went, oily and obsequious, through the door to see who it was in the shop. He hadn't expected to see Frau Drecht there – or the exceptionally large man standing behind her who, even as Kusselmann looked at him, turned round the card that read CLOSED and, pulling down the blind, slid the bolts across.

'Herr Kusselmann,' Frau Drecht purred with more menace in her voice than he'd ever heard before. 'I'd like to have a little talk with you about a diamond.'

Chapter Four

What Klaus had done after Liesel opened the door to the priest was very simple.

From the kitchen, he'd heard the sound of voices in the hall, and then footsteps going up the hard wooden stairs. He'd stood listening, with one eye on the gloom of the staircase and the other on the back of the door that led to the street. When he was quite sure they weren't going to come back, he'd crept quietly along the passage, lifted the latch and, opening the door no more than was necessary to slip through, carefully pulled it shut behind him. The only thing to show what he'd done was a trail of water on the dark of the stone floor.

Once he was in the street, he ran as though Frau

Drecht herself was after him, but the water he'd swallowed was like hard, sharp stones in his chest and stomach. He made it as far as the end of Bergenstrasse; then, throwing himself down one of the dark side alleys, he was sick as a dog into the gutter. He stood with his hand on the alley wall, spitting and shivering and trying to work out what on earth he was going to do next.

Frau Drecht had gone to see Kusselmann about the diamond. Klaus had understood that much, head full of water or not – and Kusselmann would know that it was he who'd told her. When he got back he was going to get such a beating.

He waited until the stitch in his side had let up a little and then, with an awful dread of what was going to happen when he got there, he started back across the town bridge and along the streets that led towards Kusselmann's shop. He went a longer way round than he needed to, partly because he didn't want to run the risk of meeting Frau Drecht again, but mostly because he didn't want to get there at all.

But when at last he stood at the corner of the street looking across at the shop, something didn't seem quite right. The blind had been pulled down, and the card that said CLOSED was still in the window, but the door was very slightly ajar, which was strange. He watched for a few moments, half expecting to see Frau Drecht or someone else come out, as though Kusselmann had just opened the door for them and they were still talking on the other side of it. But no one came out. And there was no lamp lit in the shop either, and that was strange too, because the afternoon was closing in and it would have been too dark for Kusselmann to work in there without one. The longer Klaus stood looking at the door, the more wrong it seemed.

Finally he crossed the street and, standing in the doorway, cautiously pushed the door open. It grated over something hard on the floor. For a moment he thought that a small stone had got caught underneath, but then he realized that there were other stones on the floor. They crunched under his feet as he stepped on them.

Only they weren't stones.

They were teeth.

The floor was covered with teeth.

The glass of the cabinets against the walls had been smashed, and every tooth – hundreds of them – emptied over the floor. He could see here and there broken blue and white shards that were all that was left of the delicate porcelain bowls. As he stared around him, his mind slowly made the connection between what he'd told Frau Drecht and what had happened here. His mouth went very dry. He picked his way carefully across the shop, the teeth and glass cracking underfoot as he trod on them.

Then he saw the black, shiny, polished tip of Kusselmann's boot poking out from behind the counter.

Klaus froze.

In that moment of absolute silence he could hear the sound of the enormous watch in Kusselmann's waistcoat pocket going *ticker-tick, ticker-tick, ticker-tick.*

Very slowly, afraid of what he was going to see, Klaus put his hands on the edge of the counter and peered round.

Kusselmann lay on the floor like a dropped rag doll – but a doll someone had taken pains to smash before they'd let it fall. There was blood everywhere. It was dark and clotted on Kusselmann's face, and in his hair, and on the front of his white shirt, and on his clean white cuffs. But even as Klaus looked down at him, Kusselmann let out a low, quiet moan.

'Herr Kusselmann?' whispered Klaus.

With the sound of teeth and glass crunching

under his feet, Klaus dipped round the counter and knelt down beside him. 'Herr Kusselmann!'

This was worse than he could ever have imagined. What Kusselmann would do to him now he couldn't even begin to think, and it was all his fault. He'd told Frau Drecht about the gold and the diamond.

He tried to sit Kusselmann up. Maybe if he helped him, that might make it better, but Kusselmann was too fat and heavy for Klaus to move, and the front of his coat was soaked with blood. It was wet and sticky on Klaus's hands. Klaus shuddered and, without even thinking, wiped them on the front of his own shirt, then realized that all he'd done was smear Kusselmann's blood all over himself as well. He let out a whimper as a wave of panic rose inside him.

He didn't know what to do: he looked wildly around at the smashed shop, at the broken glass – and that's when he saw it. It was lying only a couple of feet away on the bare floorboards beneath the counter, in the small space where he unrolled his rag bed at night.

At first he thought it was just another piece of glass, but as he moved his head, it caught what little light there was, and it sparkled like a cold flame.

It was the diamond.

Maybe it had fallen, or maybe Kusselmann had thrown it to the ground and it hadn't been seen. But there it was. Frau Drecht hadn't found it.

He glanced quickly back at Kusselmann. 'Herr Kusselmann!'

But Kusselmann didn't move; his eyes were closed tight, the lids like fat apricots with the skin all swollen and split.

Klaus hesitated. He couldn't just leave it there, he knew that. Somebody would come, and if they found it they'd be sure to take it. But maybe if he looked after it, then perhaps Kusselmann wouldn't be so angry – not if he was able to say, *Look, Herr Kusselmann, I've got the diamond.*

He looked at it again, more carefully this time.

It lay on the wooden boards in a dark thread of Kusselmann's blood – like a little shard of malice, or poison waiting in a cup. And suddenly some cold instinct, more felt than understood, told him not to touch it; told him to pass it by like a man might pass by a snake in the grass.

Only Klaus didn't listen.

Even the ticking of Kusselmann's watch seemed to stop as, hesitantly, he reached out his hand and picked it up.

It was centuries since a child had last held that diamond.

It was heavier than he thought it would be, more like a small lead weight, and as his fingers closed around it, it seemed to flush blood-red, mirroring Kusselmann's broken face.

He turned round and held it up for Kusselmann to see. 'Look, Herr Kusselmann,' he said. 'I've got it. It's safe.'

But Kusselmann didn't move. He'd gone very still indeed.

'Herr K-Kusselmann?' said Klaus in a small voice. Then, louder, 'Herr Kusselmann?' He shook him, but Kusselmann didn't move.

Slowly Klaus stood up and backed away. In the heavy silence of the shop he could hear the sound of the watch, but nothing else, and he realized he was holding his breath. He looked down at the wet blood on his hands and shirt, and suddenly knew that no one would believe that he'd just found Kusselmann like this.

Frau Drecht would make sure of that.

Without stopping to think, he began to back slowly out of the shop until he stood in the doorway, then pulled the door closed behind him. He could hear the little bell going *ting-a-ling* on the other side. Pushing his hands deep into his pockets so that no one would see the blood on them, he began to walk away – not too fast – and with every step he took he expected someone to shout after him to stop. But no one shouted. In the gathering gloom, he walked slowly to the end of the street, and without turning round he slipped into the dark warren of alleys and passages that led down to the river and the cold stone bridge.

It was only when he was in the dark of the alleys that it dawned on him.

Deep in his pocket, he was still holding the diamond tight in his hand.

Frau Drecht thumped on the front door of the house in Bergenstrasse.

She had two voices – the one she used to shout for the girl: 'Liesel! Get your arse to this door!'

And the other, buttery and sickly sweet, which she used when she spoke to the dark-haired young gentleman she'd pulled up the steps with her: 'She takes such a time, sir,' she said to him in the one, and then—

'Liesel!' she shouted again at the door in the other.

He couldn't help but notice the difference between the two. His name was Markus Brennen. He was assistant to the Professor of Anatomy at the Anatomy School. Being chosen for that post had been a conspicuous honour, but a deserved one. He was a fine anatomist – better than any of his peers – and curious as a cat. He never forgot a detail, never forgot a face. It was widely agreed that a great future lay in front of Markus Brennen. But that was the future, and this was now, and an assistant is just an assistant, however great the honour.

One of his duties was to supervise the porters when they collected bodies from the city morgue and brought them back to the school for dissection. He'd been on his way there with the open cart and two of the porters when Frau Drecht had spotted him from across the road.

'A good job I saw you,' she said, tapping him lightly on the arm. 'Save you all that trouble, I can. Two of them, like I say – poor souls – one last night, one this morning. Both still fresh as daisies, and you can't ask for better than that in your line of work, can you, sir?'

51

'I suppose not,' Markus had agreed rather coldly, trying not to look at her, or at the huge crop-haired man who'd followed them up the steps. He didn't like Frau Drecht. Maybe that came across a little too clearly in his manner and his voice, because Frau Drecht gave him a hard look and brushed at an all but invisible thread on her sleeve.

'Of course, I could just have them taken down to the morgue, sir,' she said in a wheedling voice. 'You could collect them from there. But I think they charge a bit more, don't they? All those papers to sign. All that waiting around. And then there's the clerk's fee to pay as well.'

She knew her business, he had to give her that.

They'd had bodies from Frau Drecht before. In fact, come to think of it, they'd had bodies from Frau Drecht with such regularity that . . .

Well, maybe it was best not to ask too many questions, and people did die, there was no escaping that fact.

Just more often, it seemed, at Frau Drecht's house than at others.

He looked at her awkwardly. 'That won't be necessary,' he said.

'Mmm,' said Frau Drecht knowingly. 'I thought not.'

She was about to yell at the door again, but before she could, it was opened by Liesel. Liesel, pale-faced and hollow-eyed. Markus smiled at her encouragingly, but she didn't smile back.

'Took your time, girl,' growled Frau Drecht, and Liesel could see in her face that she'd been marked down for punishment later. But for the moment Frau Drecht just pushed past her and bustled into the hall, dragging Markus behind her. Like the priest's before him, Markus's face wrinkled as he caught his first breath of the house – of the vermin and the damp.

'Mutzi Putzi,' said Frau Drecht in her false girlish voice. 'Show the nice gentleman where they'll be. Top room and loft.'

The big man jerked his head towards the stairs, and Markus, hat in hand, beckoned to the porters to follow. The four of them – Mutzi, Markus and the two porters – disappeared up the staircase into the darkness.

But Liesel didn't move; she stood waiting at the bottom of the stairs.

'What d'you think you're staring at?' said Frau Drecht acidly.

Liesel swallowed and, bobbing a small curtsey, glanced anxiously towards the closed door of Frau

Drecht's parlour. 'Visitor, gnädige Frau,' she said.

Frau Drecht looked at the door and frowned. 'What d'you mean *visitor*?'

'Gnädige Frau,' said Liesel, and bobbed again.

Still frowning, Frau Drecht grasped the handle and pushed the door open.

Sitting quietly at the little table was the tall thin priest.

He didn't stand up as Frau Drecht came into the room but, unhurriedly taking the cloth from his pocket, breathed on the lenses of his thick wire-rimmed spectacles, polished them clean and, setting them back on the bridge of his nose, looked up at her with those pale, water-clear eyes.

'Frau Drecht, I presume?' he said in a voice like ash. 'My name is Father Henriquez, and I wish to discuss some business with you.'

On the table in front of him, just where Frau Drecht had left them, were the broken plaster remains of Herr Siger's teeth.

Chapter Five

'These are curious things, are they not?' said Father Henriquez, rolling the little pieces of broken plaster beneath the tips of his fingers.

'Little knick-knacks,' said Frau Drecht, eyeing him suspiciously. She didn't like churchmen – they were all preaching and words. Only this one wasn't like that, she could see it at once. He sat there in the chair – her chair – coldly looking at her with those pale, colourless eyes.

What kind of churchman looked like that?

For a moment she felt the beginnings of uneasiness under that unmoving gaze; then she remembered that Mutzi was only a shout away, and Mutzi was more than a match for any priest. Even one like this.

'You said you had some business, Father?' she said in a tone that was less than welcoming.

The priest looked down at the pieces of plaster and then up at her. 'I would like to know where I might find the man who pulled these teeth,' he said. 'They are teeth, are they not?' He raised one hand in a vague gesture towards the door. 'I would have asked his boy, but he'd already gone.'

Frau Drecht shot a dark glance at Liesel where she stood in the open doorway; it was full of the promise of punishment. But when she turned back to Father Henriquez, her voice was suddenly all butter and oil. That was an awkward question, and it was going to need careful answering.

'I hardly wanted to say what they were, sir,' she said. 'Not the sort of thing you like to talk about – teeth.'

'Quite,' said Father Henriquez.

'But I'm not sure I even know what his name was, come to think of it,' she continued. 'Came with his bag. I just get a boy in the street to fetch a puller if we need one.'

'Then maybe the girl can remember,' he said.

'What, little Liesel?' said Frau Drecht, turning round and looking at Liesel again.

She reached out her finger and thumb and pinched Liesel's cheek playfully, but Liesel could see the warning look in her eye and feel the sharp edge of Frau Drecht's thumbnail as she dug it in. She knew exactly what Frau Drecht meant: *Don't – you – dare – say – a – word.*

'Hardly remembers her own name from one moment to the next, do you, pet?' said Frau Drecht. 'Let alone the name of some strange tooth-puller.'

'Yet here they are,' said Father Henriquez, passing his hand over the plaster teeth. 'All broken and pulled apart. One might almost think there had been something in them.'

He looked carefully at Frau Drecht as he said these words, and if she had been wondering whether perhaps he didn't really know what had been in them, that look was enough to tell her that he did.

And that was very interesting.

'One of life's little mysteries, sir,' she said.

'So it is,' he answered. 'But in my experience, little mysteries always have a price.'

'Indeed they do, sir,' said Frau Drecht slyly. 'Else everyone would be knowing them, wouldn't they, and then they wouldn't be little mysteries any more.' She cocked her head to one side. 'What price was it you had in mind for this one, sir?' she asked.

If the priest wanted to find out who'd pulled the teeth – and a fat lot of good that would do him – then he was going to have to pay for the information. At least, that was what Frau Drecht thought.

Only she was wrong.

Liesel had been watching the priest while Frau Drecht spoke, and she saw a sort of stillness come over him as Frau Drecht said those words.

He shook his head slowly and leaned forward. 'No, Frau Drecht,' he said quietly, but even to Liesel's ears there was something unmistakable in that dry as dust voice now – something dangerous. 'You misunderstand me . . . It is you who would pay the price.' He looked at her unwaveringly with those pale, colourless eyes. 'Tell me who pulled the teeth and what has become of what was in them.'

Frau Drecht heard it too. It wasn't what she was expecting, and it seemed to Liesel that it took a moment for her to understand just exactly what the words meant. Then her face hardened. 'I don't take threats in my own house,' she said.

But what the priest might have said next Liesel didn't get to hear, because there was the sound of movement and boots on the stairs outside – of

Markus and the porters coming back down. Of Mutzi coming with them.

Frau Drecht's lips parted in a thin smile. 'I have other things that I need to be about now, sir,' she said. 'So you mustn't let me keep you. The girl will show you out.'

Father Henriquez looked icily at her, but he'd heard the noise from the hall too. He stood up. 'I shall come back,' he said, 'if I do not find what I am looking for.'

'You do that, sir,' said Frau Drecht, and she stood aside to let him pass.

At the door he turned and looked at her. 'I hope, Frau Drecht, for your sake, that I won't need to.'

As he turned again, he walked straight into Markus in the hall outside. The two men quickly stepped apart, and Father Henriquez inclined his head in a stiff bow of apology. Then, with Liesel going before him to open the door, he went out and down the steps into the street.

Markus stood for a moment watching him go. He'd heard those last few words through the open parlour door, but wasn't sure he could have heard correctly because they'd sounded so very much like a threat. He was still watching after the priest, wondering what it was that had actually been said, when Frau Drecht herself appeared in the doorway of the little parlour. She had a sly smile on her pink powdered face as she looked up into the darkness of the stairs and listened to the sound of the men's hobnailed boots coming down.

Then she turned and looked at Markus. 'Collecting for the poor,' she said, as if in answer to the question he hadn't asked. 'Lord knows, we try our best, don't we, sir?' She sighed. 'But it's not as though we couldn't do with a little help ourselves.'

She looked at him pointedly. 'Which reminds me, sir,' she said. 'We need to speak about money too, don't we? Usual note, I trust?'

Frau Drecht's 'usual note' wasn't a business long in the doing. While the porters carried their canvas-wrapped bundles out into the street and loaded them onto the hand cart, pulling the worn black leather cover over them, Markus wrote out the short note for Frau Drecht to take up to the Anatomy School. It said merely: *Two cadavers (less teeth) for dissection.* Then he signed it and gave it to her.

As the front door closed behind him, the simpering smile that Frau Drecht had worn for Markus while he'd written the note dropped from her face as though it had been shot. She folded the piece of paper and tucked it into the top, most private, part of her dress. Then, with an altogether different smile, she turned and looked down the passageway towards the kitchen, where Liesel had quietly slipped away into the dark.

'Liesel!' she bawled. 'Get me some coffee.' And then she added in the voice that Liesel had dreaded, 'And put the smoothing iron to the fire while you're at it, girl. You and me need to have a little talk with Mr Iron, don't we?'

In the foul little kitchen, Liesel took the coffee pot and, filling it, hooked it over the fire. Then, with a hand that she couldn't stop from shaking, she set Frau Drecht's small black smoothing iron close up to the grate. She looked at it for a few moments, then moved it just a little further away from the flames, hoping that Frau Drecht wouldn't notice, and that it wouldn't get quite so hot or hurt quite so much when the gnädige Frau spat on it and pressed it down onto the bare skin of her arm.

While she waited for her coffee to be brought through, Frau Drecht sat herself at the small square table. Mutzi leaned against the doorway watching her. There was a look of satisfaction on her face as she pulled a small wrap of baize cloth from the folds of her dress; sweeping the broken pieces of plaster to the floor with the back of her hand, she set it down just in front of her on the table. 'Shall we see what we've got, Putzi?' she said silkily.

She undid the ribbon and opened the cloth. As she lifted it, the golden teeth fell onto the bare wood like a handful of dropped stones. She looked at them for a moment, but slowly the smile on her face began to fade and was replaced by a frown. She turned the cloth upside down and shook it, smoothed it through her fingers, then spread the teeth across the table so that she could see each and every one of them.

There was no diamond.

It simply wasn't there.

And that was when she remembered something – and that something was a very small sound: the sound of something dropping onto the wooden floor in Kusselmann's shop as she'd tied up the wrap of baize cloth, the one that Kusselmann had so wanted to give her after Mutzi had started talking to him. It hadn't seemed important at the time, that little sound – there'd been other things to watch – but now she had a good idea what it had been.

Maybe that's why she'd noticed it – that little sound: something in her head, realizing what had happened, was desperately trying to draw her attention to what she'd done.

She'd dropped the diamond.

It was on the floor behind Kusselmann's counter, she was sure of it.

Then, just as quickly, another thought pressed itself on her. Liesel had let the boy go. There was only one place he was going to make for – Kusselmann's shop. He'd find Kusselmann and, sure as eggs were eggs, the diamond too, if he had eyes in his head. And what about the priest? If he asked anyone around here for a tooth-puller, that's where they'd send him: Kusselmann's shop – she'd as good as told him where to go.

She slapped the table and swore. The golden teeth jumped on the wood.

This was going to need to be put right quickly if it was going to be put right at all. Only that was easier said than done. She couldn't have Mutzi and his big boots tramping all over the shop. He'd made enough of a mess of it and Kusselmann already. And this time there might be people who'd see him go in. Get caught in there now and there'd be a rope around his neck – and hers. No. It needed someone to slip in and slip out. Someone nobody would notice, someone who'd do exactly what they were told – and Frau Drecht knew just who that could be.

'Liesel!' she yelled. 'Get in here!'

It was dark by the time Frau Drecht and Liesel reached Kusselmann's shop. They stood in the alleyway opposite and looked along the narrow street – it was the alleyway where Klaus had stood earlier that day, only now lamps had been lit in all the windows of the houses: there were cracks of light to be seen through the shutters – all the shutters, that is, except Kusselmann's. His shop was completely dark. In one hand Frau Drecht held a small lantern; it was closed so that only a glimmer of light came from it. With the other, she held tightly onto the cuff of Liesel's coat.

When she was satisfied that no one would see them, she pulled the girl to her, pressing her face so close that in the dark Liesel could smell the rose-perfumed red grease on Frau Drecht's lips.

'Now, remember,' Frau Drecht hissed in a whisper. 'It's on the floor somewhere, behind the counter. Get it and come straight back. That's all you have to do. Understand?' She gave Liesel's wrist a sharp twist to make sure that there was no misunderstanding about what might happen to her if she didn't do exactly as she was told. 'Understand?' she hissed again.

Liesel nodded, but she knew that if it really was as simple as that, Frau Drecht would have gone in there and found the diamond herself. So there had to be more to it; had to be some reason for her not wanting to go back in. She could see that the shop was very dark, and there wasn't even any sound coming from it. Liesel began to have an uncomfortable, crawling feeling inside.

Frau Drecht pressed the lantern into her hand and stepped back into the shadows of the alleyway, leaving her standing alone in the street.

Liesel looked at the shop again and hesitated.

'Go on!' hissed Frau Drecht from the darkness behind her.

She took a deep breath and started across the narrow street. There was no one about. A single lamp was burning at the far end, but somehow that made the street seem even longer and emptier. As she got nearer to the shop, she could see in Kusselmann's window the white smudge of the card that said CLOSED. She put her hand on the door, hoping it would be locked, but when she turned the handle and pushed, it opened. On its spring behind the door the little bell rang in the darkness.

Liesel stood stock still, but nothing moved. Everything was dark and silent. She squeezed through the gap and closed the door behind her as Frau Drecht had told her to do. The little bell rang again, only this time she reached up and stopped it with her hand. Then, fumbling with the shutter of the lantern, she opened it and held it up in front of her. The lantern gave only the weakest yellow beam; everything to either side of that pale, butter-coloured light was pitch black.

There was a scurrying movement, and as her heart leaped into her mouth, she saw the tail of something small and black, like a cat, at the edge of the lantern light. Then it was gone. Underfoot the broken teeth and glass crunched as she stepped forward.

'Boy?' she whispered. 'Are you there?'

She'd already thought that if he'd come back to the shop he might still be here, and that would be a help if nothing else was. She'd at least have him.

But there was no sound. She lifted the lantern

again and looked nervously around at the broken cabinets and shelves.

'It's me, Liesel. Frau Drecht's girl.'

Something quick and soft brushed against her leg. She jerked the lantern down, and this time caught sight of a long, liquid black tail curling round the end of the counter. And she saw something else too, on the floor.

The shiny black tip of Kusselmann's boot.

And there was a taint in the air, stale like the trays of meat in a butcher's shop. It was the smell of the pool of cold, congealing blood on the floor beneath Kusselmann's head.

Now Liesel knew why Frau Drecht hadn't wanted to go back in. Why she hadn't wanted to risk being found there. This is what she'd done, and now she was waiting outside for Liesel to bring her the diamond.

She began to shake. The palms of her hands were damp, her mouth dry.

Then she thought that maybe Kusselmann wasn't dead.

With the lantern trembling in her hand, Liesel put out her foot and kicked at the toe of Kusselmann's boot.

Nothing.

She could hear the cat moving in the dark behind the counter. Almost mechanically she leaned slowly forward and peered round. As she did, the light from the lantern crept along Kusselmann's body to where the cat sat with its back to her on Kusselmann's chest.

Only it wasn't a cat.

It was a small black monkey.

It turned its head and stared at her with golden yellow eyes, and as it stared, its quick, busy little hands were searching Kusselmann's coat and pockets. It bared its dirty teeth at the lantern light and hissed; then, without taking its eyes off her, it dipped its black-nailed finger into the wet blood on the floor and licked it clean with its little pink tongue.

She could feel the scream start inside her, but it never came out, because that was the moment when, out of the shadows behind her, a hand closed firmly over her mouth.

Chapter Six

It happened so quickly. Liesel dropped the lantern with the shock of it, clawing at the hand at her face, but the lantern didn't go out. It rolled like a bottle on the floor at her feet. Shrieking, the monkey leaped from Kusselmann's chest onto a high shelf, bared its teeth and hissed again. In the rolling lantern light she could see it rocking backwards and forwards, watching her like a golden-eyed demon.

She could taste sweat and tobacco on the hard skin of the hand over her mouth. It was a man's hand. She kicked and struggled, but he cupped his palm away from her biting teeth and, with his fingers, pinched her nose shut so tightly that she couldn't breathe at all. She tried to dig her nails into his eyes, but he turned his face away and pulled her tight against his chest. She had no air to breathe. A bright wheel of light began going round and round in her head, and she could hear the blood hammering in her ears; then, suddenly, the world was full of swimming dots, soft and feathery, as though she were floating in it.

The man opened his fingers as he felt her go limp, and just for that moment there was air – the smallest breath of air – but to Liesel it was like a hard jerk on the end of a rope, and with it the world came back, real and sharp and full of pain. But that little breath was all that he let her have. He pinched his fingers shut and the air was gone again.

The monkey was still on the shelf above her, rocking on its haunches, eyes wide with attention, tail wrapped round its body.

The man moved his head. The sharp bristles of his cheek rubbed against her face as he put his mouth to her ear. 'If you want breathe,' he whispered, 'you stop.'

The voice was foreign, but unlike anything she'd ever heard down by the wharves, and they said you could hear the whole world there. He'd spoken each word without expression, as though they were learned by rote in a language that wasn't his.

But he was waiting for an answer.

She nodded her head – she could only just move it, he was holding her so tightly.

He opened his fingers again and let her breathe, but only through her nose. She stood trying to fill her lungs with air, and all the while he held his tobacco and sweat hand hard over her mouth. He only gave her a moment, then he pulled her towards the back of the shop and through the door that led into Kusselmann's private rooms. No light from the dropped lantern reached there; it was pitch dark, but she sensed at once there was someone else. She could smell the wax of a candle not long blown out. For a moment she thought it might be the boy, that he was in there. There was a scratching as a match was struck, and a little flare of light as the candle was lit again. But it wasn't the boy. In the long dark shadows thrown by the candle, stood the priest. Father Henriquez.

He lifted the candle and, holding it towards her, looked carefully at her face. The small bright flame glinted in the lenses of his thick wire-rimmed spectacles.

'Ah,' he breathed quietly. 'The girl from the

house. Now, what brings her here, I wonder?'

The man still had his hard-skinned hand over Liesel's mouth. With a small movement of his head, Father Henriquez signed for him to take it away. He did so, but he still held onto her. The priest leaned closer, until the candle was beneath Liesel's chin. She could feel the pricking heat of the flame.

'What are you doing here, child?' he asked in that voice, cold as ashes.

Her heart was racing, her tongue fat and dry in her mouth. 'I was looking for the boy, sir,' she said in a rush of words.

It was the first thing she could think of, maybe because in part it was true – she *had* been looking for him.

But in the dark and the shadows, Father Henriquez looked at her with those pale, colourless eyes. He knew that this was only part of the truth, and only part just wasn't good enough.

'What is your name, child?' he asked softly.

'L-Liesel,' she said, like a little girl caught out telling a lie.

He nodded smally, as though remembering now that that was the name Frau Drecht had used. 'Liesel,' he repeated quietly.

He looked at the candle in his hand, and moved it slowly beneath her chin. She tried to turn her head away, but the man gripped her more tightly. She could feel the real heat of the flame now, and it was beginning to hurt. Her breath started coming in shallow little gasps as she suddenly realized what the priest meant to do.

'Why are you here, Liesel?' he said.

'F-F-Frau Drecht,' she stammered.

He raised his eyebrows as if to let her know that he was wanting more than that, and moved the candle a little closer.

'She – she sent me.'

'Why?'

She was trying to think what she could say, but Father Henriquez didn't give her the chance. He lifted the flame so that it folded around the curve of her chin and onto her lips.

'The diamond!' she whimpered, trying to turn her face.

He moved the candle away, and held it just in front of her so that she could see it and know what it meant.

'She dropped the diamond,' cried Liesel.

Through tears of pain and fear, she saw him

unhurriedly look down at the floor. Then he looked back up at her. 'Where?' he said.

'Behind the counter. She sent me in.'

Without any sign of hurry, he turned away from her and went back towards the shop. She saw the dim thrown light of the candle disappear down the passage, and heard the sound of the broken teeth and glass being trodden underfoot. After what seemed like a long while but could only have been moments, the light grew brighter again as he came back.

The diamond wasn't there.

So where was it?

Father Henriquez stood in the doorway, candle in his hand, as though turning the question carefully over in his cold, clever mind. He looked sideways at the dark of the shop and then back into the dark of the room.

The tooth-puller had had a boy, that's what the girl had said. So where was the boy?

He came back towards Liesel. She tried to flinch away, but the man held her tight. Father Henriquez leaned towards her with the candle. 'What is his name?' he said.

Her eyes widened with the panic of not knowing

who it was he meant, but knowing exactly what it was he would do again if she didn't answer him. Only this time he could see that she didn't understand.

'The boy,' he said quietly, his voice full of menace. 'Where is the tooth-puller's boy?'

She shook her head. She hadn't the faintest idea.

'But you know his name, don't you? What he looks like?'

She nodded. She didn't know his name, but she knew what he looked like. How could she ever forget that?

Father Henriquez reached down and took her firmly by the wrist. His hand was bone-thin, but it had a grip like a vice.

He said something to the man in a language she didn't understand. The man let go of her, and took the candle that Father Henriquez held out to him. In its flickering light she could see that the tanned skin of his hands was covered with patterns of feathers and eyes. He went back into the shop where Kusselmann's cold body lay on the floor. Father Henriquez didn't wait for him to come back though. Still holding Liesel tightly by the wrist, he turned and led her quietly through the dark rooms to the very back door of the shop. She was too terrified now to do anything but follow. He opened the door and, pausing for a moment on the step to listen, led her away across the little yard and down the dark alleyway beyond.

On the other side of the building, Frau Drecht stood waiting with growing impatience for Liesel to come back. But as she stood there, she gradually became aware of the smell of smoke in the air, of burning. For a moment it meant nothing to her, but then, eyes widening with disbelief, she saw from across the street flickers of flame taking hold of the blinds that hung inside Kusselmann's window, and wisps of smoke curling from the iron grille above the door. The shop was on fire.

The stupid girl had set fire to the shop.

She looked wildly one way, then the other, then ran across the street to the door and turned the handle, but it didn't open. The bolt had been slid across on the inside; it wouldn't move. Furious, she swore at Liesel, thumping on the wood and hissing her name, just loud enough for it to be heard inside. 'Liesel!'

But the door didn't open.

All Frau Drecht wanted was the diamond; she

didn't care about the girl. But if the shop went up in flames she'd never find it. She yanked and pulled on the handle, but it wouldn't move. The fire had taken fierce hold inside the shop now; it was starting to cast a bright orange light out into the street. Frau Drecht shouted Liesel's name and kicked the door hard. But other people had seen the fire now, and her chance had slipped away. There were shouts, the sound of people running. A man pushed her aside and threw his weight against the door, shouting Kusselmann's name, but the door didn't move. Someone else was calling out for picks and tools – something to break the door down – but even as they tried it, the glass in the windows shattered, and with a roar the spitting flames leaped up and out into the dark sky, driving them back, their hands shielding their faces from the heat. Glancing either way to see whether she'd been noticed, Frau Drecht moved to the back of the gathering crowd and stood watching as the shop burned.

In a while, the fire-pump was brought clattering up the cobbles of the street. Men from the crowd put their backs to the handles, and slowly, under the play of the hoses, the fire was beaten down. At last there was nothing left of it but the sharp acrid smell of wet ash and burned wood. A man with a lantern went into the shop. The crowd fell quiet and waited. He came back grim-faced, and called for others to help him. Together they went back in, and after what seemed like a long time they came out again carrying between them on a broken door the charred and burned body of Kusselmann, which they set down in the street.

Frau Drecht waited for them to go in again and come out with the girl. But though she waited, no one else was brought out.

She pushed her way to the front of the crowd and, like some innocent bystander, asked whether there hadn't been a girl? Hadn't Kusselmann had a girl?

No. His neighbours knew he'd had a boy, but they hadn't found him. It was only Kusselmann in the shop – face up on the floor behind the counter. And that's when the whispers started. What was he doing there like that? One of the men who'd been inside said the back of the shop had been opened – and there was a dropped lantern on the floor. With that, the whispers went round and round – maybe the boy had let someone in? Maybe it was the boy who had set fire to the shop? But Frau Drecht knew exactly what had happened. She knew why the back of the shop was open.

Liesel.

Fat little diamond in her thieving little pocket, Liesel had dropped the lantern and slipped out the back.

Well, my girl, thought Frau Drecht darkly. *When I find you – and find you I shall – you're going to wish – oh, you're going to wish it so much – that you hadn't done that.*

Pulling her coat around her, she elbowed her way through the crowd and began the walk back towards Bergenstrasse.

The senior porter – old Keltzer – was ringing the bell to announce the start of the dissection class. It was his daily duty. The gentleman students were idling in groups in the entrance hall, and Keltzer, shabby in his black stuff coat and reeking of stale schnapps, was pushing his way bad-temperedly between them, ringing the big brass hand bell for all he was worth. 'Gentlemen! Gentlemen!' he bawled as he went.

He was an old crook, was Keltzer. He knew more than most about the things that went missing from the storerooms. In the past the school had always turned a blind eye to his little thievings, but all that had changed now that Markus Brennen was 'Herr Assistant'.

Keltzer didn't like Markus Brennen one bit.

The gentleman students paid seemingly not the slightest attention to Keltzer or his bell, but finally, slowly and still talking, they began to make their way past Herr Hilpfer, the registrar of the school – standing there all pompous and fat – and through the dark panelled doors that led into the dissection theatre where they took their places on the raked wooden terraces above the plain slab table that stood in the well at the bottom, the cold daylight falling onto it through the glass panes of the roof.

They were still talking noisily when the porters brought in the first of the bodies from Frau Drecht's house and laid it, covered by a linen sheet, on the slab. It had been washed and dried, and was ready for the knife.

But the noise quietened completely as the Professor of Anatomy, Professor Karolus, walked into the room, with Markus following a few steps behind him. They knew better than to speak then.

Professor Karolus was a brilliant man, slightly built and with dark eyes; it was often said of him that he had a dark heart as well, and brilliance and darkness make for a dangerous combination. He was not a man who welcomed interference by others in his affairs. Things had a way of not ending well for those who didn't understand that, and in consequence he was feared just as much as he was respected. He was widely travelled – in the New World as well as the Old. As a younger man he'd been almost burned to death in a fire on board a ship at sea. One side of his face still bore the scars of it to this day. And he was a hater of the Church. To Karolus, religion was a superstition that the discoveries of science would one day eradicate.

'Good morning, gentlemen,' he said coldly, and there was a mutter of respectful acknowledgement.

What happened next was always the same. Markus would take Professor Karolus's coat, with its black coral buttons, and help him into his leather apron. Then Karolus would address the theatre – but whatever the subject of that day's instruction, he would always ask them first the same question, one to which there was simply no answer.

'Where does life go, gentlemen?' he would say. 'When we have breathed our last, where does it go?'

It was more than just a habit, or a reminder to his

students of their own mortality and ignorance. That question was a statement of intent, Markus knew it. He'd heard Karolus whisper it under his breath a thousand times, over every cold corpse, over every body newly cut down from the hangman's rope for dissection.

'Where does life go?'

It was the thing that Karolus most wanted to know – a truth of so very dark a lustre. And it was this more than anything else – that science might one day provide an answer – that had drawn curious, clever Markus Brennen to Karolus in the first place. Drawn him like a moth to a candle.

As Karolus was speaking to the students, Markus would draw back the linen sheet and, with a scalpel sharper than the sharpest razor, open the body in one long cut from throat to navel. It was known as 'the assistant's incision'.

And so it was on this day.

While Professor Karolus talked, Markus drew back the sheet to reveal the body he'd brought from the little room at the top of the stairs in Frau Drecht's house. It was grey and colourless now, like turned meat. Laying his hand on its chest, he pushed in the blade and drew the sharp scalpel through the cold flesh in one neat, well-practised cut, then stood back.

Karolus finished what he was saying and moved forward to take up his own instruments. As he did so, Markus saw him glance at the face of the dead man. It was only a cursory look, but something must have caught Karolus's eye because having passed on, he suddenly stopped and turned back to look at the face again, only this time with real attention. He lifted the arm, and looked at the thin winding tattoo that ran from wrist to elbow. Letting it drop, he pushed his fingers into the man's mouth and hooked it open.

'The teeth had already been sold,' said Markus.

It wasn't unusual for that to happen, but Karolus preferred a corpse to be complete, and Markus always thought that there was perhaps the unspoken assumption that it was he who'd sold them. After all, an assistant's salary wasn't that much.

But Professor Karolus didn't answer. After what seemed to Markus to be a moment's hesitation, he wiped his fingers clean on the linen sheet and, picking up his instruments, cut through the bone of the ribs and opened the corpse to its heart.

'Observe, gentlemen . . .' he said, and the lecture had begun.

But it was a strange start.

It was Markus's place to make careful notes as Karolus worked. But watching him this time, Markus couldn't help but see some distraction in Karolus, as though his thoughts were elsewhere. More than once he caught him glancing at the dead man's face, and suddenly he had a realization – it was no more than intuition, but the more he thought it, the more certain he was.

It was a very simple thing, and by the time Karolus had finished, Markus was almost sure he was right.

Whoever the dead man on the table might have been, somehow or other, Professor Karolus knew him.

Chapter Seven

By the time Karolus was done with the dissection, his arms were blood-red to the elbows. He soaped and rinsed them clean in a bucket while the students filed out.

As he flicked the last drops of water from his fingers, he turned to Markus. 'Do you believe that the essence of a man's life lingers after his death?' he asked.

'You know I do, Herr Professor,' answered Markus. 'How else do hair and nails continue to grow on a corpse?'

Karolus nodded. 'Quite so, Markus,' he said. 'But can it be preserved? Have you ever asked yourself that?'

Markus frowned. 'Yes,' he said.

The professor looked down at the blood-stained water in the bucket. 'I wonder if you recall where the body we used this morning came from?' he said.

He didn't look at Markus as he asked the question, and it might have been a thing of no importance. Only Markus realized by that very pretence of indifference, that in some way, it was, and he was really curious now.

If Karolus had recognized the man, why hadn't he said anything? There'd been at least one past occasion when he had – it had been a street vendor, and while Karolus, like some clinical butcher, had reduced that man's body to muscle and bone, he'd remarked almost conversationally to Markus that he'd often seen him on the corner of Marienplatz with his little tray of ribbons and wooden dolls.

But not this time. Karolus had said nothing, and that was strange. It was more than strange.

'Frau Drecht's house, on Bergenstrasse, Herr Professor,' said Markus.

He held out a clean linen towel, and Karolus took it and dried his hands. But there was clearly still something on his mind, because he hesitated as he did so.

'Herr Professor?' said Markus.

Karolus looked thoughtfully up at him. 'You have duties today?' he asked.

'A class to take this afternoon, Herr Professor.'

'Nothing until then?'

'No, Herr Professor.'

'Then there is something I would like you to do for me.' Karolus smiled smally as he said it, as a man does when asking a favour of a person he knows hasn't the power to refuse it. 'I would like to know who removed the teeth. His name. His address.'

Markus couldn't help the puzzlement showing on his face. 'Of course, Herr Professor,' he said.

But if he'd thought that Karolus might say more, might explain why it was he wanted to know, then he was disappointed.

'Good,' was all Karolus said, and he picked up his coat with its black coral buttons from the table beside the door. 'I shall be in my rooms this after-noon,' he said. 'When you have finished your class, come to me with what you have found.'

And that was all.

Markus carefully arranged the notes he'd taken, and the porters began clearing the table of the mess – all that was left of the body from Frau Drecht's house. He stood for a while watching them as he gathered his thoughts. If he went straight away to Bergenstrasse, did it now, there'd be time to get there and back before his class, and it shouldn't be a difficult thing to do – to find out who'd pulled the teeth.

And besides, Markus was curious.

It was a cold, clear day. The two huge, gilded spires of the Marienkirche shone in the winter sun as Markus made his way across the town bridge. They were the highest points of the town. From their two golden crosses could be seen the tiled and leaded roofs below, the streets and the squares, the winding river and, out beyond them – beyond the fields and the far distant farms – the low silver line of the coast with the sails of ships, like little toys on an ocean.

Markus crossed the bridge, past the wharves where the moored ships were lifting on the rising tide, and on towards the rat's nest of alleys and yards that led to Bergenstrasse.

When he arrived at Frau Drecht's house, it took a while for the door to be opened. He could hear the tugging of the bolts and the scratching of the latch but the door didn't move. He imagined the thin-faced girl he'd seen the day before struggling on the other side of it, but when it finally did open, it wasn't that girl at all. It was another one altogether, smaller and even paler than the last. She didn't seem to know what she was supposed to do next. She looked at him uncertainly, and then glanced fearfully back into the gloom of the house. He heard Frau Drecht's loud voice from the parlour, demanding to know who it was. The girl turned and looked at him again, almost pleadingly this time. Trying not to breathe the verminous, damp smell of the place, Markus stepped past her and, tapping lightly on what he knew from yesterday to be Frau Drecht's parlour door, pushed it open.

Frau Drecht hadn't been expecting a visitor. The ringleted wig she usually wore lay in front of her on the table like a small dead animal. Her scalp was pale and white, covered with a thin furze of iron-grey hair. She had a small book of accounts before her. She looked up as the door opened and saw Markus.

'Good morning, sir,' she said, but there was nothing welcoming about it.

'I trust I am not disturbing you?' he said awkwardly. He was trying not to stare at the wig or her bald head, but it was difficult not to look at one or the other.

She paused just long enough for him to understand that, yes, he was disturbing her. 'Household accounts, sir,' she said. 'Always needing to be done.'

She closed the book with a snap. 'How might I be helping you today, sir?' she said.

Markus told her.

As she listened to him, her face hardened. She sat back and looked at him with what was an unmistakably hostile curiosity. 'Now, why would you be wanting to know that, sir?' she asked.

Markus wasn't used to being questioned by people like Frau Drecht. He was more used to having them do what he told them, so he said, 'I'm not sure that is any business of yours, is it?'

He saw the pinched corners of her mouth tighten, and realized at once that he'd made a mistake – that if he was going to find out anything from her, he would have to be a lot more civil than that.

'Forgive me, gnädige Frau,' he said politely. 'I meant no offence. Professor Karolus has asked me to find that out for him – it may be that he wants the teeth for some medical reason. I really don't know.'

It was the best he could think of, and though he didn't really believe it himself, it had – if not the ring of truth about it, then at least one of possibility. And he thought that the name of Professor Karolus might just sound important enough to impress Frau Drecht.

She looked at him suspiciously. Did he know what had been in them? She meant to have that diamond back, and she wasn't going to have anyone get in her way. But then, she didn't want to go offending the Anatomy School either – there was cheap money to be had out of them.

'Well, if that is your reason, sir,' she said, 'you're not going to have much joy of it – I can tell you that for nothing.'

'Why not?' asked Markus.

'Because he's dead, sir. Last night. His shop boy smashed his head in and ran off.' She shook her head sadly. 'You can't trust anyone these days, sir. Poor Kusselmann.'

'Dead?' said Markus.

'Yes, sir. And burned to a cinder too. Set light to the shop, the boy did. You can go and see for yourself if you want. Anyone can tell you where it is. So if your professor is just wanting the teeth, I'm afraid

91

he's going to be disappointed, 'cos he's not going to get them neither.'

It was clearly all she meant to say on the matter. She opened the book of accounts again, and looked pointedly down as though casting the figures. 'Now, if that was all you were wanting of me, sir . . . ?' she said without looking up.

Markus had been wondering whether to ask if she'd known who the dead man was, or known anything about him, but now there was quite a different question on his lips, though he suddenly thought better of asking it. Instead, he said, 'Yes, that is all. Thank you, gnädige Frau.'

She glanced up. 'Always a pleasure to help the Anatomy School, sir,' she answered. 'Don't mind, though, will you, if I ask the girl to show you out?'

'No. Not at all,' said Markus.

Frau Drecht bent her head over her book again, and Markus closed the parlour door behind him. He stood for a moment in the damp dark of the passage, but the girl was nowhere to be seen. Only it wasn't the girl that he was thinking about.

What exactly was it that Frau Drecht had just said? 'He's not going to get them *neither.*' She was talking about the teeth – about somebody else having asked about them too. She hadn't meant to let that slip, he was sure of it. But who else could possibly want the man's teeth?

Then, maybe because he was standing just where they'd collided the day before, he suddenly thought of the priest, and as he did so, it occurred to him that perhaps it was what that conversation had been about as well.

Now he was more curious than ever.

He looked up at the staircase and then back at Frau Drecht's closed door. He was wondering whether there might not be some explanation of it all in the man's room.

He looked at her door again.

It would only take him a moment.

As he began quickly and quietly to climb the stairs, he suddenly saw the girl. She was watching him through the banisters of the landing. He put his finger to his lips and, taking a small coin out of his pocket, put it into her hand as he slipped past onto the darker, narrower stairs that led up to the very top of the house. At each of the landings he could hear people moving behind the closed doors of their rooms, but no one came out or saw him.

When he reached the topmost landing, he stood

93

for a moment outside the dead man's door, then turned the handle and pushed it open.

The room was just as he'd seen it the day before. Nothing had been moved. The man's clothes were still lying on the floor and the rumpled, greasy sheets were still on the bed. The room smelled stale and cold. There really wasn't anything to see – no cupboards, no drawers. He poked at the clothes with his foot. Nothing would have possessed him to pick them up. He stood looking at the bare room. If Frau Drecht found him now, it would be hard to explain just what it was he thought he was doing at the top of her house if all he'd wanted was the name of the tooth-puller.

He stepped back onto the narrow landing, and quietly pulled the door closed. But as he did so, the door behind him on the other side of the landing opened, just a crack. He turned round at the sound of it. An untidy old woman was staring at him through the gap.

'I was just . . .' His voice trailed guiltily away as he tried to think of some believable excuse, but she didn't wait to listen.

'Have you come for the letter?' she said in a quick whisper.

He was still too startled at having been caught coming out of the room to follow what she'd said. 'I – I'm sorry?' he said. 'I was—'

'The letter,' she said again, and this time he heard her.

'What letter?'

She was peering at him, wild-eyed. A long wisp of grey hair trailed into her mouth, and she spat it out. 'The letter,' she hissed, nodding as she did so. 'Are you the one come for the letter? He give it me when he got ill. He said, *Give it the man who comes for the letter.* I got it now. You wait.'

Before he could say anything, she'd closed the door – at least she'd pushed it shut behind her but it didn't quite latch. It swung slowly open again, and Markus could see into the filthy little room as she went quickly about trying to find whatever it was she was looking for. A wicker cage hung from a hook in the low ceiling, and an ill-looking songbird stood miserably on the hardened hill of its own mess and dropped feathers. A blackened pan was boiling on a small stove.

'Here!' she said. She turned round clutching something to her chest, like a secret, and came back to the door, the loose wisps of hair trailing around her face. In one quick movement she put whatever it was into Markus's hand. '*Give it the man when he comes,* he told me. *Give it the priest.*'

Markus looked down. It was a folded letter, more like a packet. 'But I'm not a priest,' he protested.

He tried to hand it back to her, only she wouldn't take it. It was as though she hadn't even heard him. She stood, looking eagerly up into his face, nodding her head. '*Give it the man,*' she said, and she shut the door. This time it stayed shut.

Markus stood for a moment in the gloom of the landing, holding the letter. Then he knocked on the door. And knocked again. But it didn't open.

He went down a few stairs and turned the packet towards the dim light from below. There was something written on the paper, but he couldn't make it out. He took another few steps down, and then he could read it. Just one word – a name.

Henriquez.

He looked back up at the closed door, but there was nothing he could do. Frau Drecht might come out at any moment. He slipped the packet into his coat pocket and quietly made his way back down the stairs.

As he came to the last flight, he went more

carefully still. The girl had gone, but the front door was open now. He could see the spill of light across the hall. He stood in the shadows of the landing and looked down over the banister. He saw the top of Frau Drecht's head. She was leading a scrawny boy out of her room, holding him tightly by his shock of thick red hair. He could hear what she was saying:

'. . . and you find where she's gone, or I'll do for you, Spitzel. You understand?' She twisted her fingers and yanked the boy's hair sharply. 'Yes?'

'Yes!'

'And you tell me.'

'Yes!'

She pulled him towards the open door and pushed him out through it. Then she slammed it shut. Markus leaned back into the darker shadow and watched her as she crossed the hall and went into her parlour. He heard the door close.

He came quietly down the last of the stairs and, opening the front door, let himself out into the street. Then he pulled the door shut behind him.

In her parlour, Frau Drecht looked up as though she'd heard a noise. She walked over to the door, opened it and peered out into the hallway, but everything was dark and empty. She stood for a moment listening to the sounds of the house, then she shrugged and, closing the door again, went back to her table.

Markus walked quickly away. It wasn't until he'd rounded the corner of Bergenstrasse and was out of sight of the house that he stopped. He looked back along the street to make certain that no one had seen him leave, then he took the packet from his pocket and looked at it again.

It was no thicker than a letter, and it wasn't sealed, just folded shut.

He wondered what was in it.

Then his curiosity got the better of him. There couldn't be any harm in just looking.

He untucked the end and shook the packet open. A paper ticket fell out, creased and greasy, as though much-thumbed. He smoothed it flat. It was a pawn-broker's ticket. It didn't say what had been pawned – they never did – but the amount of money the man had got was written next to the ticket number. It hadn't been that much either – pawnbrokers drove a hard bargain, and this was barely enough for a week's food; yet small as the amount was, the man had never redeemed the ticket. Markus thought of the stale cold room in Frau Drecht's house – and realized that he had probably been too poor to ever go back.

So what was it that he'd pawned – a cheap ring, the tools of his trade?

But there was something else in the packet as well. He shook it again, and this time a single long, iridescent blue feather, like a flight quill from a bird's wing, dropped into his hand.

He stood looking at the feather and the grubby ticket. They were hardly things worth leaving for the priest. Certainly nothing that made anything any clearer.

Or maybe the man had been so ill by the end, so gone in the head, that he'd thought they were something else – something of importance. The old woman wouldn't have known any different. She'd have just done as she was asked and given the packet to the priest, come what may.

Except Markus wasn't the priest.

But the priest had come, and that was curious too, because it wasn't the packet he'd been asking about. It was the man's teeth.

Which brought him to the tooth-puller again.

He put the ticket and the feather back into the packet and stuffed it into his pocket.

He'd taken as true what Frau Drecht had told him – that the tooth-puller was dead – but if he wasn't, maybe there'd be some explanation to be got from him.

He tried to remember what she'd said the man's name was.

Kabelmann? No. Not Kabelmann.

Kusselmann.

He shouldn't be so hard to find.

Chapter Eight

Liesel was chilled to the bone and shivering in the damp air. In the grey half-light of morning she walked numbly between Father Henriquez and the broad-chested man. His name was Ramos. At least that's what she thought it was. Henriquez had called him something like that more than once, but when they spoke together it was in another language and she didn't understand a word of it. All night they'd been looking through the dirty warren of streets and alleys for the tooth-puller's boy.

Ramos had never walked far from her. Sometimes he put his hand on her arm as a reminder that he was there, and she didn't like that. When he was that close, she could smell the sweat and tobacco on his clothes and skin, and remembered his hand across her mouth. He frightened her even more than Henriquez did – Henriquez had hurt her, but Ramos had nearly killed her, and he was so strong. If she'd thought she might be able to run away from Henriquez – duck down some dark alley – she knew there was no running from Ramos. He'd have caught her before she'd gone a dozen steps. At some point in the cold dark hours of the night he'd pulled a handful of dried leaves out of his pocket. He'd put some of them in his own mouth, then made her chew and swallow the rest. The taste of sweat and tobacco had been on them too, and the leaves had been so bitter, she'd almost gagged on them. They'd left her tongue feeling fat and numb in her mouth, but they'd had a strange effect. For a while after she swallowed them she hadn't felt tired or cold at all. Then that had worn off and the tiredness and the coldness had come back, only worse because she felt sick now, and the bitterness of the dried leaves was like bile in her mouth.

The black monkey rode on Ramos's shoulder. Even when she couldn't see it, she knew it was there in the dark because she could smell its fur – rank and unclean, like a filthy tomcat. It scared her too, with its dirty yellow teeth, and golden eyes that were full of malice. It was like something that had crept from a grave. It had leaped down from Ramos's shoulder only once in the night, disappearing out of sight after something it had heard in the dark. There'd been a scuffling in the gutter, and it had come back with a live rat struggling in its fist. It had killed it and eaten it – licking its fingers like it had done when it had dipped them in Kusselmann's blood. Liesel tried not to look at it, but it was always there.

Every bundle of sleeping rags they'd passed in those passages and alleyways Ramos had stirred awake with his foot, and Father Henriquez had bent forward and held the lantern to the sleep-grimed face for Liesel to look at it. She'd been one of these children once. These were the very streets she'd lived on before her brother had died, before Frau Drecht had taken her in. Some of the faces she'd even recognized. But none of them had been the tooth-puller's boy, and she'd wondered each time what she would do if it was – pretend not to know him? But how was that going to help her?

And now it was morning.

She was cold and tired and walking along with her

eyes half shut. The one thing she couldn't have expected at all was that, instead of her finding the tooth-puller's boy, the tooth-puller's boy would find her.

Klaus had washed Kusselmann's blood from his hands and, as far as he could, from his shirt too, in the ice-cold water of the river where it lapped against the steps below the town bridge. Then he'd spent the night shivering and wet on a ledge beneath the bridge itself, high above that dangerous churning water, listening to the roar as it shot between the stone arches in the darkness below him. He'd been safe here – it was a place he knew well. There were better places to sleep during the hard, cold nights of winter, but no one would think to look for him here. There'd been maybe half a dozen other children sleeping on the ledges, but he'd kept clear of them. He'd found a place of his own and, drawing his knees up to his chin, set himself to wait for the morning to come.

In the dark night, Klaus had had plenty of time to think. He'd tried to pretend that everything would be just like it was before Kusselmann had found him – only he knew it could never be like that again, because Frau Drecht had beaten Kusselmann's head in, and the diamond she'd killed him for was in Klaus's pocket. If anyone found him with it, they'd think he'd stolen it. And if they thought he'd stolen it, it was only one little step to them thinking he'd killed Kusselmann too. Who'd listen to him?

And then they'd hang him. It wouldn't matter that he was just a boy.

He'd put his hand into his pocket and drawn the diamond out. It had been like a darker shadow in his palm. For a moment he'd thought that the only thing to do was throw it away; throw it as far out into the river as he could. He'd even stood up and drawn back his arm to do it, but that was as far as he'd got.

Because it was a diamond.

It might be the only fortune he'd ever have. It could buy him a thick coat, and food – as much food as he could eat. How could he just throw it away? That would be madness.

He'd looked at it again. It caught the moonlight, and gleamed wickedly – the edges green like the leaves of a forest.

How could he throw it away?

In his mind's eye he saw the floor of Kusselmann's shop covered in glass and teeth, and wet with blood

– a hangman's rope like a serpent winding its way across it towards him – but it was a fortune that he held in his hand, and his fingers had closed around the diamond and he'd put it back in his pocket.

He'd sat cold and alone in the darkness, listening to the sound of the water churning through the arches of the bridge, only the longer he'd listened to it, the less it had seemed like the sound of water; it was more like the sound of a wind coming through trees – until finally there was no bridge and no river, only bright daylight all around him, and a thick canopy of branches overhead, lush and green, with sunlight streaming in ribbons through it. The air was hot and humid. He could feel sweat trickling down his face; his shirt was damp and sticking to his skin. There were birds screeching and calling, though he couldn't see them – they were in the trees high above him – and in his hand he was holding the diamond. He knew it was the diamond even though he couldn't remember taking it out of his pocket. It was half hidden in a rolled ball of something soft and sticky like mud. As he'd rubbed the mud away with his thumb and uncovered it, the diamond had flashed so brilliantly in the sunlight that it had left a burn mark in his eyes that he could still see even when he blinked and looked away. It was like the shape of a kneeling man, and it was hard to tell whether it was just a mark in his eyes or a real man – he could see it so clearly. If it was a man, he was covered with feathers, but not like a bird – the quills had been pushed like needles into his skin – and his hands were folded over each other and fixed to the ground by a single silver spike driven through the back of them. There was a staleness in the air too. He could taste it on his tongue like old meat. It clung to the feathers and to the man's skin.

It was like the smell of the slaughterhouses by the river. Like the wet smell of the floor beneath Kusselmann's head.

Klaus opened his eyes with a start.

For a moment he didn't know where he was and he stared dumbly about him. The sky was just colouring with the half-light of dawn and a mist lay across the river. There were beads of dew like tiny pearls on the sleeve of his jacket. Everything was still. He could hear the soft stirrings of the pigeons roosting in the stonework above him, and the roar of the river below. Then a single feather from the roosting birds drifted past him, turning slowly in the air until it settled like a little boat on the eddies of water.

And then he remembered the forest and the feathered man, like a picture opening in his head.

He rubbed his hands over his face. It had all been so vivid, so real. He almost imagined that he could still see the outline of the man when he blinked.

Then he realized that he *could* – like a bright burn left by sunlight.

He screwed his eyes shut and opened them again, but it was still there. He could see the outline of the man's back, all ruffled with feathers.

He blinked again.

He must have hurt his eye when Frau Drecht shoved his head into the bucket, scratched it maybe, and the dream had turned it into something else, mixed it all up – at least that was what he told himself.

Only it didn't feel like that. It didn't feel like a dream at all.

Still blinking, Klaus looked uneasily about him. In places he could still see the trees, faint and indistinct against the stones of the bridge – as though he were seeing stones and trees at the same time, the one through a tear in the other.

He turned himself round and began to scramble down from the ledge, barking his shins as he lowered himself over; but as he did so, he stopped and looked at the stonework again – at the wide cracks and joints – and an idea came to him.

He didn't have to throw the diamond away at all. He could leave it here, hide it in one of the cracks under the bridge. It would be safe there, and no one would find it.

Balancing himself, he reached into his pocket and pulled out the diamond. It sparkled in the morning light. Carefully making sure he could remember which crack it was, he slipped it between the stones, then scrambled down, still blinking at the little burn of light that felt like a shard of glass in his eye.

It was still early. Klaus made his way up through the narrow streets, away from the river. He was hungry. His stomach grumbled and ached. The early service was being rung from church towers in different parts of the town. The sound of the bells carried on the cold, damp air. On the street corners, stalls were being made ready for the day, and in the houses shutters were flung open and night pots tipped into the gutters beneath.

But for all the starting of the business of the day, that dream wouldn't go away. Every time he blinked,

Klaus could see the shape of a feathered man in the corner of his eye; see the faint, indistinct ghosts of trees in the dark mouths of the alleyways and passages as he passed.

And there was something else too.

The cold dawning on him that Frau Drecht hadn't meant to leave that diamond in Kusselmann's shop. How could she have?

And she'd know who'd taken it. Who else would have gone back to Kusselmann's shop but him?

He began listening for the sound of her little buttoned boots; began looking for her powdered face round every corner. Maybe that's why he saw Liesel before she saw him – because he was looking so hard.

She was on the other side of a street. He watched her for a moment, not sure it was her, but then she turned her face and he saw that it was. He had to tell someone about Kusselmann, and she'd helped him once already. When he was sure that Frau Drecht wasn't anywhere to be seen, he crossed the street. Liesel was walking with her eyes half shut. She'd lagged a dozen steps or so behind Father Henriquez, far enough for Klaus not to realize that they were together. Ramos was even further away, his attention all on a boy sitting by the gutter, head resting on his folded arms.

Liesel didn't hear Klaus when he spoke to her; she was too tired. He had to reach out and catch hold of her arm before she even realized he was there. But as she turned round and saw who it was, every last bit of sleep fell away from her and her eyes widened. She looked quickly round at Father Henriquez: he still had his back to her. 'Go away!' she hissed, trying to pull her sleeve out of Klaus's hand – but he didn't let go.

'I just wanted to thank you,' he said.

She pushed him away, jerking her sleeve free. 'Get out of it!'

Only this time Father Henriquez saw the movement out of the corner of his eye. He turned round, and the expression on Liesel's face told him at once who this boy was.

'Run!' she screamed.

But Klaus just stood looking confusedly at her. She pushed him again as hard as she could. He lost his footing on the wet cobbles, and that was what saved him, because it was at that moment that Father Henriquez tried to grab hold of his collar. Klaus slipped and fell, the cloth ripped in the priest's hand, and this time Klaus didn't need any more telling. Scrambling to his feet, he took to his heels as fast as he could.

'The boy!' shouted Henriquez.

Ramos spun round. The priest was pointing after Klaus – who was already hurdling a stack of baskets, going hell for leather into the dark of the nearest alley. Liesel took her chance: she picked up her skirts and ran for all she was worth after him.

Henriquez was shouting something at Ramos, holding out the piece of Klaus's torn collar. Ramos snatched the cloth and, with the monkey clinging to his back, its arms tight around his neck, leaped over the baskets and plunged down the dark alley after them.

Liesel ran blindly between the narrow walls towards the river. At their end was a deep slipway and a thin plank, the water black and thick beneath it. Klaus took the plank at a run, the wood springing and bouncing under his weight. Liesel followed, and it twisted beneath her. Even as she leaped the last few steps onto the splintered wood of the wharf, it dropped with a splash into the dirty water below. She turned and looked back. Ramos hadn't reached it before it fell. He teetered on the edge of the slipway, but she knew it would take him only moments to find another way round. She didn't stop. She could see that Klaus was still running.

From nowhere, a huge dog on a chain leaped out at him. It took him completely off balance. He sprawled heavily face first onto the splintered planks of the wharf, the dog barking and snapping at him, its chain rattling on the wood. Liesel was only a dozen steps behind. She kicked the dog as hard as she could and grabbed hold of Klaus's coat to pull him up, but there was blood everywhere. His face was thick with it. A splinter from the wharf, wide as her hand, sharp as a knife, had sliced right through his nose: it was hanging by a thread of skin. She looked around desperately. Between the poles of a wooden jetty she could see Ramos trying to find a way onto their side of the wharf. The dog was still barking and pulling at its chain. She kicked at it again and dragged Klaus to his feet. The wharf in front of them was spread with fish ready for gutting. At a dead run, they scrabbled and slipped across it. The gutting women in their leather aprons shouted and swore at them. One of them grabbed Liesel by her hair and swung her round, but Liesel kicked her as well, and with a howl of pain the woman let go. Liesel heard the blade of the woman's gutting knife whip past her face, but she didn't stop. Still holding onto Klaus's coat, she pulled him after her, across the rows of fish, and then there was hard stone beneath their feet. Klaus was trying to run and hold his face at the same time, but he could barely breathe.

Ahead of them were the big warehouses of the wharf; some had their doors open. It was the only place Liesel could see to hide. She dragged Klaus into the nearest one, pulled him down into the shadows, and looked at his face. 'Oh my saints!' she breathed.

She tipped his head back and, tearing a strip from the hem of her skirt, she put it to his face and held it there, but she could feel his nose move under her fingers as she touched it. She looked around in the darkness. She could dimly make out rows of stacked sacks and wood. The air smelled of sugar and tar.

Pulling Klaus with her, she began to creep into the deeper dark, away from the light of the door. They could hear the men working in the warehouse, and then something else – footsteps running past the doors outside – and as she looked down at the floor, Liesel realized that Klaus's blood must have left a trail along the wharf behind them.

They heard the footsteps stop and come back.

Liesel put her finger to her lips. Some of the nearby sacks had been pulled out, and there was a gap through to the other side of the row. Without a sound they wormed their way through to where it was darker still. Then she leaned slowly forward and peered down the row. She could see the doorway. Ramos was standing against the half-light, listening. As she watched him, he swung the monkey down from his shoulders and let it drop to the ground. It skittered away into the darkness.

She leaned back and held her breath.

They could hear the sound of the workmen close by now, but they couldn't see them. Leading Klaus by the sleeve, Liesel edged along the row of sacks and into the dark, then stopped and listened again. The voices were suddenly closer, and as they crouched down, one of the sacks above them was pulled away, and in the light of a lantern Liesel saw the face of a man. He saw her too. She tried to sign to him not to say anything, not to give them away, but there were rats and thieves enough in that warehouse already and he wasn't going to have two more.

'Get out of there!' he roared, and swung at them

115

with the end of the hook and chain he'd pulled at the sack with.

They ducked away into the narrow passage, running along a line of high stacked timber, but they could hear Ramos's voice calling to the men. They'd almost reached the back of the warehouse; there was nowhere else to hide.

And then Klaus saw a door – at least saw the crack of light around its edge and realized what it was. It was low down in the back wall only a dozen yards from them. He pulled at Liesel's coat, pointing at the light, and as he did so, the monkey – teeth bared and eyes like lamps – dropped out of the darkness above them onto the piled sacks by Liesel's face.

She couldn't help herself. She screamed.

The monkey shrieked and leaped around them. There was the sound of running, but the door was only yards away now. In one tumble they reached it and pulled at the latch. It swung open, spilling them out into the grey daylight, but even that was bright after the dark. They didn't look back. In the few moments it took Ramos to find the place, they were gone, and there was nothing for him to see but an empty alleyway and an empty yard beyond it.

Ramos stood calmly looking out into the yard,

and then he looked down at the ground at his feet.

In the dirt and mud were dark spots of blood.

Like a little clockwork toy, the monkey sprang out from the doorway behind Ramos and onto his shoulder.

Ramos crouched down and, winding Klaus's torn collar around his finger, dipped it into the blood, then rubbed it onto the monkey's gums. It tried to pull its head away, but as it tasted the salt of the blood, its eyes widened; it grasped Ramos's finger with its black leathery hands and began greedily licking at the cloth.

Then he swung it down onto the ground, the cloth still clutched tightly in its fist. When it had licked it clean, it began casting about for more. It found another spot of blood, then another. Ramos let it go, and followed it as, spot by spot, it made its way along the alleyway and out across the empty yard.

Chapter Nine

Klaus was trying to run. He was holding the torn strip of Liesel's skirt to his face, but blood filled his mouth and throat. He could hardly breathe. Liesel was pulling him along by the arm, but he just couldn't do it any more. He shook himself free and folded over, spitting and gasping for breath.

'Come on!' Liesel pleaded. She tried to pull him again, but he wouldn't move. She could feel the clammy damp of sweat on her skin. She didn't know what to do.

She glanced back down the empty street. There was no sign of Ramos or the priest but they might be coming at any moment – they might be just round the corner. She looked at Klaus again. His face was grey and there was a thick, dark ribbon of blood hanging from his chin. She could leave him, she knew it; all she had to do was run and she'd be safe. But what about him?

She bit at her lip, looking around desperately.

There was a pile of hay against a wall. They could hide in that, she thought, but then she saw the flight of steps above it. It led up to the open door of a hayloft from where the hay had fallen. That was a much better place.

'Come on!' Liesel said. 'Just to there!' She took hold of Klaus again. He tried to push her away, but this time she wasn't going to let go. She dug her fingers into his sleeve and dragged him towards the flight of steps.

The loft was dark and narrow, and sweet with the smell of hay and horses. Klaus crawled into the deep hay. Liesel followed and, kneeling down, looked at his face.

Just like her brother's. Even the colour of his hair.

She tore another strip from the hem of her skirt and folded it into a square. Then, very carefully, she peeled away the sodden rag and laid the clean piece in its place. She lifted his hand and pressed it down over the dry cloth. 'Hold it like that,' she said.

119

There was nothing else Liesel could do. There wasn't even any water to wash him with. She wiped her hands clean on the hay, then on her skirt. Her heart was thumping in her chest. She crept back to the door of the hayloft and peered down into the street below. There were people about now – a woman was sweeping her step and some men stacking planks of wood on a cart. But there was no sign of Ramos or the priest. They'd lost them.

She glanced at Klaus. 'They think you've got it,' she whispered. 'That diamond the puller took. That's what it's all about. That's what they want.'

He didn't answer. Huddled against the wall, he sat with his eyes shut and his knees drawn up to his chin. His face was a mess.

Liesel looked back down into the street. It was a moment before she realized that Klaus hadn't said anything, even though he must have heard. She turned and stared at him. He'd opened his eyes just a crack, but as she looked at him he closed them again.

And the truth of it dawned on her. 'You have, haven't you?' she breathed. 'You've got it.' She scrambled back through the hay until she was next to him. 'You've got to give it back,' she whispered, 'or they're going to skin you.'

Then something else dawned on her. Something just as bad.

Frau Drecht would think that she'd taken it. Would think that's why she hadn't come back, that she'd run away. There'd be no telling her any different because Frau Drecht wouldn't believe a word of it. Liesel felt for the burn marks on her arm. They'd be nothing compared to what she'd get this time. Frau Drecht would beat her brains out if she got hold of her and she didn't have that diamond.

Just like she'd done to Kusselmann.

Liesel felt her mouth go dry. 'You've got to give it to me,' she said. She held out her hand. 'I've got to give it to Frau Drecht. Let them get it off her.'

'I haven't got it,' Klaus mumbled.

She didn't believe him. 'You can't keep it,' she hissed.

'I haven't got it!' he snapped.

Liesel leaned forward. 'You know what happened to Kusselmann – you saw him, didn't you? Well, that's what you and me are going to get if you don't give it back.'

Fear lent a hard edge to her voice, and though

Klaus tried to stare her down, he knew she was right and it scared him. He could still hear the sound of the scattered teeth and broken glass crunching under his boots. Could see Kusselmann on the floor behind the counter. You just don't get to keep a diamond that isn't yours. That was the mistake Kusselmann had made, and it had got him killed. It's what Klaus had known right from the start as he followed Kusselmann back from Frau Drecht's house – you don't need to hide something unless someone else is looking for it. Only they knew who had it now – and maybe Frau Drecht did as well.

He took a breath. He could taste the salt of the blood in his mouth. 'I hid it under the bridge,' he said.

Liesel put her hands to her head in desperation.

'I didn't know what else to do,' he protested. 'It was just on the floor of the shop. I didn't mean to take it.'

'Then we've got to go and get it,' she said.

Klaus closed his eyes and let his head fall back against the wooden post behind him. His face was ashen. There was no moving him, she could see that. Maybe if he had some water and a rest he'd be able to do it then?

There was another door from the loft. It looked out onto the stable yard on the other side. Liesel scrambled through the hay and peered down. There was a pump and a trough in the middle of the yard.

She came back and knelt beside Klaus. 'Look, I'll help you,' she said. 'I had a brother once – he was like you, and he was everything to me – but I didn't help him when I should have done, and I know what that's like, see? We've got to help each other, or we're done for. I'm going to get you some water, clean you up. There's a pump down there.'

Liesel looked about her. There was nothing even vaguely like a cup or a bowl to carry it in. She'd just have to find something on her way.

'You stay here,' she said, putting her hand on his shoulder. 'And when I get back, we'll sort what we've got to do. All right?'

Before he could say anything, she'd ducked under a low rafter and was gone.

Klaus leaned his head against the wooden post and listened. In the dark he could hear the horses shifting their feet in their stables below, but there weren't any voices, and he realized that the stable lads must be at their breakfast. He closed his eyes and pressed the cloth to his face.

What if the girl was lying? He wanted to believe her, but she was a Bergenstrasse girl, wasn't she? What if she was just trying to get the diamond for herself? What would he do then?

He sat in the dark thinking of a warm coat and hot food – everything that a diamond could buy for him.

And then he had an idea.

Maybe, when they got to the bridge, he could just pretend he couldn't find it . . . She wouldn't know any different. He could say it wasn't there any more.

Only that was the way to end up like Kusselmann, dead on a floor with his face beaten in.

He felt sick. The cut ached right into the bone. He tried to make it hurt less by moving the cloth a little, but that only made it worse, and he could feel his nose move.

Klaus gritted his teeth and opened his eyes.

He could still see that bright little burn mark – sharper and clearer now against the darkness of the loft: the flash of the diamond, like the shape of a feathered man. He could almost believe that the shape was moving. That each time he blinked, the man's face was actually slowly turning towards him.

And then he realized that it was.

The air grew warm and damp about him. There were trees above him, sunlight flooding through their branches, only this time he could feel the dirt of the ground beneath him as well: it was thick with fallen leaves. He closed his fingers around them, and they folded and creased in his hand.

He could *feel* them.

And all the while, blink by blink, the face of the feathered man slowly turned towards him – Klaus could even hear the quills on the neck and back rustling, hear a whispering of voices in the trees above his head.

He couldn't stop it. Slowly, the feathered man was turning to look at him, and there was blood on the ground.

Klaus opened his eyes with a start. His heart was racing.

There was no forest, no trees – only the dim shapes of piled hay, and the rafters of the roof. He could still see the little bright flick of light, but that's all it was – a flick of light as he blinked – and the loft was silent but for the shifting of the horses in the stalls below.

His skin was damp with sweat and his breath was

coming in gasps. He stared into the dark and the shadows.

Where was the girl? How long had she been gone – five minutes? Ten? There was no way of knowing, but it had been long enough for him to fall asleep.

Then Klaus realized that there was something in his hand. It was difficult to see what it was in the darkness. It felt hard and rough.

He lifted his hand to his face and opened his fingers.

They were leaves, all withered and brown. Like in the forest.

He frowned. They must have been in the hay.

He turned his head to look down, and that's when he saw the man – a real man, in a coat and boots – sitting in the shadows of the loft, watching him.

Klaus let out a gasp. He would have scrambled away, but he was already against the wall and there was nowhere for him to go.

The man sat looking steadily at him. 'I wondered when you'd see me,' he said in a low whisper.

'I haven't got anything,' said Klaus quickly. People take things if they think you've got them. They don't tend to trouble you if you haven't. Not unless you're really unlucky.

The man grinned as though Klaus had said some-thing funny, and Klaus didn't like the look of that.

Almost lazily, the man got up and, stooping beneath the low beams, crouched down in front of him. He couldn't have been more than twenty. In the half-light from the loft door Klaus could see his hard face. He was wearing a corporal's coat – weather-stained and muddy; his hair was tied back in a soldier's queue, but the ribbon was all loose and dirty.

'You got a name, boy?' the man said.

Klaus glanced towards the open doorway. The corporal's eyes followed his look, but the girl was nowhere to be seen.

'Klaus,' he said. The word almost dried in his throat.

The corporal nodded. 'Well, Klaus,' he said. 'Let me learn you two things you're going to need to know if you're going to go hiding up in barns.' In the half-dark he held up a finger in front of Klaus's face. 'One,' he said, 'you always make sure they're empty.' He held up another next to it. 'Two, you're right careful what you say in them until you have.'

It took Klaus a moment to understand what he meant.

He meant that he'd been there all the time.

Which meant he must have heard every word they'd said, even about the diamond.

Especially about the diamond.

Klaus felt himself go cold inside. 'It's not a real one,' he blurted out. 'We was just pretending—'

The corporal smiled and shook his head. 'No,' he said. 'It's real enough, isn't it, Klausy boy? Real enough for you to have to go hiding away up here. And you've got it hidden under a bridge, haven't you?'

He reached forward and Klaus flinched away, but the corporal was only reaching for the cloth on Klaus's face. 'It's all right, matey,' he said. 'I just want to see what you've been up to.'

There wasn't anything Klaus could do. He held himself stock still as the corporal peeled back the cloth and drew in a long breath.

'That's handsome,' he said. 'Saw a captain of horse get his nose sliced clean off like that once. But then he was an unpleasant git, and had it coming.'

He put the cloth back, and placed Klaus's hand carefully on it. Then he turned his head towards the door. 'We'll just wait for Maidy to come back with that water, shall we? Then we'll get you cleaned up proper.'

He must have seen the look of doubt on Klaus's face. 'It's all right,' he said. 'I'm not going to hurt you, am I? You're the one knows where that diamond is. And you're not worth a fart if I let your face fall off, are you?'

The man sat back on his heels watching the little door. It looked as though he could have sat like that all day if he'd had to. Only he didn't have to. It wasn't more than a few moments before Klaus heard footsteps on the ladder.

The corporal heard them too. 'That'll be Maidy with the bucket,' he said quietly.

Unlike Klaus's, Liesel's eyes weren't used to the dark any more. She couldn't see where Klaus was. She ducked under the rafters, and cautiously stepped into the shadows. He had to be hiding in there somewhere – that is, if he hadn't run away. When she was in the yard, she'd begun to think that maybe she'd made a mistake leaving him like that – that he wouldn't be there at all when she got back – and without him how on earth was she going to get that diamond back to Frau Drecht? That might be the only way of saving her skin. Saving both their skins.

'Boy?' she whispered. 'Where are you?'

Klaus could see *her* though. She was carrying the drinking bowl from the trough.

The corporal could see her too. 'Call her,' he whispered.

Klaus hesitated. The man put his hand on Klaus's arm. 'Call – her,' he said.

'I'm here,' breathed Klaus in a whisper he almost hoped she wouldn't hear.

'Louder,' said the corporal.

'Here.'

She heard him this time. She came under the rafters, and it was only at the very last moment that she saw the corporal. She stopped dead.

'It's all right, Maidy,' he said in a low, singsong voice.

Liesel looked at Klaus and back at the man. She didn't know who he was but she didn't like what she saw. 'What do you want?' she said.

He held out his hand. 'That little bowl of water – then I can clean him up.'

She hesitated, and looked at Klaus. Klaus nodded.

She handed the bowl over, and the corporal set it down in the hay at his feet. Then he went through his coat pockets until he found what he was looking for – a square of dirty cloth. He dipped it into the bowl and, tipping Klaus's head back, let the water drip onto his face.

Liesel sat watching him as he cleaned the blood away – she could see the torn weather-stained coat and the soldier's ribbon in his hair, but he wasn't a soldier – or if he was, what was he doing here?

And then she guessed. She'd seen people like him before, hiding up in dark places. Then they were gone the next day. 'You're a deserter, aren't you?' she said.

The man didn't look at her. He dipped the cloth in the water again. 'That's a hard word, Maidy, for a fighting man,' he said.

She glanced nervously at Klaus. 'They hang deserters,' she said.

The corporal grinned, but he still didn't look at her. He tipped Klaus's head back again. 'Only if they catch them. But don't you go getting any ideas like that, Maidy, not when I'm cleaning up your friend here, 'cos that wouldn't be what I'd call civil, would it now?' He shot her a hard sideways glance, then rinsed the cloth again. 'And we've all got our reasons for hiding, haven't we, Maidy?'

He cleaned Klaus's face as well as he could, then

131

unwound the neck scarf he wore round his own throat and, passing it over the square of torn skirt, fixed it tightly in place with a knot behind Klaus's head. 'You're going to need that sewn, boy,' he said.

He turned as though to speak to Liesel, only instead of looking at her his gaze seemed to go right past her to the door. 'Now, there's something you never see,' he said.

She thought he was making fun of her, or that it was some trick. Then she realized that he actually *was* looking at something behind her, and she turned round.

On the handrail at the top of the stairs, squatting on its haunches and bobbing its head to peer into the dark of the loft, was a little black-nailed monkey.

Chapter Ten

Liesel let out a cry of panic. Klaus was already scrambling into the darkness.

The monkey heard the movements in the hay. It stood upright on the handrail, bobbing its head this way and that, trying to peer into the gloom. Liesel caught hold of Klaus and pulled him out of the hay. All she could think of doing was running. But the corporal was instantly alive. He grabbed her by the wrist and held her.

'What is it?' he asked.

'They're coming – the man's coming!' she said.

She was desperately trying to pull herself away from him, but he didn't let go. He shot a glance at the door, then back at her. He could hear footsteps now, climbing the wooden flight of stairs. 'In the hay,' he said quickly.

He pushed her away. Whimpering with the fear of it, she ducked down into the dark after Klaus.

There was a pitchfork leaning against one of the beams. The corporal took hold of it and began covering them both with hay. He'd only just finished when Ramos appeared at the top of the stairs. The monkey jumped, soft pawed, onto the floor of the loft and skittered away into the shadows. Ramos stood in the doorway, his hand on the frame, his eyes adjusting to the darkness.

The corporal was singing now, making a large pile of hay with the fork. It looked for all the world as if he was supposed to be there; as if this was what he did. He took no notice of Ramos at all. From where Liesel was hidden she could see the corporal standing in the light that came from the door over the stable yard. But he was between them and Ramos, and that wasn't by accident. She dug herself deeper into the hay and came up against Klaus. He was lying absolutely still. She could hear his breathing. It was so loud.

'Sssh,' she whispered, but he couldn't do anything different. His whole body was already rigid with the effort of being quiet.

The corporal was still singing. Through a gap in the hay Liesel saw him turn round and look at Ramos as though he'd only just realized he was there.

'What can I do for you, matey?' he said, still turning the hay with the fork.

Ramos didn't answer. He was peering past the corporal into the darkness of the loft. Then he looked down at the chaff and dust on the floorboards where the daylight slanted in through the door.

There were dark, wet spots of blood in the dry dust.

The corporal looked at them too. 'That'll be that boy,' he said indifferently. 'Right mess he was.'

Ramos looked up at him.

In the dark Klaus pulled himself deeper down into the hay and held his breath.

'Where?' said Ramos in that shapeless way people say words that aren't their own.

'Oh, you've missed him, matey,' said the corporal, turning the fork into another pile of hay. 'Sent him on his way, face like that! Must have been five or ten minutes since.'

But whatever was said next Klaus didn't hear,

because a soft weight dropped onto the hay just above him. He could feel it moving about like a cat, only he knew at once what it was. He lay absolutely still. Something hard scratched against his face. Instinctively he put his hand to it and felt the nails and leathery skin of the monkey's paw. It was pulling at the corner of the wet rag. It drew its paw back the instant he touched it, and in the dark he could hear it licking the blood off its fingers. He tried to turn his face away, to bury it in the hay, but the monkey only shifted and wormed its fist in again. It was tugging at the rag. Then it bent forward and pressed its face right up against Klaus's and began to lick at the cloth. That was more than Klaus could bear – he could smell its dirty fur and its damp, rank breath on his face. Before he even knew what he was doing he'd dug his fingers into its face and pushed it away. It gave a shriek and leaped backwards. Ramos turned sharply, ducking his head and looking into the dark, and as he did so, he saw the bowl of water and the blood-stained cloth on the floor at the edge of the light.

But that was all he saw, because the corporal hit him.

It was all one movement – Ramos didn't even see

136

it coming. The blunt end of the heavy pitchfork handle caught him like the butt end of a pistol on the side of his head. His world exploded into a cascade of light and he stumbled to his knees. But he was strong. He tried to stand up, turning his head dumbly towards where the blow had come from, and the corporal hit him again. Only this time he measured it first and, with a crack of wood on skull that split the handle of the fork, Ramos dropped face first into the hay and lay still.

Liesel saw it all.

She saw the corporal, his face set, turn the fork round in his hands, ready to drive the spikes straight through Ramos's back. But all of a sudden he stopped and looked sharply at her, then down at the man at his feet. He was breathing hard, and she knew at once what he was thinking – that if he killed him, he'd have to kill her too. Couldn't leave someone who'd seen.

His face broke into a slow grin. 'No need for that now, is there, Maidy?' he said in a low, dangerous whisper. 'Don't want you getting me two ropes, do we?' And he stepped away from Ramos and threw the broken pitchfork down into the hay.

The monkey was shrieking and leaping from

rafter to rafter above them, but the corporal took no notice of it. He pulled Klaus out of the hay.

Klaus was staring at Ramos. 'Is he dead?' he said in an unsteady voice.

The corporal glanced over his shoulder as though it didn't matter to him one way or the other. 'No, he's not dead, boy. But he's probably going to wish he was when he wakes up, so we'd better be moving smartish, hadn't we?'

Liesel looked at him, then at the boy. 'We're not going with you,' she said.

'Well, that's a matter of opinion, Maidy,' he answered. He picked up his hat and brushed it down.

'I'm not called Maidy,' she said angrily. 'I'm called Liesel, and we're not going with you.'

The man put his hand on Klaus's shoulder and looked coldly at her. 'Well, Liesel,' he said quietly, and there was that dangerous whisper in his voice again. 'You can do what you want, but Klaus here is coming with me.'

She hadn't known the boy's name until then.

She went quite pale.

The corporal picked up a handful of dry hay and gave it to Klaus. The torn cloth and scarf that bound up his nose were already sodden with blood. 'Use that,' he said.

Liesel stood watching dumbly. For a moment she didn't know what to do.

If she let Klaus go, she wouldn't have a hope of getting the diamond back. It was under the bridge, she knew that, but she couldn't even begin to know where. And if she hadn't found it before Frau Drecht got hold of her, what happened next wasn't even worth beginning to think about.

But she didn't like the look of the corporal at all – not one bit.

'Where you taking him?' she asked.

Klaus's face was turned towards her. He was willing her not to leave him alone. She could see it.

So there wasn't really a choice.

'I'm coming as well,' she said quickly.

'Well, that's just fine, Maidy,' the corporal said.

But he didn't wait for her. He took Klaus by the arm and steered him through the door and down the flight of stairs.

'I'm coming too,' she called after him, and she picked up her skirts to follow.

At the top of the stairs she turned briefly and looked at the unconscious man in the hay. As she did, the monkey dropped from the rafters above her. It landed on the floor next to him and began hesitantly pawing at his face. But he didn't move. It sat down and wrapped its tail around its body. Then it turned towards her and, with a face full of malice, bared its dirty teeth and hissed.

She fled down the stairs before it could move again.

The corporal had already started along the street. He was holding Klaus by the top of the arm. There was something purposeful about it that wasn't right if he was just trying to help – Liesel saw it at once. She had to run to catch them up. Klaus was clutching the scraps of hay to his face, using them as a cloth. He looked wide-eyed at her.

This wasn't right.

'We don't need you any more now,' she said, falling into step with Klaus. 'We'll be all right now. We can manage.'

But the corporal didn't answer her. He just kept walking.

She tried again. 'Come on, Klaus,' she said.

It was the first time she'd said that name for a long while, and it felt so strange. It made her giddy. She tugged at his sleeve, trying to pull him away, and at that the corporal caught her so tightly by the wrist that it hurt.

'Ow!'

'Now, listen, Maidy – Liese – or whatever your name is . . .' He put his face so close to hers that she could see the stubble beneath his skin. 'You're not the one that's actually needed here, see? So if you want to come along, you're going to have to shut up, or I'll find some dark little place and I'll leave you in it. Do you understand me?'

She looked from him to Klaus – and suddenly she understood.

She wasn't needed because it was Klaus who knew where the diamond was, and somehow the corporal knew about it – she could see it in his face. It felt as though the ground was opening up beneath her. If he got hold of it, that would be the end of it. There'd be no getting it back then.

It was pointless pretending that she didn't under-stand what he meant. Maybe if she could explain . . .

'It's not ours,' she said. 'We've got to give it back—'

But he shook his head before she'd even finished. 'Don't give me that, Maidy,' he said.

There was a knowing look in his eye, and she

knew what he meant: that the only reason she'd been helping Klaus was because she wanted the diamond for herself.

'I've got to give it back,' she said quickly, 'or she'll skin me.'

But the man only grinned. 'Cart before the horse, Maidy,' he said. 'Got to find it first, haven't we? Then who's going to have it is quite another business. Maybe your friend would like to buy it back?'

'She's not my friend!'

He let go of her wrist and she stood rubbing it, glaring at him angrily, but there was nothing she could do and he knew it.

'So' – he pushed his hat more firmly onto his head – 'if we all understand each other, we can be getting on.' He looped his hand back through Klaus's arm. 'Come on, Klausy boy,' he said, and he started him along the street. 'You've got something to show me.'

The town bridge spanned the river in wide stone arches, the deep water folding beneath it like muddy glass. As they made their way through the alleys and narrow streets back down towards it, Liesel was desperately trying to think what to do. Finally she leaned closer and whispered in Klaus's ear, 'Pretend you can't find it.'

It was the only thing she could think of. She wasn't sure he'd even heard her, but she couldn't say it too loudly or she knew the corporal would. He was still holding Klaus's arm on the other side, and he wasn't going to let him go.

The ledge that Klaus had slept on was on the far side of the bridge. They crossed over and made their way down the flight of steps that led to the water's edge. The last steps were green and slippery, and there was a large rusted iron ring with a barge chain set into the stone, but they didn't go that far down. Klaus had them inch their way round a corner, and then they were on a part of the bridge that couldn't be seen – the part where he'd climbed up onto the ledge to sleep. Just below it the water was churning like brown snow between the pillars, the noise echoing off the stones of the arch. Liesel could feel the cold spray on her face.

The corporal stood looking up at the narrow ledge and at the joints and cracks, then turned to Klaus. 'Where'd you put it, boy?' he said.

But Klaus had heard Liesel when she'd whispered to him, and now he had to decide what to do.

It was a diamond. His diamond.

It was warm beds and hot food. It was dry boots and a carriage.

He glanced at her and she shook her head – just a tiny movement. He wouldn't even have noticed had he not been looking for it.

He looked up at the curve of the stones. 'It's up there,' he said.

But he didn't look at Liesel as he said it, and she didn't know whether he was telling the truth or not. All she could see was that he had no colour in his face at all now. Behind the scarlet smear of blood he was as grey as a ghost. He could barely stand. It had only been the corporal holding onto him that had kept him going this far. He wasn't even able to scramble up onto the ledge by himself.

'I'll put you up,' said the corporal. He made a stirrup with his hands for Klaus's foot and hoisted him up onto the ledge.

Klaus stood unsteadily for a moment, looking blankly at the wall. Black dots were swimming in front of his eyes. That little flick of light hurt, it was so bright and hard. He could see the ghost shapes of trees behind the stones. He wasn't even sure if he could remember which crack he'd put the diamond in, and there was a noise in his head like the roaring of a wind. He began to work his way sideways along the ledge – then stopped and stared at the stones, because they weren't just stones, they were the trunks of trees, and the cracks were crevices in the bark – only they were stones as well; he could see the two at the same time and he couldn't tell which was which, and the air was both warm and cold. He stuck his fingers into one crack, and then into another. He could feel something hard and smooth in it, like a pebble, and suddenly he knew what to do. He worked it free with his fingers and stood swaying on the narrow ledge, staring at the thing that he held in the palm of his hand.

Liesel's heart sank.

'You got it?' called the corporal. 'Then you bring it down now.'

Only Klaus didn't move.

'Come on, boy,' said the corporal again, beckoning to him this time.

Klaus turned his head and looked down at him and Liesel.

Then he began to edge away.

Liesel wasn't sure what he was trying to do. And then she saw. The part of the bridge that she and the corporal were standing on went only halfway across

145

beneath the arch; the ledge that Klaus stood on ran the whole width of it. If he was quick, he could get under the bridge and out the other side before they could even reach him.

He was going to keep the diamond; he was going to run and leave her behind.

'No . . .' she whispered.

'Come on, boy,' the corporal was saying. He was still holding out his hand as Klaus edged away. 'Don't make me come up and get you.'

Then he realized what Klaus was up to as well. 'Oh, no you don't, matey,' he said. He scrambled up the stonework onto the ledge and began to work his way carefully along it.

Maybe Klaus had thought he could run away. Or maybe he'd thought that the corporal wouldn't try to follow him because the ledge was so narrow. But it was far too narrow for games like that, and as Klaus tried to turn round, his foot missed it. Liesel gasped as he grabbed wildly at thin air and dropped like a stone into the churning water below.

He didn't even leave a mark in the foam.

One moment he was there.

The next, he was gone.

Chapter Eleven

Professor Karolus sat at his desk.

About him in the room, scattered amongst his papers and books, were the oddities of his years of scientific travel, all the things he'd collected and kept. There were pale specimens floating in large spirit-filled jars, and small statues and stone carvings from the Americas – Inca cups and figurines studded with jade and coloured stones.

The afternoon was closing in and the lamps had been lit. In the shadows cast on the wall behind him hung three rows of wax masks. They might have been the faces of sleeping people were it not for the coil of rope around each of their broken necks. It was a customary gift to the surgeon at a hanging –

a wax mask of the man it had been his job to make quite certain was dead. But they weren't all men; there were women too. There was even one smaller one, of a child.

Markus had grown used to them as just things on the wall, but as he stood there telling Karolus that the tooth-puller was dead, he couldn't help thinking that Karolus's face, scarred as it was, was every bit as dark as any one of those wax masks.

Maybe even more so.

What kind of man could watch the hanging of a child, then have a mask of its dead face on his wall?

Karolus listened while Markus talked. Then he leaned back in his chair. 'You are certain,' he said, 'that the tooth-puller is dead?'

Markus nodded. 'I went to his shop, Herr Professor. There's barely anything left of it.'

'And his boy, you say, is presumed to be the cause of it all?'

'Yes, Herr Professor,' said Markus. 'But only because he can't be found.'

Karolus frowned at him. 'I would say that was proof enough, wouldn't you?' he said.

He pushed his chair back and stood up, then walked to the windows. He looked out at the last streaks of colour in the sky. It was as though he was pondering the news, but it seemed to Markus as if he wasn't that surprised.

'The man whose body we dissected,' he said, turning to look at Markus again. 'He died in the boarding house, you say?'

'Yes, Herr Professor,' said Markus.

'Did he leave any things, do you know? Any possessions?'

Markus hesitated. If he'd had any remaining doubts that Karolus had actually known who the man was, he didn't have them any more. But the man had been a pauper – anyone could have seen that. All he'd owned was the lice in his clothes. So why would Karolus ask?

He shook his head. 'No, Herr Professor,' he said. 'The room was quite bare.'

Karolus said nothing for a moment; then, 'The boy, the one who is missing – do you think you could find him for me?'

Markus shook his head again. 'I'm not sure I would know where to start, Herr Professor.'

'But I would like you to do it all the same,' said Karolus coolly. 'There is something I would like to ask him. It is only a small matter. I'm sure

149

he will be happy to tell me when you find him.'

But what that matter might be, the professor didn't say.

He waited until Markus had closed the door, then rang the bell for his clerk.

Karolus's clerk, Menz, was a little man, prematurely bald and with an oily skin that shone on the top of his head like sweat. He was loathed by the students. Too often they'd find him listening in doorways, in places where he simply wasn't wanted. Menz, in his threadbare brown tailcoat and greasy neckcloth. 'The professor's little dog', they called him, and he paid them back in kind whenever he had a chance. There was no rumour or piece of malice concerning them that wasn't told to Karolus by Menz.

'Ah, Menz,' said Karolus as the clerk opened the door. 'I have a little task for you.'

As Markus made his way through the darkening streets back to his own rooms, he tried to make sense of the day, but it was beyond him. How was he supposed to even begin to find the boy? He didn't even know what he looked like, let alone what it was that Karolus wanted to ask him.

Then, from nowhere, he thought of old Keltzer, the senior porter.

What Keltzer didn't know about the back streets of the town could probably be written on a pin. If anyone knew how to go about finding a boy, it was Keltzer. If he was sober, that is. It was always possible.

Markus stopped at a market stall and bought some cold meat and bread – you got nothing for nothing from Keltzer, he knew that. Then he made his way down the side streets to the dirty tenement houses behind the Marienplatz where Keltzer lived. He knew the way – he'd been to see Keltzer once when the man was ill. If he was lucky, Keltzer might just remember the favour, but he wouldn't count on it.

There was a lantern alight in the hallway of Keltzer's block. Some painted girls were standing beneath it getting ready for their night's work. Markus pushed his way past them and climbed the narrow stairs to the landing where Keltzer's room was. There was no answer when he knocked on the door, so he tried again.

'Keltzer!' he called. 'It's Herr Brennen from the school.'

There was a moment's silence, then the scraping

of a chair on a wooden floor and the slipping of the bolt and chain.

Over his coat, Keltzer was wrapped in a blanket against the cold; he stood in the doorway looking at Markus with watering, red-rimmed eyes. 'Well, well,' he said. Markus could smell the waft of stale onion and schnapps on his breath. 'Herr Assistant, is it?'

'How is your chest, Keltzer?' asked Markus.

Keltzer looked at him suspiciously, and not without reason. Maybe Markus had finally come about all those little things that had gone missing. Then he saw the loaf of bread and the cold meat. 'What do you want?' he said.

'I want your help,' said Markus.

They sat on either side of Keltzer's bare little table. Keltzer poured a tin cup of schnapps for Markus and one for himself; then he cut the bread and the cold meat and began stuffing it into his mouth as though he hadn't eaten all day.

Markus watched him. 'I want to find a boy,' he said at last.

Keltzer glanced up from the bread and meat.

'A boy who is hiding,' Markus went on. 'Where would I begin to look?'

Keltzer frowned. 'Why do you even need to ask?' he said. 'Go to the market on Diebenplatz. Give any boy a schilling, and tell him there are ten more to be had. You'll find your boy quick enough that way.' He stuffed more bread into his mouth. 'Why do you want to find him?' he said.

Markus shook his head, glancing around the small, dirty room – the unmade trestle bed; the cold empty stove. 'I wish I knew,' he said.

Then he had a thought. 'You'll know all the pawn-brokers round here?' he said.

Keltzer's face became suspicious again. That was where a lot of those 'little things' that had gone missing had ended up. 'What if I do?' he said.

Markus reached into his coat and drew out the little folded packet. He opened the end and shook the greasy ticket out onto the table. The feather fell out with it. 'Whose shop is this?' he asked, pushing the ticket towards Keltzer.

He thought Keltzer might recognize the writing. But Keltzer wasn't looking at the ticket, he was looking at the feather.

'I had feathers like that once,' he said. 'Whole bagful of them. Sold them too. Dressmakers used to pay good money for feathers like that.'

Markus looked down at the thin, shining feather on the table. Surprisingly, he hadn't thought that it might actually be worth something. Maybe that was what the man had pawned – a bag of feathers like this . . .

'Brought them back from the Americas,' said Keltzer as though Markus had asked him where he'd got them from – which he hadn't. His eyes became vacant with remembering. He took a drink from his tin.

'What were you doing there?' asked Markus.

Keltzer gave a hollow laugh. He gestured to the cold bare room. 'Making my fortune,' he said. 'Time was when a young man could – new worlds, new places. You could do what you wanted in those days. Not like now.' He looked at Markus. 'Your Professor Karolus was there when I was,' he said. 'You should ask him to tell you all about it when you have your cosy little talks.'

He didn't like Markus.

He crooked his finger mockingly round his tin of schnapps, as though politely drinking coffee from a cup. This wasn't the first bottle Keltzer had had today, Markus could see that.

But Markus was all attention now. 'Where would

that have been, then?' he said.

'Where what?' said Keltzer.

'Where you were, with the Herr Professor?'

'In the mountains – a gold mine. I was the store-man. He was doctor to some expedition while I was there – measuring and collecting things, that's what they did. Doctor to the mine as well for a time. It hadn't got one, you see.' He sat cradling the tin of schnapps, his eyes distant again. 'Stories I could tell you . . .' he said.

The tin was almost empty. Markus filled it again from the stone bottle on the table.

'Stories like what?' he asked.

'Hmm?' said Keltzer.

'Stories like what?'

'Like what they did to the workers in the mine.' He shook his head as though he couldn't be bothered to say any more. 'Their lives weren't worth a piss – not that anyone cared.'

Then he looked up at Markus again. 'But there were things to be had from them that you wouldn't believe – precious things. They'd give anything, do anything, to get to an easier place. Gave that bastard Siger little bits of Indian gold – old stuff, old as the hills. Made no difference. He still screwed them all

155

the same.' He grinned at the remembering.

But the name had meant nothing to Markus. 'Siger?' he said.

'The mine foreman,' said Keltzer. 'And you know what he did with it – all that gold they gave him?' His eyes were glazing over and his words were getting slower. He leaned forward across the table, put his finger to his mouth and tapped. 'Teeth,' he said. 'Had them made into golden teeth.'

Markus was quite still.

So that was it.

That's how Karolus had known the man. He'd been the foreman at the mine when Karolus had been the doctor there. The teeth had been made of gold – and the tooth-puller had pulled them.

'What happened to him?' he asked.

'That's another story,' said Keltzer thickly.

He picked up the pawnbroker's ticket and, barely even looking at it, tossed it back across the table. 'That's one of Laub's,' he said. 'Corner of Schwanplatz. That's where you'll find him.'

Markus took the ticket and put it back in the packet. 'What happened to him?' he said again when he saw that Keltzer wasn't going to answer. He knew where the foreman had ended up, he was sure of that. But he was curious to know how he'd got there.

Keltzer shook his head. 'Disappeared,' he said. 'None of the workers would say a thing. It was as though they'd all agreed not to. It was your Doktor Karolus – that's all he was then – took men out to search for him. But they never found him. So they hanged ten of the workers to find out what had happened, but even then no one would say. They could have hanged them all and it wouldn't have made them talk. That's what your Karolus wanted to do. Ten wasn't enough for him – he'd have hanged every last one of them.'

'And that was it?' said Markus.

Keltzer shrugged. 'Story was that Siger had got his hands on something more than they were prepared to let him keep. But that was just a story.'

'And Karolus hanged the men?'

'Oh, yes,' said Keltzer. 'In cold blood. You'd better watch out for him, Herr Assistant.' He grinned unpleasantly and took another drink from his tin. 'But where's the fun in being careful, eh?' he asked. 'Even you, Herr Assistant.'

He emptied the tin and, filling it again, held the

bottle unsteadily out for Markus, but Markus shook his head. He didn't want any more. Besides, he'd already learned more from Keltzer than he could ever have hoped for.

He took the feather and dropped it back into the packet; then, standing up, he drew some coins from his pocket and laid them on the table. 'That'll buy some wood for the stove,' he said. 'You need a fire in this weather – chest like yours.'

Keltzer looked at him coldly. 'I don't need your charity, Herr Assistant.'

But Markus left the coins where they were. At the door he stopped and turned. He was thinking about what Keltzer had just said about the foreman, about Siger.

'What was it he was supposed to have taken – what was it they wouldn't let him have?' he asked.

Keltzer gave a little laugh into his tin, then laughed again at the stupidity of it. He looked up at Markus. 'An angel,' he said. 'They said he'd stolen an angel.'

In the warmth of his own rooms, with the fire lit, Markus sat quietly rolling the quill of the long blue feather between his fingers. He'd thought he understood it all while he was sitting at Keltzer's table – the teeth, the tooth-puller – but as he walked back through the cold dark streets, he'd become less sure, and it was the feather and the pawnbroker's ticket that were the cause.

The foreman – if that was him – had known that the priest was going to come. He must have done, because he'd left him the packet. Only the packet wasn't anything to do with the teeth.

So maybe it wasn't the teeth that Karolus really wanted at all. What if it was something else – something he'd been ready to hang all those men for?

Markus leaned forward and picked up the pawnbroker's ticket from where it lay on the table in front of him.

Perhaps he'd been wrong. Perhaps the ticket hadn't been a mistake after all. Maybe that was what Siger had wanted the priest to have.

Well, there was an easy way to find out what it was.

All Markus had to do was go to Laub's shop on the corner of Schwanplatz, and buy it back.

Chapter Twelve

Laub's shop was still open. It was the time of day for men to come and raise money for their night's drinking, or wives to buy back their bed sheets with their day's wages. Whatever Laub lent, he took back double. But where else were people to go if they were poor?

Sometimes, you see, there just isn't any choice.

The shop was only a couple of streets from Frau Drecht's house on Bergenstrasse. Markus had to walk past the house to get to Schwanplatz. It made sense if he thought about it. The man would have chosen the nearest place to pawn his things.

There were fewer lanterns lit on the street corners in this part of the town, and Markus had made sure before he set out that he was wearing his thickest coat and carrying his heaviest stick. You could never be too careful on Bergenstrasse.

The brass bell behind Laub's door rang as Markus pushed it open. The shop was dimly lit. Laub didn't spend more money on lamp oil than he had to. There was a plain floor and a wooden counter. Curving around the counter was a line of wooden booths with doors like church confessionals. Even poor people liked their privacy when dealing with Laub. Even poor people have their pride. In the gloom of the ceiling and on the walls hung all manner of things, each with a ticket and a price – boots, saws and hammers, kettles, fire irons, pots, mirrors – each to be redeemed or sold as their owner's fortune would have it. The more expensive things were safe on the other side of the counter, where Laub's two big dogs lay on the floor.

Markus went into the first of the booths and closed the door behind him. It was like a little cabin, narrow and fusty. At first he could see no one behind the counter, so he rapped on it with his stick. As he did so, he realized that the man was just round the curve. He had his back to Markus and was talking to someone in another of the booths. There was a little

161

set of jeweller's scales on the counter in front of him, and the glint of gold.

'You think on it for a moment,' Laub was saying, as though he'd just made an offer that wasn't quite what had been hoped for. Then he turned and made his way along the counter towards Markus.

His hair was thin – rat-tailed and grey. It had left a line of grease where the ends lay on the shoulders of his black frock coat.

'Sir?' he said in an obsequious voice. He was already deciding how much Markus might be worth. Young gentlemen tended to have such expensive troubles. 'How can I help you?'

'I'd like to redeem this,' said Markus, taking the ticket out of the packet and pushing it across the counter.

Laub hesitated momentarily. He knew all his customers, and Markus wasn't one of them. So what was he doing with one of his tickets?

He pulled a pair of wire-rimmed glasses out of his coat pocket and, putting them on, turned the ticket round and read it. Then he looked up. 'Oh, there's no redeeming this, sir,' he said. 'It's past its date, you see. It's bought stock now.'

Markus shook his head. 'I'm sorry,' he said. 'I don't understand.'

Laub put his finger on the writing on the ticket. 'Has to be redeemed by this date, sir. You see? Or it's sold as stock.' He gestured to the hundreds of things hanging from the ceiling and the walls.

Then Markus understood. 'But I can buy it back, surely,' he said. He looked at the ticket. 'For two schillings.'

Laub smiled thinly and shook his head. 'It's not like that, sir,' he said. 'What I buy at and what I sell at aren't always the same, you see? There's the risk on the loan, so there has to be a commensurate profit on the sale. Intelligent gentleman like you must see that, sir?'

Markus saw it only too well, and he could see exactly where this was leading. 'So how much would I have to pay for it?' he asked.

Laub looked at him knowingly. *If you want it that much, hookey,* he was thinking to himself, *the answer is going to be quite a lot.*

But he said nothing.

Behind him on a row of shelves were a number of ledgers. He pulled a set of low steps towards him with his foot and, running his hand along the shelf until he found the ledger book he wanted, took it down and laid it flat on the counter in front of Markus. Licking his finger, Laub slowly turned the pages over until he found the entry that matched the ticket.

'Laub!' The woman in the other booth was growing impatient at being left, and suddenly Markus realized that he'd heard that voice before.

It was Frau Drecht's.

He drew himself back a little from the counter, so that there was no chance of her seeing him.

'A moment,' said Laub, unperturbed. He read the entry on the page and looked up. 'I'm afraid it's already been sold, sir.'

'Laub!' Frau Drecht was getting more impatient still.

'Who bought it?' said Markus in a low voice, one that Frau Drecht wouldn't hear. He was already thinking that maybe he could buy it back from them.

But Laub had closed the book. 'That's a matter of the strictest confidentiality, sir,' he said. 'I'm sure an intelligent gentleman like you will understand that. Can't have disgruntled customers going looking for their things once they've been sold as stock, can we? All sorts of trouble might be caused by doing that.'

It was all he was going to say on the matter. Done business was done business.

He tore the ticket through and threaded it onto a long skewer that hung on a length of string from the back of the counter. Then, like some thin ghost, he bowed to Markus and made his way back to the other booth.

'My dear,' he said in an oily voice. 'Have you thought?'

Markus stood in the fusty-smelling booth. There was nothing more he could do. He turned to lift the catch on the door – and then stopped.

Laub hadn't put the ledger book back on the shelf. It was still on the counter where he'd left it.

Markus looked quickly along to the other booth. Laub had his back to him. He was deep in an argument with Frau Drecht. He was trying to placate her but she was having none of it. She wanted to watch him weigh whatever she'd brought in again. She didn't believe he'd done it fairly the first time.

Markus reached across the counter and drew the ledger book back into the booth. One of the dogs stirred on the floor. It lifted its head and looked at him warningly, but Markus ignored it. Balancing the book against the edge of the counter, he began quickly turning the pages, glancing up at Laub's back all the while. There was the page for the ticket. He ran his finger down to the entry. There it was – a date and the name: *Siger*. Then another date and the name *Frau Rassler* – that must be who'd bought it. And an address. There was the money lent and the money paid as well.

But it was what was written in neat copperplate pen between the two that made Markus stop. He had to read it twice just to be sure he wasn't making a mistake; then he quickly closed the book and pushed it back onto the counter.

That was when Laub turned and saw him. 'Hi! What you doing!'

Markus didn't so much as look round. He opened the door of the booth and began to walk out of the shop. Laub was shouting and swearing. It was only when Markus turned the handle of the door to the street that he realized Laub was doing something more than just that.

He was setting the dogs on him.

Breathless and sweating, Markus stood at a street corner looking at the tears and rips in his thick coat. If he hadn't been carrying the heavy stick, things would have gone far worse for him. Even so, he wasn't going to forget Laub's dogs in a hurry. If he ever got the chance to give them a good kick, he wouldn't pass it up.

As he'd run across the square with the dogs at his heels and Laub shouting into the night after him, he thought he saw Karolus's clerk, Menz, standing beneath the lamp at the corner. He hoped to goodness he hadn't or it would be all over the school in the morning – Herr Assistant chased out of a moneylender's shop by the moneylender's dogs – what a good story Menz would make of that. Come to think of it, Markus was almost sure he'd seen him earlier as well, in the street near Keltzer's room. That little turd got everywhere.

But Menz was the last thing on his mind now, because Markus had seen what was written in Laub's book – he knew just what it was that Siger had pawned. It was the one thing they weren't going to let him keep – he could almost hear Keltzer laughing into his tin of schnapps as he'd said it.

What Laub had got for his two schillings was an angel in a dark leather box.

So what exactly was it? A little statue, a figurine?

Maybe it had been taken from a church, and

that's why Siger had wanted to give it back to the priest – his conscience had got the better of him after all those years. Only before he could do it he'd had to pawn it just to buy food.

But then Markus stopped.

Why would a man with a mouthful of gold teeth need to pawn anything? Why couldn't he have just sold *them*?

He hadn't thought of it before, but now he realized that it was the first thing he should have asked, and there wasn't an answer to it.

But he could find out exactly what the angel was. He hadn't been chased halfway around Schwanplatz by Laub's dogs in order to just give up on it now. Frau Rassler's address had been in the book. It had to be around here somewhere.

And he was right. It was.

Frau Rassler lived in a tall tenement house that leaned brokenly into a little courtyard around a well. Markus had to go beneath an archway to get to it, then tread in the dark through the filth and mud to the stone steps up to the open door. At the top of the steps, beneath a lantern, a small boy was holding a sagging cat in his arms. It was almost as big as he was. Behind him, other children were sitting in the gloom of the wooden staircase. When Markus asked the way to Frau Rassler's rooms, they pointed up to the landing on the first floor.

He climbed the stairs, and there, painted neatly on the wall outside the door, was a little sign. It said simply:

FRAU RASSLER — DRESSMAKER
FEATHER AND LACE TRIMMING DONE

Markus knocked at the door and waited. He could hear voices and sounds from the rooms above. He could smell cooking. It dawned on him that he hadn't eaten.

Someone came and poked their head over the banister of the landing above, curious as to who it was below. Then the head disappeared again.

Frau Rassler's door opened. A woman dressed in a neatly-made brown cotton dress stood looking at him.

'Frau Rassler?' he asked.

She nodded distractedly. She had the air of someone to whom something very disagreeable had happened, and for an instant Markus was inclined to say that he would come back another time. But then he thought that maybe that was just the way she always was – and anyway, he was here now. Besides, he'd already decided what he was going to say.

'I wonder if you could help me?' he started. 'It's about the item that you recently bought from Herr Laub. I was thinking that it might be a pair with something I already have, and I wondered whether I could see if it was . . .?'

He'd got the rest of a story worked out too, but he never got to say it because the woman's face, which was already pale, went paler still. She glanced back into the room and put her hand anxiously up to her mouth, then beckoned him to follow her in. Markus took off his hat and stepped through the door.

The room was lit by bright lamps. The wicks had been trimmed short. They burned as brightly as it was possible for them to do. A large table stood in the middle of the room. It was spread with cloth all cut and pinned, and there were dressmaker's dummies with half-finished work on them. In the lamplight the dummies cast hard, sharp shadows against the walls.

In the middle of the floor next to the table lay a large leather box. It was easily the size of a travelling trunk. It took Markus a moment to realize that it was the box that Frau Rassler was staring at.

'Take it!' she whispered. 'I don't want it. You can have it.'

She edged nearer to the wall, as far away from the thing as she could get, and wiped her hands on her dress, as though trying to wipe the touch of something away.

She reached out and took hold of Markus's sleeve. Her hand was shaking and her eyes were wide. She was almost beside herself. 'It bleeds,' she said in a broken whisper. 'When you pull the feathers, it bleeds.'

Markus looked back at the box.

There were a handful of feathers on the floor beside it, where Frau Rassler must have dropped them. They were long and iridescent blue, just like the feather in the packet. That was why she had bought it, he thought – for the feathers.

He lifted her hand from his sleeve and took a step towards the box. This wasn't what he'd been expecting at all, and there was something very wrong about it.

The lid was made of thick, hard leather. He reached down and lifted it, and as it opened he caught the smell of something stale and old.

Like meat.

At first he couldn't grasp what he was looking at. In the shadow cast by the bright lamps the box just seemed full of darkness and feathers.

He took one of the lamps from the table and brought it nearer. Then he could see.

Inside the box was the figure of a man, large as life and made of dried, transparent skin – hollow like old parchment. It was pierced with thousands of iridescent feathers, each of the quills sharpened to a point like a needle and pushed through the skin as though they were growing from it.

He couldn't see the face – the figure was kneeling with its head bent down and its arms stretched out in front of it, a single metal spike driven like a nail through the back of its crossed hands, fixing them together.

As Markus moved the lamp, he saw the broad curve of the feathered back, the neck and head, the soles of the feet where the skin was puckered and dry.

It wasn't like anything he'd ever seen before.

He reached out and touched the feathers on its back. As he did so, his fingertips brushed the skin and he felt the familiar pattern of pores – like the skin of his own back.

He drew his hand away in disgust.

It was real skin.

He pinched the quill of one of the feathers and worked it free. As he did, a single bead of dark blood rose through the dried skin, and the curved back shivered as though it had taken the shallowest of breaths.

'Holy God . . .' whispered Markus.

It was still alive.

Chapter Thirteen

Liesel ran to the edge of the stones and looked down into the churning snow of water, but Klaus was gone.

'Klaus!' she shouted.

Her voice was lost in the roaring noise.

The corporal was standing on the ledge above her, holding onto the wall, peering out towards the middle of the river and the turning skin of water that had cleared the bridge. She saw him pull off his coat and boots, and jump; then he was gone too into the rush of water and foam. She stood there, not daring to take her eyes off the place where they'd gone in, but she couldn't see anything.

Then the corporal appeared again – just his head above the rush of water as it swept him out into the middle of the river. The current was turning him round and he was struggling against it, but he looked down into the water as it swept him along. He was already drifting out of Liesel's line of sight around the far pillar of the bridge when she saw him lift his shoulders and take a gulp of air, saw the white skin flick of his feet as he upended, and then he was gone again.

Whimpering under her breath, she turned and fled back up the stone steps, taking them two at time. She reached the top and ran blindly out between the carts and the carriages on the road, the drivers swearing at her as their horses shied and reared, then down the steps on the other side, half falling, slipping on the wet stones, until she stood, breathless, on the long strand of mud and grit of the river shore.

Hands to her mouth, breath stopped up inside her, she stood watching the water. Then some movement made her turn her head and look much further along the shore, and there was the corporal.

Waist deep in the water, his hair plastered to his face, he was dragging behind him the sodden bundle of rags that was Klaus. She ran along the strand, then waded out into the shallows. The water was ice-cold. Her skirt wrapped round her legs like a heavy blanket, making her stumble and fall. She scrambled to her feet again, soaking wet, and, grabbing hold of the back of Klaus's jacket, she and the corporal pulled him out and dropped him, coughing and retching, at the water's edge.

'You stupid little bastard!' shouted the corporal, and he kicked Klaus, sending a spray of water into the air.

Liesel tried to stop him, but he pushed her away and she fell backwards into the freezing shallows.

'Leave him alone!' she shouted, struggling to her feet.

The corporal glared angrily at her, and she hesitated. She watched as he took Klaus's hands, first one, then the other, and bent the fingers open to see if he was holding the diamond. But Klaus's hands were empty. The corporal half dropped, half threw him back into the shallows at the edge of the water and kicked him again. 'You stupid little bastard!' he shouted.

Still glaring at Liesel, he turned away and stalked back towards the bridge. She watched him go, his hair plastered in rat-tails across his face, his wet shirt sticking to his skin.

Her lip was bleeding where he'd pushed her away. She hadn't realized it until then. She wiped it on the back of her hand and stood watching the corporal, wanting to make sure that he really had gone and wasn't going to come back. Then she squatted down beside Klaus. He was lying in the mud, half in, half out of the water. He was alive, but the diamond had gone, and whatever hope Liesel had had – that had gone with it. There was no saving her from Frau Drecht now.

She sat back in the mud and put her face in her hands. There was nothing she could do.

She looked down at Klaus. He was coughing up water. His face was white and bloodless, the rag sodden and loose around his neck, his nose hanging by a thread. He was shivering. So was she.

They couldn't stay there, Liesel knew that. They had to find somewhere warm and dry, and someone to look at Klaus's face. If she took him to the Pauper's Hospital on Veergarten, maybe they'd sew it. After that they'd just have to trust to luck.

She stood up, trying not to think about Frau Drecht, or how Klaus had ruined everything for her. Instead, she tried to picture her brother, but all she could think was how much she missed him. How much she needed him now. It was like a pain.

'Come on,' she said softly. She tied the loose bandage around Klaus's face, pulled him to his feet and, looping his arm around her shoulders, led him back along the shore to the wet stone steps.

'What on earth did you go and do that for, Klaus?' she said in a voice thick with despair.

But Klaus didn't answer. He just closed his eyes and tried not to see the feathered-man-shaped burn of light, or the outlines of trees that he just couldn't make go away – it felt as though there were tears in the air, and he was seeing the river and a forest all at the same time, the water of the river piercing the roots of the trees like a fine scarf of painted cloth.

Frau Drecht sat brooding in front of her dressing-table mirror. She finished rouging her face, then dipped her finger into the pot of red, rose-perfumed grease. Puckering her lips, she smeared them into the shape of a small cupid's bow.

Then she had a thought.

A man who hid gold and a diamond in his teeth might just hide other things as well. Maybe that's why he hadn't always paid his rent on time. Maybe he'd hidden all his money too. If you were going to hide one thing, it stood to reason you'd hide another.

She looked up at the ceiling, as though trying to see through the wooden floorboards and timbers right up into Herr Siger's room. Then she pushed back her stool, went out into the hall and climbed the dark, narrow stairs.

As she stood outside Herr Siger's room, Frau Drecht heard the door behind her open just a crack – and then close again just as quickly as she turned her head to see who it was. As she looked at the door, it opened again, no more than a slit, as though the mad old woman inside were watching. Frau Drecht didn't have time to be bothered with that. She pushed open the door to Herr Siger's room.

First she pulled the mattress off the bed and shook it. Then she shook the dirty pillow and the greasy sheets, then his clothes and boots. But there was nothing to be found. She stood looking around the room. There was nowhere else to hide anything – unless of course he'd hidden it under the floor? She stamped on each of the floorboards in turn with her little black buttoned boots, but none of them was loose. Breathless from her efforts, she looked up and saw again through the open doorway the crack of the door across the landing, and a new idea popped into her sharp, suspicious little mind.

What if what had been there had already been taken?

What if some interfering, mad old bag had already looked around the room and found it . . . decided to keep it for herself?

Now, there was a thought.

Maybe she wasn't so very mad after all?

Purposefully now, and still looking at the other door, Frau Drecht crossed the room. As if confirming what she'd thought, when she reached the landing the little crack closed, but that wasn't going to stop Frau Drecht. She turned the handle and pushed the door open.

The old woman, Frau Eber, was standing in the middle of the room. In a suddenly anxious lather when she saw Frau Drecht, she quickly stepped back and began stirring something in her little cooking pan. In the cage above her head, her songbird hopped from perch to perch with quick flicks of its wings.

Frau Drecht stood quietly in the doorway watching her. She'd been right: guilty, if ever she saw it.

She crossed her arms and leaned against the

doorpost. 'Where'd you put it, dearie?' she said in a voice like sharp glass and honey. 'Herr Siger's little thing you took from across the way?'

The old woman hesitated just for a moment, then, head still bent over the pan, began stirring even more furiously.

'Hmm,' said Frau Drecht dangerously. She looked about the little room, and then her eyes fixed on the wicker cage.

She stepped forward and, unhooking the door, drew the bird out in her closed fist, its head just poking out at the top. It tried in vain to peck at her.

Frau Eber stopped stirring. Her face was full of alarm now, her eyes fixed on the little bird in Frau Drecht's hand. It was the only thing she had. She made a small frightened noise.

Frau Drecht held the bird up, rocking her fist just a little. Then she smiled and, loosening her grip, drew one wing out between her pinched fingers and gave it a little experimental tug. 'Where'd you put it, dearie?' she whispered.

Frau Eber moved her hands helplessly in the air as though trying to reach the bird, then bit her thumbs. 'I didn't take it,' she said quickly, shaking her head, her wild eyes fixed on the little feathered

181

wing. 'He gave it me. I just did what he asked. He said it was a secret. Not to tell.'

'Course he did, dearie,' said Frau Drecht. 'But now you're going to give it to me, aren't you?'

The old woman shook her head desperately. 'No!' she said. 'I give it to the priest.'

At that, Frau Drecht stopped. She leaned forward, frowning, the wing still pinched between her fingers. 'You did what?' she said.

Frau Eber's eyes were fixed on the bird. 'He said, *Give it the priest*. So I give it to the priest.'

She reached out her hand, but Frau Drecht moved the bird away. This was getting more interesting by the moment. 'Gave what?' she said carefully.

'A little packet. It was just a little packet.'

'Was it, now?' said Frau Drecht. *You could hide a whole fortune of diamonds in a little packet* was what she thought.

But whatever she might have been going to say next was interrupted, because there was a sound of footsteps running up the stairs and, breathless and flustered, the small, pale-faced girl appeared in the open doorway.

She bobbed a frightened curtsey to Frau Drecht. 'Please, gnädige Frau,' she said in a trembling voice.

'Spitzel's come. Says to tell you he's found her.'

Slowly Frau Drecht turned round and looked at her. 'Found Liesel?' she said. Things were getting better and better. 'Well, well . . .'

She dropped the bird. It fell to the floor in a broken-winged flutter of feathers. Frau Eber gave a little cry and leaped forward to pick it up, but Frau Drecht didn't bother to look. She was already on her way through the door and back down the stairs to the hall.

The red-haired boy was waiting nervously for her at the bottom of the stairs. Frau Drecht caught him hard by his ear and dragged him into her small parlour, swinging him to a halt in front of her, and slamming the door shut with her boot.

'Well?' she demanded.

'I see'd her,' he said. 'She's gone in the Pauper's.'

'The hospital?' said Frau Drecht, as though she couldn't see how that could possibly be right. 'You sure it was her?'

The boy nodded his head furiously. 'She was in the line waiting at the gate,' he said. 'She'd got Kusselmann's boy with her too.'

She eyed him suspiciously. 'Kusselmann's boy?'

He nodded again.

What did Liesel have to do with Kusselmann's boy?

'Where'd she go then?'

'She's still there,' he said. 'They was only just opening the gate. I come as fast as I could, gnädige Frau.'

Frau Drecht looked at him coldly. 'She see you?' she asked.

He shook his head.

'Well,' breathed Frau Drecht with a malicious smile on her face. She wound her fingers in his hair and, pulling it tight, leaned her face close to his. He could see the white threads of spittle joining at the corners of her red greased lips. 'If that's how it is,' she whispered, 'what you do now, is this . . .'

The Pauper's Hospital stood in Veergarten, a narrow street between Bergenstrasse and the market on Diebenplatz. It was one long whitewashed room with a bare wooden floor and bare wooden benches. At the far end, a row of trestle beds were separated one from the other by low boards. The beds were always filled and the air was thick – it smelled of stale bodies and unwashed clothes.

The people who were lucky enough to get

through the door – and not everyone did – took their places on the benches and sat waiting for their turn to be seen. Klaus and Liesel were almost the last ones in and they were right at the back. Klaus's face was still bleeding. Someone gave him a square of cloth, but he just sat holding it, staring vacantly into space. It was Liesel who took it and wiped the blood away.

She didn't know what they were going to do now. He'd as good as done for both of them. 'You shouldn't have taken it,' she hissed. 'You should have pretended you couldn't find it. That's what I told you to do. Now we've got nothing.'

For the first time since he'd been pulled out of the river, Klaus seemed to hear her. 'I never took it,' he mumbled.

She could have slapped him. She thought he was trying to pretend again – that he'd never even had it, never taken it from Kusselmann; but then he slowly turned his head and looked at her. His eyes were watery and bloodshot, and he was squinting as though there was something painful in them, but he had the ghost of a smile on his face.

'I never took it,' he said quietly.

And suddenly she realized what he *actually* meant:

he'd never taken it out of the crack. It had been something else – a stone or a pebble. He hadn't even had it in his hand when he'd fallen in. He hadn't meant to fall in, but he hadn't taken it either. It had been a trick, and it had fooled her too. The diamond wasn't in the river, it was still there beneath the bridge.

She stared dumbly at him. But before she could speak, a man in a long drab coat moved her aside so that he could stand in front of Klaus and look at his face.

'He fell in the river,' Liesel said brokenly, because she was still thinking about the diamond and what that meant.

It was still there.

'You have a mother?' the man was saying to Klaus. 'A father?'

Klaus slowly moved his head.

'Are you his sister?' he asked Liesel.

'Yes, that's right,' she said quickly, almost without thinking. And then she realized what she'd said, and it felt wrong.

'He'll have to have this sewn,' the man said to her. 'Come back to the gate this evening.'

'Can't I stay with him?' she said.

But the man shook his head, and it didn't matter how much she argued, he wasn't going to let her stay. Finally he said, 'If you don't go now, I will not sew it at all.'

There was nothing more she could do. She leaned close to Klaus. 'I'll come back,' she whispered. 'You'll be all right here. They'll see to you. Stitch you up. Then, when you're done, we'll go and find it. Right?'

He didn't answer, but he nodded his head. He'd closed his eyes and was sitting with the cloth pressed to his face.

With a last glance back at him from the door, she left him on the bench and went lightly down the steps and out across the little yard to the iron gate that led to the street.

Everything had changed. She didn't even feel tired any more. It was going to be all right. At six she'd come back for Klaus and they'd get the diamond. Then Frau Drecht would leave them alone.

She could have danced.

But as she came out through the little iron gate, someone caught at her sleeve. She turned round quickly. It was one of the boys from Bergenstrasse –

187

she knew him at once – ragged and pinched, the one with the red hair. 'Spitzel', they called him. As she looked at him, he glanced anxiously over his shoulder back down the street.

'Don't go that way,' he said urgently. 'She's going to get you, Liesel. She knows you was here. I had to tell her.'

Suddenly she felt very cold. She didn't need telling who he meant. All the joy of the moment before was gone like a candle blown out by an icy breath.

He looked behind him again. 'She'll skin me if she knows I told you,' he said. 'You've got to get away.' He pulled at her arm. 'Come on!' he said. 'She'll know for sure if you go that way.'

Liesel looked back down the street, but Spitzel was already pulling her after him.

'I give her the slip,' he said. 'If you go this way, you'll be all right. Come on!'

There wasn't time to argue. There was an alley on the other side of the street. Still holding her arm and glancing back over his shoulder, Spitzel dragged her towards it. 'You'll be all right this way,' he said. 'But you've got to be quick.'

It was a narrow alley, darker and narrower still the

further they went. They'd gone most of the way down when Spitzel stopped running, and stood looking back towards the light of the street. But there was no one there; no one had followed them. He looked at Liesel. They were both breathing hard. He was still holding onto her sleeve.

She pushed her hair back from her face and caught her breath. 'Thanks,' she said, and tried to move her arm away; it felt awkward, him holding it now.

But he didn't let go. He was still looking at her. She tried to pull her sleeve away again, but he held on, and suddenly she realized that there was something about all this that just wasn't right – the alley was too dark, and there was no one to hear or see.

'Sorry,' he said.

'What do you mean?'

From the darkness of the doorway right next to her came a faint, familiar fragrance of rose-perfumed grease.

'Hello, Liesel.'

Chapter Fourteen

You don't cross Frau Drecht.

Locked in the dark little yard at the back of the kitchen in Bergenstrasse, Liesel sat on the damp cold stones with her eyes screwed shut and her arm under the spout of the big wooden pump. She let the cold water drip onto the burns Frau Drecht had made with the hot iron.

It must have been hours since she'd been shut in there, but she was still shaking.

She could hear Frau Drecht in the kitchen talking to Mutzi – at least she could hear the sound of their voices rising and falling on the other side of the door. It had to be Mutzi: the sound of his voice was like a low growl, and she'd heard him come –

his hobnailed boots on the hard stone floor.

They would be talking about Klaus. About going and getting the diamond. She knew it because she'd told Frau Drecht where it was, and they wouldn't be able to find it without Klaus. They'd have to go and get him from the Pauper's first, when the clocks struck six. Only she didn't want to think about what they'd do to him when they had the diamond. He knew what they'd done to Kusselmann. They'd close up his eyes for good, she was certain of it.

And it was her who'd told on him. But it was the only thing she could have done.

Sometimes you just don't have a choice.

She opened her eyes. In the darkness she could see a thin crack of light at the edge of the yard door. She pulled herself up and, creeping quietly across the worn stones, carefully laid her ear to the crack.

It was Frau Drecht who was talking. She'd lit a cigar – Liesel could smell it through the door, bitter like the smoke from old rags.

'. . . be cleaner this way,' she was saying. 'We'd only need tell him she's back here – he's not to know she isn't.'

Liesel frowned. This was the end of something that Frau Drecht was saying, not the beginning, and it was about her. She pushed her ear closer to the door.

There was a long silence. She could smell the cigar, and hear Mutzi shifting on his chair.

'You wouldn't have to do it,' said Frau Drecht. There was a nightmarish quiet to her voice.

'I'll see to it. You just make sure of the boy and I'll be along when I've done.'

Done what? thought Liesel.

Then, cold as a chill breath, she realized what Frau Drecht was going to do. Liesel was the only other person who knew what had happened to Kusselmann. So Frau Drecht was going to close up *her* eyes too.

She heard the scrape of Mutzi's chair as he stood up.

'I'll give you a letter,' said Frau Drecht. 'They won't argue with a letter. Six is when the gate opens. They're punctual, so just you make sure you're there in good time. I'll see to what needs to be done here.'

Their voices grew fainter as they went out into the hall and along to Frau Drecht's parlour.

Liesel had as long as it took Frau Drecht to write that letter, and then Frau Drecht was going to come back.

She pulled at the door. It was bolted fast. She tried to dig her fingers into the crack along the doorpost, but she couldn't get them through. She felt a cold sweat rising on her skin. She pulled at the door again, but it wouldn't move.

She stepped back and looked hopelessly at it, and as she did so, she heard the sound of hard wooden pattens on the kitchen floor. Small. Not Frau Drecht's. She put her eye to the crack.

It was the pale-faced girl, the one who'd taken her place. She'd come into the kitchen carrying a jug.

'Here! Come here!' Liesel hissed through the crack.

The girl stopped and, with a startled look, turned slowly round to see who'd spoken.

'Here!' hissed Liesel again, even more urgently. 'Come here!' Liesel put her eye to the crack to see what the girl was doing.

She was looking at the door now, then anxiously back over her shoulder towards the hall.

'Come here!'

The girl didn't move.

'Please! You got to let me out!'

But she just stood there like a startled rabbit.

Liesel banged at the door in frustration and put

193

her mouth to the crack again. 'I'll get you something. I'll get you a doll.' It was the first thing she
could think of. 'You want a doll? I'll get you one. Big
one. But you got to let me out or you don't get it.'
She put her eye to the crack again.

The girl was backing slowly towards the hall.

'No! Don't go!'

With a flick of her skirt, she vanished.

'No!'

Liesel pulled wildly at the door. In a blind panic
now, she looked around at the dark brick and stone
walls, the pump, the little trough, the slop hole, but
there was nowhere even to hide.

Then she looked up at the small piece of sky and
saw a little ledge about twelve feet up the wall. It
took a moment for her to realize what it was. It was
the first-floor landing. There was a dirty pane of
glass there. That had to be it. She'd hardly ever paid
it any attention, never thought what it looked out on
– it was as brown as the plaster of the wall and let no
light in. But that must be it. It must look out onto
the tiny yard.

If she could get to that . . .

She started looking at the wall beneath it,
running her hands over the damp stone. The bricks

were uneven. They'd never been properly pointed, just roughly laid. But try as she might she couldn't find a handhold on any of them. More desperately now, she tried somewhere else. She found a place where she could put her foot, but she still couldn't reach anything higher, so she tried again, and this time her fingers closed around a hard jutting edge of brick.

But time was running out.

Once she'd written the letter, Frau Drecht came back into the kitchen. She glanced at the yard door. It was still shut. She drew a last deep breath on her cigar, laid it down on the edge of the table and, from the wall by the stove, took a heavy black iron poker. Sliding back the bolts of the door, top then bottom, the heavy poker in her fist, she stepped into the darkness of the little yard.

'Come here, Liesel,' she said in a voice of soft velvet.

There wasn't a sound.

Frau Drecht stood still for a moment, her eyes adjusting to the dark, peering into each of the corners.

Then, from the wall above her head, she heard a scraping sound, and looked up.

In the dim light she saw Liesel clinging to the ledge, saw the white patch of her face as she looked down. And in the same moment the dirty pane of glass that Liesel had been working free with her fingers fell with a smash on the stones in front of Frau Drecht.

She stepped quickly back. 'You come down here, Liesel!' she said, her voice hard and threatening now.

But Liesel knew better than to do that.

With one last look at Frau Drecht, she pulled herself in through the little square window and fell face first onto the hard floorboards of the landing.

'Oh, no you don't, dearie,' said Frau Drecht quietly.

She went quickly back through the kitchen and, with her face turned up towards the landing above her, the iron poker in her fist, she began to climb the stairs. 'Come here, Liesel,' she said in a dangerous singsong. 'You come to Frau Drecht and we'll forget all about it.'

But there was no answer.

She stopped and listened. From the dark above her she could hear the sound of Liesel running up the stairs.

She started to climb again, her voice like broken glass and honey. 'Come on, Liesel. Come to Frau Drecht . . .'

Up on the landings above her, like a moth beating against a light, Liesel was trying each of the doors. But they were all locked, and those that were opened showed only a crack and then shut again just as quick when they heard the sound of Frau Drecht calling.

'Please!' Liesel whispered, pulling at the handles.

But the doors stayed shut.

She held her breath. She could hear Frau Drecht coming – the staircase creaking with each slow step.

'Lieeeesel,' called Frau Drecht softly.

Through one of the broken banisters, Liesel looked down onto the staircases below. She could see the top of Frau Drecht's head and the iron poker in her hand.

Then, from out of the dark behind her, someone gripped Liesel by the wrist.

'Ah!'

She tried to twist herself free and, turning, saw the wild hair and mad thin face of Frau Eber.

'Sshh!' said Frau Eber, her bony finger crooked to her mouth. She glanced past Liesel into the darkness of the stairs; then, still gripping her by the wrist, pulled her back along the landing and into her own room. She closed the door. 'The window,' she said.

Liesel stared blankly at her. They were at the top of the house. There was nothing now but the loft and the tiles of the roof.

Frau Eber still had her by the wrist. She pulled her towards the dirty little window and, lifting the catch, opened it as wide as it would go. 'Out,' she said.

Liesel peered out over the sill. There was a stomach-shrinking drop beneath her. She could feel the cold damp air on her face, see the little alley courtyard and the wet line of the open sewer that ran beneath an archway and out into Bergenstrasse proper. She could see the broken tiles of the tenement roofs, the skylights and chimney pots – all below her – weeds and bushes growing high up in the gaps. Out beyond it all she could see the uneven roofline of the town, and the silver curve of the river.

But there was something else.

Along the wall below the window ran a narrow tile ledge. It was spread with crumbs and crusts left by Frau Eber for the birds.

Liesel looked back into the room: surely she couldn't mean that. But there was nowhere else, and from out in the hall she heard Frau Drecht's voice calling her name.

Sometimes you don't have a choice.

'Out!' said Frau Eber.

Liesel took a deep breath. She scrambled up onto the windowsill and, holding tightly to the frame, made herself turn round. Looking back into the room rather than down at the giddy drop, she reached for the narrow tiles of the ledge with the tips of her shoes. Then Frau Eber closed the window.

Liesel crouched among the crusts and crumbs, not daring to move, her face pressed to the cold damp plasterwork below the windowsill. She could feel the emptiness of the drop behind her. Then, faint through the glass of the window, she heard Frau Drecht's voice in Frau Eber's room, and realized what a stupid thing she'd done. Frau Drecht only had to open that window and look out and she'd see her.

Liesel turned her head very slowly and made herself look along the ledge. It ran only a few feet more, then it stopped, broken and crumbled against the wall. Just as slowly, she turned her head until she could look the other way. In that direction the ledge ran further, and there was another roof, joining the side of the building, a lower one with a chimney stack. A desperate idea began to form in her head. She shut her eyes and, pressing herself closer to the wall, began to creep backwards along the ledge, one small step at a time.

She could still hear Frau Drecht calling her name – the sound was getting louder, and all at once the filthy skylight in the loft roof just above her head was thrown open. Liesel froze stock still. Frau Drecht shouted her name.

'Liesel!'

But she hadn't seen her.

She must only have looked out along the tiles of the roof because a moment later the skylight shut again with a slam that rattled the panes of glass, and her voice grew faint.

Liesel took a breath and moved again, working her way along to the end of the ledge. When she was above the ridge tiles of the roof below, she looked down. The drop was more than she'd thought – at least twice her height – and the tiles were black and wet. She hesitated. She looked along the ledge again. For an instant she thought of going back, of climbing in again through Frau Eber's window. But Frau Drecht lay that way.

As she hesitated, from over the roofs of the town, from the different towers and churches, the carillons of clocks began to strike the half-hour. Liesel heard them, and for a moment they meant nothing more than the sound of bells. Then she looked at the reddening sky, the closing signs of the day. It had to be half past five.

And she thought of Klaus.

It left her only half an hour.

Manoeuvring herself against the wall, she lowered herself to her knees and jumped. She felt the tiles break and slip as she landed on the hard roof below, and then all at once she was sliding too, feet first, down towards the edge and the drop to the street. She scrabbled wildly at the tiles and felt herself slowing. With a heart-stopping jolt she came to a halt with her feet resting on the rusted iron gutter-work at the roof edge. It creaked and moved, but she'd stopped. For a moment she couldn't work out exactly where she was – everything looked so different from up here. She turned her head sideways. To her left she could see what could only be the catslide roof of the laundry at the end of

Bergenstrasse, and she realized what had happened. She'd come down the roof to the other side of Frau Drecht's. This was the back of the next house. If she could find her way down onto that catslide roof, then she could get down to the street. But it was still a long drop.

Shuffling sideways, she began to work her way along the edge of the roof, putting her weight on the old gutter only when she absolutely had to. Each time she did she felt it move. The tiles were wet and cold. It took so long. With a final scramble, she found herself at the top of the long, sloping laundry-house roof. She could stand now. She could see the laundry-house yard below her, the big boiling pots, the washed sheets hanging on ropes, the women all unawares with their sleeves rolled back on their pink arms. She was almost down.

She took two steps and then lost her footing.

In a confused tumble of arms and legs, she came down the sloping roof and dropped the last ten feet onto a pile of stacked baskets and crates. But for them she'd have broken her neck. For a moment she lay there, every atom of breath knocked out of her body. She could hear the shouts of alarm from the women who'd seen her drop like a shot crow from the roof. They crowded round her, but Liesel ignored them. She got unsteadily to her feet, pushed them aside and, deaf to their words, her hands leaving dirty black marks on the clean hung sheets, she weaved through the coils of steam and vats of water out onto the street. As she did so, she heard the clocks striking the three-quarters of the hour. Without another thought she took to her heels and ran.

Down the darkened alleys, out across the busy crowded streets. Past the porters from the market, the fish stalls and the baker's windows. Liesel didn't stop. She thought her lungs were going to burst, but she didn't stop – not for more than a moment at one corner to catch her breath again. As she came into the last street, she heard the clocks chiming the hour.

The little iron gate of the Pauper's Hospital was open. There were people filing through. She slowed to a walk. She couldn't see Mutzi or Frau Drecht.

She pushed herself into the queue, ignoring the complaints. Worming and elbowing her way to the front, she ducked through the gate and ran across the yard to the big wooden door that led into the Pauper's Ward. More cautiously then, she slipped inside. Candles had been lit in alcoves along the walls but there was little other light. In the gloom there was a quiet murmur of voices, and that stale unwashed smell. She looked about but she couldn't see Frau Drecht or Mutzi.

She had to find Klaus before they did.

She began working her way along the row of beds, but with a sinking feeling in her stomach that grew with each step, she reached the end and still hadn't found him. She looked back at the benches by the door.

She could see the whole room.

She was too late.

Klaus had gone.

Chapter Fifteen

For a moment Liesel could do nothing but stand dumbly looking at the shadowed room – the rows of beds, the benches, the people – a sick panic rising inside her.

Only it didn't matter how much she looked, because Klaus wasn't there.

She bit her lip, trying to tell herself that there had to be something she could do. But there was nothing, not now, and she knew it. She was too late.

She looked down the ward towards the big door that led out onto the steps and the street. As she did so, it opened and more people came in, roughly dressed and poor. The last was a man carrying a small child. He stepped through, then turned and held the door for someone else, a big man. Mutzi.

Instinctively, Liesel pulled herself back into the shadows of the wall. For an instant she thought he'd come looking for her because he stood uncertainly just inside the door, peering into the dimness of the ward. But as she watched him, he stopped one of the passing men and handed something to him.

Her eyes widened. It was a letter – the letter Frau Drecht had written. It had to be. Only that meant that Mutzi hadn't got there before her after all. So where was Klaus? She looked quickly around the room again.

The man Mutzi had handed the letter to called to someone else. He came over, but Liesel was too far away to hear what was said. Keeping to the shadows, she began to move as close as she dared. But she still couldn't hear what they were saying. The three men stood talking, then the letter was given back to Mutzi. He took it. She watched him stuff it into his pocket. Then he turned and went back out through the door that led to the street.

Puzzled now, she looked at the room again, and suddenly she realized what must have happened. Klaus had gone without her. He hadn't even waited.

Stepping out of the shadows, she caught up with the man who'd spoken to Mutzi.

'Please?' she said, pulling at his sleeve. 'I'm looking for my brother. He was here, but he isn't here now.'

She stuck to her story – tried to explain how she'd brought Klaus in, how the man he'd been talking to just now had been asking for him as well, but it came out so confusedly that it didn't make any sense, and he wasn't really bothering to listen to her anyway, she could see it. Then, all of a sudden, he stopped and looked down at her, as though he'd just realized what she was actually saying.

'I told your uncle,' he said, nodding to the place where Mutzi had been.

'He's not my uncle,' she protested, but he didn't pay any attention.

'Your brother went with the priest.'

At that she stood absolutely still. He must have thought she was half-witted, the way she was just standing staring at him.

'The priest,' he said again, as though the word was explanation enough. 'The one whose carriage hit him. He's been searching the hospitals for him all day, wanting to make sure he was all right. He was lucky to find him. The priest has taken him back to your home.'

'But that isn't what happened,' she said, shaking her head. 'He wasn't hit by nothing. He fell over—'

Only she'd already lost his attention again. He'd started to walk away. She ran after him, and pulled at his sleeve.

'That isn't what happened,' she said desperately.

But he wasn't listening any more.

Taking herself out of the stale air of the Pauper's Ward, Liesel sat on the steps of the hospital with her head in her hands. The street was bitterly cold now, and dark. There was an icy wind. It was going to freeze – there was already cat ice on the puddles in the wet mud of the street. She didn't know what to do.

It was never going to be enough, just giving the diamond back to Frau Drecht – why hadn't she realized that? With or without it, she was done for. Frau Drecht was going to close up her eyes because of Kusselmann. She couldn't even just walk away any more. Sooner or later Frau Drecht would find her because someone would tell on her – they were bound to, just like she'd told on Klaus.

Only she hadn't meant to.

Carefully she pulled back her sleeve and looked at the burn marks on her arm. They stung so. Even by the weak light of the lantern above the steps she could see them, weeping and raw.

She closed her eyes. She was so tired, so cold. It was hours since she'd slept – when had she slept? She couldn't even remember, and closing her eyes only made it worse. She could hear the thoughts in her head like so much noise:

The priest would have to go to the bridge, because that's where the diamond was. Klaus would tell him, and he wouldn't find it without Klaus so he'd have to take him as well. Only Frau Drecht would be there too. She'd be there, or she'd set someone to wait and then she'd come, and she'd only do that because Liesel had told . . .

In the confusion of her thoughts Liesel saw, like moving pictures, the thin priest in his black coat, and Klaus, and the bridge, and Frau Drecht's powdered face, and the hot iron – only it wasn't a hot iron any more; it was a poker. A big iron poker, and Frau Drecht was bringing it down on Klaus's head. 'No!'

She opened her eyes with a start. Her heart was racing.

No.

She couldn't just leave him alone like that. She'd done that to someone once before when he'd needed her, and she wasn't going to do it again.

Holding up her wrist between the fingers of her other hand, she blew gently on the burned skin of her arm – her breath felt clean and cold. Then she pulled the sleeve back down and, standing up, wiped the grit from the step off her hands. Almost asleep on her feet, she started walking towards the river and the town bridge, the cat ice on the mud cracking with every step she took.

Klaus remembered sitting with his legs over the edge of the table watching the man thread the bright silver needle, remembered the bowl being held for him to be sick into when it was all done; but what had happened since he couldn't really remember at all – it was just one oily confusion, and somewhere in it he'd been carried, and somewhere there'd been cold air and a carriage and the buttoned hard leather of a bench seat. But now he lay on a floor looking up at the shadows of a stone ceiling, curved and vaulted, and there were candles alight, lots of candles.

The more he looked at the ceiling, the more he realized that it wasn't just stone. There were holes pierced through it and he could see trees and leaves. He was looking up into a thick forest with sunlight between the branches. Only he could see the stones of the ceiling and the leaves and the trees all at the same time. There were brightly coloured birds and serpents amongst the branches.

He lay quietly on his back looking at the colours. He could feel the damp warmth of the air, hear the rustling of the leaves and the sounds of the forest. As he watched, the serpents glided along the branches, and the birds beat their wings. There was a little black monkey looking down at him; he could see its honey-coloured eyes – and he realized that there were other faces peering from amongst the leaves – children watching him, only their lips were bloodless and their eyes hollow and empty. They had feathers, all faded and broken, pushed into their hair, and their mouths were smeared with mud.

As he watched, from the branches above him, they began to lower silver threads, fine like silk. He could see them in the sunlight, dropping slowly down towards him, first one, then another, until there were dozens. It was only when the first of them snagged on his skin that he realized that each one was hooked with a tiny barbed pin. He tried to brush them away, but the hooks caught in his hair and his hands, like sharp little thorns. The more he tried, the more they snagged. He heard the laughter of the children as they tugged and pulled on the threads. They were hooked in his face, his lips, the skin of his hands.

'No! Stop it! Stop it!'

Only that made them laugh even more.

Then there was a different voice. A man's voice. Klaus felt the weight of a hand on him before he'd even seen who'd spoken. It was the man who'd chased them – the one the corporal had left half dead in the hay. Klaus stared at him, because it seemed as if he was still in the forest with the laughter and the little hooks caught in his skin; and the man was in the candlelit room, reaching towards him through a window in the air. The man's arms and chest were bare – Klaus could see the sheen of sweat on his skin; there were feathers in his hair too, only they were bright and clean – green and gold. There were patterns – coloured serpents, feathers and eyes – daubed across his skin. Then all that was gone, and the hooks and the laughter as well, as though they had suddenly been swallowed by silence, and he saw instead only the lit candles, and the cloth of Ramos's coat and the bowl of dark water that he held in hands that were patterned with feathers and eyes.

There was a sheen of sweat on Ramos's face. 'Drink,' he said, tipping the bowl towards Klaus's lips.

The water was bitter and cold. It made his mouth numb.

'Is he awake?' said another voice, but the words were in a language Klaus didn't understand.

Ramos put his hand to Klaus's chin and made him drink again. 'He is awake. I have brought him back.'

Klaus could see the ceiling now, all shadows and dark in the candlelight. There were no leaves, no trees. It was just bare stone. He could feel the stiffness of the stitches in his face, like little hooks.

He blinked slowly, and as he did so, the pale, bone-thin face of Henriquez leaned out of the shadows above him.

'Where is it?' The priest's voice was as dry and dead as ashes. 'Did your master take it, or the boarding-house woman? What did they do with it?'

Klaus looked from one to the other – the flat, dark face of Ramos, the gaunt, pale face of the priest. It took him a moment to understand what Henriquez was saying, but as his head slowly cleared, he realized something important.

They didn't know he'd got the diamond.

They thought it was Kusselmann or Frau Drecht who had it.

He lay there for a moment, his mind racing, thinking what to say. He only had to tell them that he didn't know where it was – that would be enough, then they'd let him go. He could keep it.

'There wasn't nothing,' he said at last. It seemed to him as though someone else had spoken the words, because it didn't sound like his voice. It sounded thick and slurred.

But Henriquez didn't let him go. He leaned closer. 'The leather box,' he said. 'Where is the man in the leather box?'

Klaus frowned. He'd thought the priest was talking about the diamond, only he wasn't. Klaus looked blankly at him. He didn't know what the priest was talking about at all. What man? What box? There hadn't been a box. Only the teeth.

He couldn't have pretended the expression of

dumb confusion on his face. It was plain for anyone to see.

'He doesn't know,' said Ramos.

'It *had* to be there,' said Henriquez impatiently.

Klaus looked from one to the other. He couldn't understand what they were saying. It was foreign talk. But he saw the priest hesitate as though some new thought had occurred to him. And he was right, because Henriquez was remembering Frau Drecht's house and the porters carrying the bodies down the stairs. If it wasn't the tooth-puller or the landlady who had found what he was looking for, then it must have been someone else.

Then he remembered the young man he'd passed in the corridor. There'd been no one else.

He bent over Klaus again, his eyes pale and colourless. 'Who took the bodies from the boarding house?'

Klaus knew the answer to that. He'd heard Frau Drecht and Kusselmann talk often enough. He even knew how much a body was worth; knew how much *his* body would be worth.

He suddenly felt very cold. Why would they want to know that?

He shifted awkwardly and looked around. There

was no Liesel. There was no one. Only the bare stones and the shadows of the room. 'The Anatomy,' he said in a small voice.

As he said this, something moved in the shadows behind Ramos; it leaped lightly onto the corner of a table, like a cat. It sat watching him, its tail wrapped around its body. Only it wasn't a cat. Klaus could see the honey-coloured eyes and dirty yellow teeth. But it had been in the forest.

He looked up at Henriquez. He didn't understand what was happening. 'Please, don't hurt me,' he said.

Henriquez straightened, took off his wire-rimmed spectacles, and carefully cleaned them on a cloth from his pocket. Then he put them back on and, reaching down, lightly brushed the fingers of one hand through Klaus's hair. 'That depends on whether you are a good boy,' he said slowly. 'What is your name?'

'Klaus.'

'Are you a good boy, Klaus?'

'Yes,' said Klaus with barely a breath.

He felt the fingers tighten in his hair as Henriquez bent down and looked into his face. 'Then tell me where the diamond is.'

* * *

Markus stood in the dark yard below Frau Rassler's window. He could still feel on his fingertips the dry, greasy touch of the skin; could still smell, even in the clean cold night air, the stale inside of the leather box.

He tried to tell himself that perhaps he'd been mistaken, or that perhaps it was only some last lingering vestige of life that had made the figure appear to move and bleed. It was what he'd spoken of to Karolus only that morning: men dead for days came to the dissection table with fresh stubble on their chins.

But that didn't explain this, because whatever was in that box had been dead for a very long time. Perhaps even centuries. Surely no life could linger that long?

The skin had been smeared with pale colours – green and blue, red and ochre. The tops of the arms were entwined with garlands of flowers, but these were all withered and faded. There were feathers too, broken and lice-eaten, pushed into the remnants of the thick plait of black hair. And the fingernails – stained and yellow against the silver of the spike – had grown curved like claws.

217

There had been a malevolence about it. Markus had felt it, like a cold breath down his spine. He'd closed the lid carefully, as if not wanting it to see him.

This was what Siger had stolen. This was what he'd left for the priest.

'Take it!' Frau Rassler had whispered, her eyes fixed on the box. 'You can have the feathers – I don't want them. Take them!'

They must have been worth months of money to her, but she'd tried to scoop them up, the ones that had fallen onto the floor, and press them into his hands. They'd felt greasy and dry, just like the skin. Markus hadn't known what to do or say.

It was only when he promised to come back that she'd let him go at all. He remembered her face even now, frightened and pale at the doorway as he looked up one last time from the bottom of the stairs.

Markus had thrown the feathers into the gutter the moment he stepped into the yard, and now he stood in the dark; a dog was barking from one of the landings, he could still feel the touch of the skin against his fingertips. He wiped his hand on his thick coat, but even then he could still feel it. He pulled the coat more closely around him and, not wanting to look back, went quickly through the arch and out into the narrow street beyond.

It was late now. There was a hard sparkle of ice on the stones. The air was biting cold.

He retraced his steps along the unfamiliar back ways that led down towards the wharves and the town bridge. He just wanted to be in his own rooms now. He'd had enough. He was tired and hungry, and not one part of this made sense any more. But he was sure of one thing. Whatever was in that box was what Karolus had wanted to find from the moment he'd recognized the dead man on the table – because it hadn't started there; it had started years ago when Siger had been the foreman of the gold mine and Karolus its doctor. And it wasn't Siger that Karolus had been looking for when he hanged all those men in cold blood. No, it was something else. He'd been looking for the thing that Siger had taken.

Markus pulled his coat even tighter around him. It was bitterly cold. The sky was dark and clear. It would get colder still. In the various doorways and alleys he passed, street children, wretched and miserable, huddled for warmth against the night.

They were too cold even to try and beg. He hardly spared them a glance. But as he approached the steps of the town bridge, he saw one child sitting alone, just at the edge of the lantern light. It struck him as a strange place to choose – all alone like that – and you couldn't be too careful at night, not in this part of town. He began to walk more slowly. But there was no one lurking in the shadows behind them, and the child wasn't looking at him, but towards the arches of the bridge.

It was a girl.

He saw the thinness of her face by the lantern light as he passed.

But it wasn't until he'd taken several more steps that he suddenly realized whose face it was, and where he'd seen it before.

Chapter Sixteen

Markus stopped and looked back.

He was very good at faces: he never forgot one.

It was her, he was sure of it – the girl who'd opened the door that first time at Frau Drecht's house. He even remembered her name – Frau Drecht had bawled it loudly enough.

So what was she doing here at this time of night?

It was only an idle thought, simple curiosity, and he'd been about to walk on again when another thought occurred to him, and that wasn't an idle one at all, because it was about the tooth-puller's boy.

He'd almost forgotten that it was actually the boy that Karolus had sent him to find in the first place, and Karolus wouldn't have done that if there hadn't been a reason. Now, here was Frau Drecht's girl. She'd have been in the house when the tooth-puller had called. At the very least she'd be able to say what the boy looked like. He'd be foolish to let the chance pass.

Markus began to walk back towards her. It was only now that he saw the rime of frost glittering on her clothes and in her hair. She was huddled against a wall, her eyes were closed. There was frost on her lashes too. He bent down beside her and saw that her lips were pale blue with cold.

'It's Liesel, isn't it?' he said.

She didn't so much as stir.

A different concern overtook him now. He put his hand to her cheek; it was as cold as any corpse, and for a moment that's what he thought she was. But when he pressed his fingers into her neck, he could feel the pulse, faint and weak.

He looked about him to see if there was anyone around who might help her, but it was late now and the path to the bridge was empty. There was only him.

Markus put his hand to her face again. It was like ice. He couldn't leave her like this – she'd be dead within the hour. And suddenly he thought of all the pale, nameless child corpses he'd seen dissected on the Anatomy School table. Some of them must have died alone, just like this, only he'd never given it a thought before. Never thought how it had actually happened.

Only he did now. It happened like this.

He looked down at the girl again. If he walked away now, it would be him, not the cold that killed her.

He bent down and shook her hard. 'Come on! Wake up!' he said sharply. 'Wake up!'

She lolled against him like a stiff doll. He couldn't get her to wake up at all.

For a moment he thought about taking her back to Bergenstrasse and Frau Drecht, but that wasn't a part of the town he cared to be in at this time of night. No, if he was going to do that, it could wait until the morning. The important thing was to get the girl warm. It was perhaps ten minutes to his rooms. The caretaker's widow, Frau Hofker, could take care of her there. That would be the simplest thing. And then he could ask her about the boy.

Markus took off his thick coat, wrapped it around her and picked her up. Her clothes were stiff and frozen. She didn't make so much as a sound. He carried her up the stone steps and out across the bridge towards Morbahn Strasse.

As he passed the shadows at the top of the steps, he didn't notice a ragged boy with red hair. If he had, he'd have remembered his face – and where he'd seen that as well.

But he didn't see him. And he didn't see the boy slipping out of the shadows of the steps and quietly following him.

Frau Hofker had a couple of cramped rooms at the bottom of the stairs in the hall. She kept a chair by her door where she would sit all day. She would sweep the staircases and sell coal and make the fires. But the chair was empty now, and there was no light showing under her door when Markus reached it with Liesel in his arms.

He beat on the door. 'Frau Hofker!'

But there was no answer – no sound of movement either. There was nothing for it: he would have to take Liesel to his own rooms.

Although Frau Hofker had left a lamp lit at the bottom of the stairs, the candle in the glass she'd left at the top had blown out. Markus stood in the cold darkness of the landing fumbling for his key, only to find when he turned it in the lock that the door had been open all the time. It happened sometimes. He'd forget to lock it. He closed it behind him, and in the dark put Liesel down on the rug in front of the unlit fire while he struck a match and set it to the dried sticks and wood that Frau Hofker had already laid in the grate. The sticks began to crackle and spit. Then, feeling in the dark for the lamp on the table, he lifted its glass and held the last gutterings of the match to the wick. It took a moment for the little yellow flame to catch; then he blew out the match and turned to look for his surgeon's bag.

And stopped.

In the shadows cast by the lamp and the small fire, a man was sitting motionless on the chair in the corner of the room.

It was the priest he'd seen in the hall of Frau Drecht's house. Father Henriquez.

Markus straightened. 'What are you doing in my rooms?' he said.

For a moment the priest didn't answer. He sat quietly regarding Markus. 'You were not hard to find,' he said at last. 'It needed only the briefest of enquiries at the Anatomy School. I did not realize, though, that you were the mine doctor's assistant.

What connected little worlds we find when we start to look.'

Markus frowned. The priest knew what Karolus had once been. 'If you mean that I am Professor Karolus's assistant,' he said, 'yes, I am. And I ask you again: what are you doing in my rooms?'

Henriquez slowly leaned forward into the half-light, and for the first time Markus saw what he was holding.

A single blue feather.

Markus glanced down at the table beside him. He'd taken the packet and the ticket with him when he'd gone out looking for Laub's shop, but he'd left the feather there. Only it wasn't there any more.

'I would like to know where you got this?' said Henriquez in that cold ash voice.

Markus hesitated. The packet, and everything that had been in it, had been meant for Henriquez, but the priest couldn't have come here for that because he wouldn't have known that Markus had it.

So what had he come for?

Markus laid the spent match on the table, his finger resting on it as he looked up at the priest. 'Since you ask, then I have a question for you,' he said. 'Why is it important?'

Henriquez took a moment to answer. He turned the feather between his fingers by its quill. It made a blue sheen in the lamplight.

Lying on the rug, Liesel felt the warmth of the little fire on her face. She thought she was still by the bridge watching for Klaus, but she could hear voices, and slowly she realized that she wasn't. The voices sounded very far away. She opened her eyes, and watching the small flickering flames she lay very still and listened.

Then she realized whose voice it was.

'You are a man of science, are you not, Herr Assistant?' said Henriquez. 'But do you never wonder about men's souls? Do you never ask yourself what becomes of them when all that is left behind is the blood and filth that you strive to understand with your knife and your anatomy table?' He was looking steadily at Markus now. 'Do you never ask yourself that, Herr Assistant? Where does life go?'

The question caught Markus quite unprepared, because it was the very one Karolus had asked a thousand times – the question to which there was simply no answer. But Henriquez was looking at him as though he was waiting for one.

'We are taught there is a Heaven and a Hell,' answered Markus. 'That the souls of the Just go to the one and the Damned to the other.'

'So we are,' said Henriquez, nodding smally. 'But where is the proof of that, Herr Assistant? What man ever came back from the dead and told us so?'

It was a curious thing for a priest to say.

Henriquez smiled coldly, as though he'd heard the thought in Markus's head. 'They are different things, you know,' he said. 'Faith and proof.'

'So?' said Markus.

He couldn't see what the purpose of this was. He turned and, bending over Liesel, laid his hand on her cheek. It was still ice-cold, but he could see that her eyes were open now, looking glassily into the crackling fire.

'Tell me, Herr Assistant,' said Henriquez. 'Do you know what Cortés and his conquistadores found in the Americas?'

At that word, Markus looked up. That was where this had all started, he knew it – with Karolus and the gold mine.

'They found a people who believed they could send a soul, as a messenger, between the worlds of the living and the dead, send it and call it back,' said

228

Henriquez. 'Do you know how they did it? No? They chose a man – it would have been a great honour for him. They fed him and celebrated with him, and then, when it was time, they killed him – flayed him alive – and dressed his still living skin with the finest of feathers so that it wouldn't disgrace them when his soul wore it again in that other place. Then they put a knife through his heart and sent his soul on its way. That was their faith.'

'Then it was a barbaric one,' said Markus.

'Do you think so?' said Henriquez. 'It's always the other man's faith that is *barbaric*, is it not? But is it so very different a thing to eating the flesh or drinking the blood of Christ?'

He looked at Markus with those pale, water-clear eyes, and in barely more than a whisper, he said, 'How do we know, Herr Scientist, that they were not right?'

The words hung in the silence of the room. Markus could hear the little flame of the lamp guttering on its wick, the sticks spitting in the grate. 'Because there can be no proof of it,' he said.

For a moment Henriquez looked at him with distant eyes, as though he were seeing something somewhere else. 'Faith grows to be an empty thing without proof,' he said.

Then his gaze hardened again. He held up the feather, turning it slowly on its quill, iridescent blue in the shadows and the light. 'Where did you get this?' he said, but there was a colder edge to his voice now.

Liesel could hear the words, but they were coming and going like story pictures in her head and none of it made sense. Henriquez wasn't talking about the diamond or Klaus, she knew that, and she would have liked to see just what it was that the priest was holding; only that would have meant turning her head, and she didn't want to do that because the fire was so warm on her face, and if she did, he might see her again, and that would be the end of her. So she lay very still.

But Markus was looking at the feather, because he knew now what was in that leather box. Only why did Karolus and this priest want it?

'It was on the floor in the house on Bergenstrasse,' he said. 'I picked it up.'

Henriquez took off his spectacles and unhurriedly cleaned them on the cloth from his pocket. He replaced them and looked at Markus again; then he glanced down at Liesel on the floor, as though seeing a child there didn't surprise him at all.

'I think we both know that is not true,' he said.

But what he said next wasn't what Markus expected at all. Still looking at Liesel, Henriquez said, 'Remind your mine doctor that there is only one way for the child to be chosen. Remind him of that, Herr Assistant. And tell him that I know where it is.'

He stood up like a knife unfolding, the feather still in his hand. 'He can find me at the convent of the Marienkirche,' he said.

Without another look, he stepped past Markus and through the door onto the dark of the landing. Markus heard his footsteps going down the empty stairs to the street.

It took a moment for him to gather his thoughts. Henriquez believed that Karolus had the leather box and the skin that was inside it – that at least was clear; that's where he thought the feather had come from. But there was something more than just that.

He looked down at Liesel. What had Henriquez meant about the child?

Liesel was staring into the fire. She'd begun to shiver now, which was good.

Still turning Henriquez's words over in his mind, Markus took a small phial of liquid from his surgeon's bag, poured it into a glass and, lifting Liesel's head, tipped it into her mouth. She tried to push his hand away, but she had no strength to do it, and besides, the liquid felt warm on her tongue and her throat. But she wanted to tell him about Klaus and Frau Drecht – that she had to get back to the bridge and watch for Klaus – only the words just wouldn't come.

'You'll rest better now,' he said, and laid her head back on the rug.

He sat watching her as her eyes closed again, but his thoughts were somewhere else.

They were on the dried skin in the leather box. He could still feel the grease and sweat of it on his hand.

The more he thought about it, the darker it became, like a solid shape in his head. He could see the bead of blood rising on its back, the shiver like an in-drawn breath.

Surely it couldn't still be alive – if it was what Henriquez had said, then it was centuries old.

He had to see it again. Had to see if there was anything else in the box; anything that would explain why they wanted it. Explain why Karolus had hanged all those men just to find it.

Only he couldn't leave the girl here like this.

Markus went out onto the landing and peered over the rail. Wherever Frau Hofker had been, she was back now. There was a light from beneath her door. Lifting Liesel in his arms, he carried her down the stairs and knocked.

Frau Hofker opened the door. Brushing her protests aside, Markus carried Liesel in. The room smelled of warm lamp oil and cooking. He took his coat from around Liesel and laid her close to Frau Hofker's little stove. Frau Hofker stood over him complaining loudly, but as Markus moved Liesel, they both saw the line of burn marks on her arm and exchanged a silent look. Without another word Frau Hofker went to fetch a bowl of water and a cloth.

Markus looked at the raw, burned skin and thought of Frau Drecht. This was why she'd been at the bridge. She'd run away.

'These need to be cleaned properly,' he said to Frau Hofker when she came back with the water. 'I'll fetch my bag.' He put his hand to Liesel's face. It was warmer now, and there was colour in her lips.

Fetching his surgeon's bag from his rooms, Markus carefully cleaned her arm, then bound it with a fine gauze of greased cotton. She moved her head a little as though in protest as he did so, but her eyes never opened and she didn't wake.

'She'll be fine now,' he said, pulling on his coat. 'Keep her warm. And keep her here – I need to talk to her when I come back. But I have to go out.'

There was an agitation about him that Frau Hofker couldn't miss. It wasn't like him at all. 'Is everything all right, sir?' she asked.

'Yes,' said Markus, perhaps too quickly. 'Yes, it is.' He smiled awkwardly. 'I just have to go out.'

Markus went down the steps and into the freezing street. The sky was bright with stars and frost. He made his way back across the town bridge. Against the clear sky he could see the darker lines of ships moored along the wharves, their masts like a forest of thin trees. Finally he found himself again beneath the arch that led to the dressmaker's yard.

The stairs were unlit, but as he looked up towards the landing, he saw a light. It spilled out in a fan across the wall.

The dressmaker's door was open. 'Frau Rassler?' he called.

But there was no answer.

He climbed the stairs. 'Frau Rassler?'

The room was all in disorder. The lamps were still brightly lit, but everything was scattered and thrown, and in the middle of the floor was the dressmaker. She was rocking slowly backwards and forwards on her heels, making a small wordless noise.

Then Markus realized that there was something missing. Amongst all the confusion of the room, the spilled patterns and cut papers, the leather box wasn't there. He cast his eyes quickly around. It wasn't there.

Markus bent down beside the dressmaker. She was still rocking backwards and forwards, her eyes wide open. He put his hand on her arm. 'Frau Rassler,' he said firmly.

She turned her head and stared at him.

'Where is the box, Frau Rassler?' he said. 'The leather box?'

She made noises, as though trying to speak; then she shot out her hand and grabbed hold of the lapel of his coat. Her grip was like iron. He tried to pull her fingers away, but she wouldn't let go. She was staring at him wide-eyed.

As he tried to pull her hand away, he noticed that

she was holding something tightly in it.

It was dark and small – a button pulled from a coat.

A black coral button.

Chapter Seventeen

Markus prised the button out of the dressmaker's hand. She didn't try to stop him. It was almost as if she didn't even know he was doing it.

He turned it over and looked at it more carefully.

There was only one man that he knew wore coral buttons like that. He saw them every time he held Karolus's coat or helped him into his leather apron. Only how could Karolus have known to come here? He looked stupidly around the room as though there might be some answer there, but there wasn't.

And then he remembered Karolus's clerk, Menz: Menz in the street outside Keltzer's rooms; Menz in Schwanplatz outside Laub's shop.

That hadn't just been coincidence. He'd been

following him all the time. That was how Karolus knew. Markus had led him here.

And Markus would never have known it but for that little black button.

Only what had happened then he couldn't begin to say.

He looked at the disorder of the room – the tipped chair, the spilled patterns, the woman's staring eyes. She must have grabbed hold of Karolus's coat like this too, and the button had come off in her hand. Had she been trying to stop him opening the box?

It had been opened: Markus could smell it. The stale odour of grease and sweat hung in the air. He could taste it on his tongue like off meat.

He pulled his coat out of the woman's fingers and her hand clutched at the front of her own dress, her fingers creasing the cloth.

'It's all right,' he said. 'It's gone.'

She turned her face blankly towards him.

He stood up and opened one of the shutters to let the cold night air in. As he turned round, he was aware of someone standing in the open doorway. It was a young girl, peering in from the gloom of the hall.

Suddenly he realized that this wasn't a place to be

238

found – he didn't want to explain what he was doing there. If Frau Rassler's neighbours came and crowded at the door like the girl, they'd think he'd done something to her. That this was his fault. He could only guess what would happen then, and he wasn't going to wait to find out.

He crossed the room to the door. The girl backed nervously away from him.

'Get your mother,' he said as he stepped past her onto the landing. 'Get her to come here and help. Do it now!'

But that was all he said. He didn't even stop. He went down the hard wooden stairs as quickly as he could and out into the freezing night.

He already knew where he was going next.

When he reached Karolus's house, the lantern was burning above the steps outside. It was as sure a sign as any that Karolus and his carriage had been out. Markus stood at the bottom of the steps looking up at the fine front door and the sashed and shuttered windows, and as he did so, a warning voice began whispering in his head, telling him to stop here; that this was some business of Karolus's that he should have no part in.

Only he didn't listen to it.

It took several minutes for the housekeeper to answer Markus's knock, and when she finally did she looked sourly at him over the light of a small candle, as if to let him know that she'd come unwillingly from the warmth of her bed.

Markus ignored the look. 'I want to see Herr Professor Karolus,' he said.

'The Herr Professor is asleep,' she answered curtly. 'It is the middle of the night.'

'Then wake him up,' answered Markus sharply.

Her mouth tightened and she was about to argue the point with him when, across the hall, another door opened and light spilled from the room.

'It will not be necessary to wake me, Martha,' said Karolus from the doorway. 'I am not asleep. You may allow Herr Brennen in.'

The housekeeper gave Markus one last hostile glance and, with a dip of her head to Karolus, retreated with the candle into the darkness of the house.

Karolus watched her go. He didn't say anything until the last glimmer of her light had gone. 'It is a late hour to be calling on me, Markus,' he said at last, without warmth.

'Nonetheless, I see that you are awake,' Markus answered.

'But hardly sufficient reason to disturb me,' said Karolus.

He turned his back on Markus and returned to the lit room. Markus, still wrapped in his thick coat, followed.

The lamps and candles were burning brightly. Here, as in the professor's rooms at the school, were spread the collected curiosities of his travels, only these were of the rarer sort – gilded masks, and stone panels carved with winding serpents and strangely shaped, angular men. Several books lay open across the tabletops, as though Karolus had broken off in the middle of some search.

'Perhaps you have found the boy?' he said, closing the heavy covers of the books so that Markus might not see the pages they'd been open at.

But Markus didn't answer. Instead, he reached into the pocket of his coat and, taking out the black coral button, dropped it onto the table in front of Karolus. It fell like a small stone onto the glass-covered leather.

Karolus glanced down at it, and then up at Markus.

'It was in the dressmaker's hand,' Markus said simply. 'She must have pulled it off your coat.'

Karolus moved the button with his finger, and then looked up at Markus again. 'How very industrious you have been, Markus,' he said coolly.

'You might have told me what it was I was *really* looking for,' said Markus curtly. He was angry at having been used.

'You found it for me without the necessity for that particular instruction being given,' said Karolus.

Markus could feel his temper rising. He wasn't Karolus's dog. 'You haven't told me why you want that boy, either,' he said. 'Or am I just supposed to blindly find him as well?'

Then he remembered what Henriquez had said. 'Or is he the child?'

The moment he said it, he realized that it was a mistake because Karolus looked sharply up at him.

'Even more industrious . . .' he said, his eyes not leaving Markus. 'Who told you that?'

The words were spoken quietly enough, but Karolus's whole manner had suddenly changed, and Markus was instantly aware of it. It was something about that boy. Something that Karolus had not meant Markus to know.

Markus hesitated.

'Who told you about the child?' Karolus asked again.

In that single moment Markus saw that everything Keltzer had said was true – Karolus had hanged those men; he'd stood and watched them choke out their lives on a rope because of this. Whatever it was, it was that important.

And now Markus had come to interfere.

And people who interfered with Karolus's business did not end well. In at least one place, Markus was sure now, they'd ended up dead.

This wasn't the time to be clever. It was a time to be very careful.

'There was a letter,' said Markus, choosing the words with care. 'A packet with a pawnbroker's ticket and a feather – only Menz will have told you that part since you had him follow me.'

'He has his uses,' said Karolus indifferently. 'But that is not what I asked. Who told you about the child? What did they say?'

There was no going back now. 'A priest,' said Markus.

Karolus frowned.

'He was at the house on Bergenstrasse the day I

collected the body. He must have been looking for the box as well. He came to my rooms tonight.'

'And that is why you went back?' said Karolus, gesturing at the button. 'To show him what you had found? I do so hope, for your sake, Markus, that it was not.'

Markus hesitated again. Why had he gone back? Why was he even here now?

He knew the answer to that: curiosity.

'What is this about?' he said quietly. 'What is in that box?'

A cold smile crossed Karolus's face. 'Ever curious, aren't you, Markus,' he said dangerously. 'Well, perhaps I'd better satisfy your curiosity.'

He picked up one of the candlesticks and, pausing in mid movement, looked at Markus again. The flames settled in the still air. 'Too much curiosity is a killing thing, Markus. I would have you remember later that I warned you of that.'

Without saying any more, Karolus crossed the room and led Markus out into the darkened hall.

Markus had been to this house only once before – on a summer's day. There'd been a single glass cupola at the very top of a deep stairwell, and motes of dust turning slowly in the long column of light.

There'd been a lantern too – in the shape of a huge bronze galleon suspended above the hall on a chain that ran up through all five floors to its fixing in the roof. Just looking up at the drop of chain from below had made Markus's head swim. A Spanish galleon, Karolus had told him, a conquistador's ship, and Markus had asked what had become of it, the real ship, and Karolus had become quiet, as though recalling a pain of his own. 'It burned at sea,' he'd said at last, and had moved on.

But now the hall was dark, save for the flickering light of the candles in the stick that Karolus carried. Markus could almost feel the bronze galleon on its long chain looming like a threat in the darkness above him.

Karolus led him through the corridors of the house until at last he stopped and held the candlestick to a plain panelled door. Taking a key from his pocket, he unlocked it and pushed it open. Even before Markus stepped through the door he could smell the skin – the staleness of the sweat and grease in the velvet heavy dark.

Karolus lit the candles in the room one by one.

The skin had been lifted out of the leather box and laid on a long table by the wall. It looked even more like a living man than it had before – a man caught in the moment of touching his forehead to the ground, his arms stretching forward in supplication; but a silver spike had been driven through the backs of his hands like a nail, fixing them for ever.

Markus saw the sheen of the feathers in the candlelight, the squat powerful curve of the back and limbs. But he could see something more now.

He could see the face as well.

Beneath the plait of the man's thick black hair – the feathers and the garlands of dead flowers – the face was twisted in an expression of inconceivable pain. This had not been a kind death. Whoever he might have been in life, the agony of his death was etched there for all eternity in the flayed skin of his face.

Markus turned and looked uneasily at Karolus.

'It is the only one left,' said Karolus. 'Who knows how many there were once, but this is the very last – Cortés and his priests burned the rest.'

Markus looked at the feathered skin again. 'My God,' he breathed.

'No, Markus,' said Karolus sharply. 'Not *your* god. Another god completely. Does yours have to be the only one?'

246

Markus looked at him. He'd heard those words once already that night. 'That's almost what the priest said,' he answered.

Karolus looked at him coldly. 'And what else did your priest say?'

'That it was a relic – an act of their faith,' said Markus.

The feathered skin had a darkness all of its own – like a nightmare. Nothing would make him touch it again, not for anything, but it held his eyes just as it had done before.

'What did they do?' he asked.

It was a moment before Karolus answered. 'They sacrificed lives to it. One to summon its soul from that other place, and one to send it back. They believed it was a messenger between the worlds of the living and the dead, Markus.' He drew his hand along the feathers of the broad back. The dry quills rustled against each other. He lifted the candles so that the feathers shone with an iridescent lustre. 'Who is to say they were not right?'

Markus looked at the skin again, the plait of hair, the feathers and the dried flowers, and this time he felt an even darker presence, as though this were an empty vessel waiting to be filled.

He stepped back. 'That is superstition, not science,' he said.

'You think so?' said Karolus. 'Then you disappoint me, Markus. I did not expect your mind, of all people's, to be so closed. Have you learned nothing? What is "superstition" – or "religion", for that matter – if not an explanation by ignorant minds of something greater than they can comprehend? And is that not the purpose of what we do, of what science truly is – to throw light into that darkness, to reveal its truth? How do you know that there is not a truth to be discovered here, Markus; something greater than we yet comprehend?'

Markus turned and looked at him. Karolus's eyes gleamed darkly in the candlelight.

'What did the priest mean – about the child?' he asked.

But Karolus didn't reply. 'Let me not detain you any longer, Markus,' he answered coldly. 'If, that is, your curiosity to see this again has been quite satisfied.'

Markus didn't move. 'You will not tell me, will you?' he said.

'Oh, I will tell you, Markus. Come tomorrow, and

you shall have your explanation. I promise.' Karolus gestured to the door. The conversation was at an end.

He led Markus back through the darkened house to the door to the street. 'Tomorrow, Markus,' he said. 'Come tomorrow.'

Karolus closed the heavy door behind Markus, and stood quite still for a moment in the silence, listening to the noises of the house. But there was no other sound.

Then, holding the candlestick before him, he went back along the hall to the library and, from a green leather box on his desk, took a long, thin steel knife, the edges as sharp as a razor. Opening a narrow door in the panelled wall, he stepped through into a smaller room beyond, where Menz, in his brown threadbare tailcoat, sat waiting.

He stood up as Karolus came in, straightening his neckcloth as though to smarten himself up before his master.

'Ah, Menz,' said Karolus with a disarming smile. 'You are still here. Good. There is one last thing I would have you do for me.'

Poor Menz.

Menz, in his shabby brown tailcoat and grubby neckcloth.

Menz, whom no one would ever miss.

Out in the freezing street, Markus walked in an uneasy confusion back towards his rooms. This had answered nothing. He was tired and cold, and there was something darkly wrong about all of this.

When he reached the house on Morbahn Strasse, he hesitated in the hall, his hand poised at Frau Hofker's door. But there was no crack of light beneath it, and he could hear the watchman calling the hours in the street outside. It was the middle of the night. There was no waking her now. That could wait until the morning.

It could all wait until the morning. He would speak with the girl then.

Chapter Eighteen

The dark little room was stale with Mutzi's night breath, and the smell of his unwashed bed and unemptied pot.

Frau Drecht shook him roughly by the shoulder, and pulled back the broken shutter at the little window. A cold grey light came in. 'Get up!' she said.

Spitzel waited uncertainly behind her at the open doorway. It didn't pay to go any nearer Mutzi than you had to. Especially if he'd been drinking the night before.

Mutzi opened his eyes and, with a groan, passed one huge hand across his face, then rubbed it through his short cropped hair.

Frau Drecht picked up his coat from the floor and threw it onto the dirty bed.

'Guess who little Spitzel's found again,' she said.

Chapter Nineteen

Someone was hammering at Markus's door.

The noise of it slowly penetrated his sleeping mind.

'Herr Brennen! Herr Brennen! Wake up!'

He opened his eyes and blinked.

'Herr Brennen!'

It was Frau Hofker's voice.

He turned his head and looked dumbly about at the room. He was sitting in his chair, still wearing the clothes of the night before, but the small fire had burned out and in its place, daylight made a hard line across the floor. He couldn't even remember falling asleep. Then, like playing cards dropped one by one into his head, he remembered the girl, and Karolus, and the feathered skin of the man.

'Herr Brennen!'

'I'm here,' he answered.

Stiffly he stood up and, still blinking at the daylight, crossed the room and unlocked the door.

Frau Hofker stood on the dimly lit landing. Gerst, one of the porters from the school, stood beside her. Even in that half-light Markus saw the grim set of his face.

'There has been such an accident, Herr Brennen,' said Frau Hofker, wringing her hands.

Markus looked up at Gerst.

'Please, come at once, sir,' the porter said.

'What has happened?' said Markus.

But Gerst didn't answer; all he did was ask again.

'Would you come at once, sir?'

Markus fetched his thick coat and followed Gerst down the stairs and out into the icy street, but he couldn't get a word more out of the man. Though he realized soon enough where Gerst was taking him. He was leading him towards Karolus's house.

When they got there, Markus found that a small crowd had gathered by the steps. They were peering curiously up at the closed door and shuttered windows. Markus and the porter pushed their way through and up the steps to the door, which opened to them when they knocked.

In the hall, the hard morning light slanted across the long iron chain of the galleon lantern, but everything else was shuttered and dark, just as it had been when Markus had left it only hours before. Only now, in the bleak gloom at the bottom of the stairs stood a handful of men, their breath making small clouds in the chill, still air of the house. They turned to look at Markus as the heavy door shut behind him. They were all men he knew, trustees of the school – and Hilpfer, the registrar, was there as well, his face fat and pale in the thin light. But there was something lying on the floor at their feet. A lit candlestick had been set beside it.

It took Markus a moment to realize that it was the body of a man. He crossed the hall, but it wasn't until Hilpfer stepped aside that he saw whose the body was.

It was Karolus.

Markus stared down at him.

Karolus lay sprawled, his eyes wide with terror, his head broken open and spilled like a dark egg across the hard flagstones.

'The housekeeper found him,' said Hilpfer. He

drew himself up self-importantly. 'There is to be no scandal about this, Brennen,' he said. 'Do you understand?'

As he said the words, Hilpfer looked around at the other men, and they nodded, as though this was something they had already discussed, already agreed upon. 'It is to be said only that he *fell*.'

That last word was so pointed that Markus realized at once why Gerst hadn't said anything – he'd been told not to.

Because Karolus had jumped. That's what Hilpfer meant – he'd taken his own life.

Markus looked up into the long dark drop of the stairs, into the motes of dust turning slowly in the slanting shaft of daylight. He could see now that one of the spars of the galleon lantern was bent downwards; a scrap of Karolus's coat hung from the end of it.

Only that didn't make any sense at all. Markus had seen him just hours before, and whatever it was that Karolus had intended to do then, it hadn't been to jump from the top of a flight of stairs. No, there had to be something else.

Or some*body* else.

What if the priest had come here?

'You have searched the house?' he said. It was the first thing they should have done.

But Hilpfer only looked angrily at him. 'The doors were locked, Brennen. It is abundantly clear, it seems, to everyone here but you, what has happened. Professor Karolus killed himself.' He hissed these last words in a whisper through gritted teeth, as though fearful that they might be overheard. 'But there is to be no scandal for the school. Do I make myself clear enough now? Herr Professor Karolus *fell*.' He turned away, and began talking in low tones to the other men.

Markus stood there for a moment. Hilpfer was wrong, he knew it. This was something to do with that feathered skin, and what Karolus had meant to do with it – he was sure of it.

He glanced back into the shuttered blackness of the hall.

Was it even still there? Or had Henriquez taken it?

Without any words, he detached himself from the group of men and quietly crossed the hall. No one paid any attention to him. He couldn't remember which of the corridors it was that Karolus had led him down, so he took the nearest one. As his eyes grew accustomed to the gloom, he saw the line of the walls, made out the darker outline of the doors. He hesitated, looked back along the cold corridor to the dim, shadow figures in the hall; then, reaching into his pocket, he drew out his match case and struck a single light.

It took him several moments more to find the right door. But at last, there it was, plain panelled, just as he remembered it. Only it wasn't locked now. It stood half open.

He stopped.

He could smell in the dark air through the open door the lingering staleness of the skin, only now there was something else as well – something cloying and familiar.

The butcher's-shop smell of an anatomy table.

He pushed the door slowly open with the flat of his hand.

He could see nothing. The room was velvet-dark and silent, but he could hear something dripping.

Drip.

Drip.

Barely breathing, he lifted the match to the darkness – the flame no more than a little orb of light at the tip of his fingers. The first thing it lit was the arm of a man, the grubby cuff of a cheap shirt.

Not breathing at all now, Markus held the match higher and the light fell on a cold, dead face.

It was Menz.

He lay across the table, eyes open and staring, a single knife wound through his heart. But his head had been tipped back over the edge of the table and his throat cut – it gaped ear to ear, deep as the bone. A bucket set on the floor beneath him had caught his blood, which still dripped from the shocking white skin of his neck.

Drip.

Drip.

There was a ladle and a cup on the floor. Sheets of paper had been scattered about; some had fallen into a pool of blood. With a shaking hand Markus bent slowly down and picked up one sheet, then another. They were notes, each one covered in Karolus's minute writing, save for one unfinished page which had only two words hastily scrawled across it, barely legible in the light of the match:

The boy.

A burned-out lantern lay broken on the floor, and next to it, lying in a pool of Menz's blood, something glinted in the darkness. Markus held the match towards it.

It was the silver spike.

Even as he realized what it was, the match burned out. He dropped it with a gasp and struggled with his shaking hands in the dark to light another, but they showered out of his fingers onto the floor until he was left with just one. He struck it and it flared into light. Shielding the flame, he held it to the empty corners of the room. He could feel the last remnants of self-control slipping from him.

The feathered skin wasn't there.

He began to edge backwards from the room, and as he did so, he saw in the weak, flickering flame, footprints through the blood on the stone floor – like those of a man walking on the bare skin of his feet.

'Hilpfer!' he shouted. 'Herr Doktor Hilpfer!'

He turned and fled back down the corridor, saw in the cold half-light of the hall the startled faces of the men turn towards him.

And then he stopped.

Because in the air above their heads, something was falling slowly through the slanting column of light, turning and twisting among the motes of dust.

He walked uncertainly forwards, his face turning upwards to watch it. Hilpfer was frowning darkly at him – but then, following Markus's gaze, he turned his head and looked up too.

They all did.

They stood watching the thing float silently down, until Markus reached up and closed his fingers around it.

It was a feather.

A single iridescent blue feather.

And finally he understood what it was that Karolus had meant to do. 'Saints save us . . .' he breathed quietly. *Come tomorrow,* Karolus had said, *and you shall have your explanation.*

This was the explanation. This was what Karolus had done.

He stared back up through the slant of daylight into the darkness of the stairs, but he could see nothing. Hilpfer and the other men were looking at him. He couldn't even begin to think of what to say to them.

'There is a dead man,' he began falteringly. 'Menz. Karolus has killed him. I think that something has gone terribly wrong.' He turned away. 'Gerst!' he shouted.

Hilpfer caught him angrily by the sleeve. 'This is neither the time nor the place for some idiotic student prank, Brennen.'

But Markus only looked at him palely. 'I wish to God it were.'

Gerst appeared out of the dark.

'Bring more light,' said Markus. 'A lantern – anything.'

Pushing his way through the men, he took the candlestick from the floor beside Karolus's body and, standing on the bottom step, his hand on the rail, he leaned out and peered up into the shadows that lay beyond the slant of daylight.

But even as Markus looked up, he felt a dark excitement flood through him like a wave. What was it that Karolus had found – that a soul could really be called back from the dead? If that was it, then the enormity of it was almost incomprehensible – it was a discovery that men could only ever dream of making, of being a part of. And yet it was here, almost within Markus's reach.

Gerst appeared with one of the lanterns from beside the street door, though it had already burned low and there was only a small greasy flame left in the glass. 'It's the best I could find, sir.'

'Bring it!' said Markus, and with a last glance at the body of Karolus, he began to climb the stairs, the candles and lantern making a small orb of light about him.

For a moment Hilpfer stood watching, but when he saw what Markus was doing, saw Gerst follow him, he came quickly up the stairs behind them, pushing past the porter. 'What the devil do you think you're doing?'

But Markus didn't answer.

Holding the candlestick before him, he crossed the first landing; the flames guttered and flickered, casting shadows along the dark unlit passages that led from it. There was a sudden clamour of voices from the hall below. Looking down over the rail and into the half-light, Markus and Hilpfer saw the appalled faces turned up towards them.

Someone had found the body of Menz.

As Markus looked down at them, he heard a different sound, almost lost in the noise from below. 'Quiet!' he shouted over the rail, his hand beating the air for silence. 'Quiet!'

They fell quiet.

In the silence he could hear a sound that he couldn't place – like the brushing of dry straw along

263

a wall. Like the rustling the quills had made as Karolus ran his hand across the feathered man's back.

Markus glanced at Hilpfer. Hilpfer had heard it too – he was peering up into the shadowed darkness of the stairs above them, trying to see where the sound had come from.

He motioned to the porter to follow.

Even more cautiously now, they passed through the slant of weak daylight that fell from the cupola across the long lantern chain, and climbed into the darkness of the stairs that lay beyond it, the candle-light casting shadow men along the wall behind them.

There was no sound now, only the creak of their steps on the tread of the stairs. Everything else was silence.

Markus's heart began to race. He could smell it now – smell the stale skin and sweat. Taste it on his breath.

Karolus had been right.

Beneath the last landing he signed to Gerst to stop and, lifting the candlestick higher, raised his head slowly above the remaining few steps of the stairs. By the flickering light he could see the bare floor and the darkness of the passage beyond. The handrail was broken – it must have been where Karolus had fallen.

Or jumped.

Suddenly cold doubt began to seize Markus.

From somewhere in the dark of that passage came a slow rasp of breath. Like a soul remembering again, after centuries of silence, what it was to breathe.

'Give me that light,' said Hilpfer to Gerst.

Markus felt more than saw Hilpfer take the lantern from Gerst, and put his hand out to stop him, but Hilpfer pushed it aside and stepped up onto the landing.

There was another long drawn breath from the dark.

'What is it, Brennen?' said Hilpfer, holding the lantern higher, but it gave barely any light at all now. 'Is it an animal?'

'No,' said Markus. 'Come away, Hilpfer. It is something that Karolus has brought back to life.'

Hilpfer looked round for a brief moment – just one glance, his face full of disbelief. Then the rustling of feathers and quills started again.

Gerst began to back away down the stairs.

'Damn you, Gerst, stay there!' hissed Markus.

But Gerst kept going.

'Gerst!'

But the porter had gone; left them alone in the dark of the stairs.

'Come back, Hilpfer,' whispered Markus.

But Hilpfer didn't move. He stood in the last light of the lantern, peering into the blackness. 'Bring your light, Brennen,' he called. 'I want to see.'

Markus took a step forward, but the light fell only onto empty darkness. There was nothing there to see – but they could still hear it: the rustling of feather quills. It filled the air all around them.

Then Hilpfer laid his ear to the plaster of the wall. He turned and looked at Markus with a wholly bewildered face. 'It's coming from inside,' he said.

They were the last words he ever spoke.

In the plaster next to Hilpfer's face two dark, feather-lidded eyes flicked open as a hand of yellowed fingernails, curved like claws, shot out of the wall and hooked themselves through Hilpfer's throat.

Chapter Twenty

Klaus's wrists had been tied with a hard, thin cord. He had no feeling in his hands any more. He sat on the cold stone floor in the candlelit dark, watching Henriquez pray.

The priest was kneeling in front of a small wooden cross, and though Klaus could hear his prayers, they were muttered so quietly, so quickly that he could hardly make out the words at all; even when he did, they weren't words he understood. In the candlelight and the shadows, all he could see was the pale skin of Henriquez's face and hands, and the glint of the silver crucifix that hung between his fingers.

Once or twice he'd heard footsteps pass outside

the heavy wooden door, but Henriquez had shut and locked it, and no one came in. Perhaps every hour – at least often enough that he'd noticed it – Klaus heard a little bell ring somewhere nearby, as though it was being tugged on a rope. But no one ever answered it, and there were no windows for him to see where it was either.

And all the while the guttering candles burned lower.

He wondered where Liesel was now. He'd been so wrong about her. She'd have gone back to the Pauper's for him, he knew that, and he knew what she'd have thought when she'd found him gone – that he'd taken the diamond and run, just left her to take her chances with Frau Drecht. Only he hadn't done that at all, and he couldn't even tell her.

But he had told Henriquez where the diamond was hidden. There'd been no not telling him that. He'd told him right down to the last mark on the stones of the bridge, and now they were waiting for Ramos to come back with it – and what would happen then Klaus didn't want to think about, because they wouldn't need him any more. So he sat shivering in the dark with his hands tied, listening to Henriquez pray.

But there was something else that frightened him as much as Ramos and Henriquez. It was the voices of the children – faint and mocking; he could hear their laughter in the darkness around him as though from a forest. Sometimes he could almost see them too – pale, empty-eyed faces, their lips dry and drawn, their mouths smeared with mud. They would lean out of the darkness towards him as if out of a waking dream – only it wasn't a dream: Klaus knew that because when they did, he really could see branches in the air above him.

And always there was that little flick of light in the corner of his eye as he blinked. Like the outline of a man.

Only it was getting closer.

And Klaus had heard a scream too. It had echoed through the forest like the sound of a pig having its throat cut in the slaughter yards, and at the sound, every bird had taken flight and the children had all fallen silent. Klaus had opened his eyes with a start and seen Henriquez looking him.

'I heard a man scream,' he'd whispered.

But Henriquez had only looked at him with those colourless eyes. 'You heard no one,' he had said in a voice like ash, but that wasn't what had been written on his face.

And Klaus knew then that the scream had been real.

And now they were waiting for Ramos.

And that time had come.

There was a touch at the door. Henriquez heard it. He stood up and, holding a candle to light his way, put in the key and unlocked it.

Ramos appeared from the dark passage and closed the door behind him. The lamp-eyed monkey that had been riding on his shoulder leaped down onto the table, one fist clutched tightly to its chest as though it was holding a secret.

'You have it?' asked Henriquez.

Ramos didn't say anything. He reached forward and tapped his finger on the table in front of the monkey. It turned its head towards him, hesitated, as though reluctant to surrender its prize; then, taking its fist haltingly from its chest, jumped off the table and dropped something hard and glittering onto the wood. Klaus saw it sparkle in the candlelight as it fell, and the gleam of it was red like Kusselmann's blood.

'It is the one,' said Ramos.

'Can you be sure?' said Henriquez, reaching forward.

But Ramos gripped his arm and stopped him. 'Do not touch it!' he said. 'Unless you want him to come for you as well.'

Henriquez drew his hand away, and Ramos looked at him almost with contempt. He picked up the stone and held it in his fist in front of Henriquez's face. 'They are my gods, Priest,' he said. 'I do not fear them.'

Still holding the stone, he swept the table clear of everything but a jug of water and, taking a leather bag from inside his coat, he untied the top. He had his back to Klaus, and it was difficult for Klaus to see what it was that he was doing, but he seemed to be tipping something from the bag into his hand, and kneading it into a shape with water from the jug. He did it several times.

Finally he turned and looked at Henriquez. 'It is ready,' he said.

'Come here, boy,' said Henriquez.

Awkwardly, Klaus stood up but didn't move.

The priest beckoned to him. 'You need not be afraid,' he said. He picked up the leather bag from the table and held it out towards Klaus. It smelled sweet, like treacle. He wet his finger with his tongue and dipped it inside the bag. 'It is chocolate.' He put his finger in his mouth, as though to prove there was no harm to it. 'Would you like some?'

There was something dangerous and unsaid in that voice, and Klaus heard it – but he was so hungry, and the chocolate smelled so sweet. He could feel his mouth watering.

But he didn't answer.

'We are going to play a game,' Henriquez said.

Klaus could see now what Ramos had been doing. On the table were seven rolled balls of dark chocolate, each about the size of a pigeon's egg. There was something almost familiar about them, as though he'd seen something similar somewhere before, but he couldn't have said where or when.

'I want you to take one,' Henriquez said. 'Only one. It is how it is done, you see. How a very special child is chosen.'

Klaus still didn't move. He didn't understand what the priest meant.

Henriquez took off his wire-rimmed spectacles and slowly cleaned them. Then he put them back on and looked at Klaus again with those pale eyes. 'It is all you have to do,' he said. 'Then you can go.'

It didn't sound right.

And Ramos was looking at Klaus as well.

But the chocolate smelled so sweet.

Hesitantly Klaus came to the table. His hands were still tied. He looked at Henriquez and Ramos again, then uncertainly back at the seven little rolled balls of chocolate.

'But only one of them,' whispered Henriquez like an uncle offering a single treat. 'You can only choose one.'

'And then I can go?' said Klaus.

It was too good to be true. But Henriquez nodded. 'Then you can go.'

Klaus looked down at the seven balls: they were identical. But if they were all the same, why did it matter which one he took?

Slowly he reached forward to touch one of them, then stopped.

No. Not that one.

He touched the one next to it, and looked up at Henriquez.

'Good,' said the priest. 'Now, you must put it in your mouth.'

Still looking at Ramos and Henriquez, Klaus picked up the little egg of chocolate.

It smelled so good. He closed his eyes and put it into his mouth.

The chocolate was rich and smooth. Only, as it melted, there was something else in it too; he could feel it hard and sharp against his tongue and his teeth, like a stone. He spat it out into his hands, the chocolate smearing down his chin, and then he realized what it was.

It was the diamond.

Henriquez and Ramos were both looking at him.

He began to back away. 'I don't want it,' he said quickly. He held the diamond out to them. 'You can have it.'

But they just stood looking at him.

He threw it down onto the floor. 'See,' he said. 'I don't want it.'

'It chose you,' said Ramos.

'There wasn't no one else to choose,' said Klaus.

Even as he said it, he knew that if he'd just taken that first chocolate ball – the one he was going to – then the diamond wouldn't have been in it.

'I could choose again,' he said, still backing away.

'It's too late for that,' said Henriquez.

They took a step towards him.

Behind them he could see the door. There was always a chance they hadn't turned the key, that it was still open. He made a wild dash to get past them, but Ramos caught hold of him and bundled him down onto the floor and held him there.

Henriquez leaned over him. He was looking into Klaus's face. 'Can you see them?' he said in a whisper.

Klaus didn't understand what he meant.

Henriquez gripped him by the face and turned it roughly towards the dark of the room. 'Can you see them?' he said again, more urgently this time.

And this time Klaus had to look, because it wasn't just the dark of the room that he could see; it was the children too, their mouths caked and smeared . . . not with mud like he'd thought – it never had been mud.

It was chocolate.

They peered down at him from between the leaves and branches of trees and their faces were all sorrow.

He stared back at them, his breath coming in short gasps. Ramos held him more tightly. Henriquez looked around into the shadows of the room, as though he knew what it was that Klaus could see and was trying to see it too. But all he could see was darkness.

'The boy can see them,' said Ramos. There was triumph in his voice. 'The dead ones have come.'

Chapter Twenty-one

Hilpfer hung pinned to the wall by the hand of clawed nails driven through his throat. He was kicking like a puppet, the heels of his shoes drumming against the floor and the plaster, but he was already a dead man. The lantern fell from his fingers, and in the last of its light Markus saw the shape of a feathered man appear from the wall behind Hilpfer like a stain soaking through wet paper – first its face, then its arms and chest – until it stood there on the landing, its back to the deeper darkness of the passage. Behind it there was a shimmer in the air, like a haze, and dimly moving within it, Markus could see patterns like the boughs and branches of trees blown by a wind.

He stood transfixed.

The figure turned and looked at him, eyes empty and black like glass, the flame of the candle reflecting from them as two single beads of light.

Then, dragging Hilpfer, its nails still through his throat, it drew slowly away from the candlelight and into the deeper dark of the passage, the sheen of its feathers becoming indistinguishable in the blackness – until Markus couldn't see it all; only the two reflected beads of light in its eyes. Then the eyes closed and he could hear the sound of Hilpfer's heels dragging across the bare floorboards. Then even that stopped, and out of the silence that followed, a rustling of quills began to fill the air.

The candle guttered out.

Markus's breath was coming in shallow, uneven gasps. Still holding the candlestick, he began to back away down the stairs, not daring to take his eyes off the walls or the dark mouth of the passage, the air about him filled with the rustling of quills. He could hear voices calling up to him from the stairs below, but he couldn't answer them. He reached the landing, turned and ran.

The men were standing waiting for him in the

hall, their faces turned up towards him, demanding to know what had happened. But Markus didn't answer. He tumbled between them, pushed his way through, his face drawn and pale, specks of Hilpfer's blood wet on his cheek and hand.

'No one go up there!' he shouted. 'I have to find the priest. Close the house! Don't let anyone in. Close it!'

With those last desperate words he was gone.

He had to find Henriquez. The priest was the only one who might know what they had to do, who might understand what it was that Karolus had begun.

He had to find Henriquez.

The streets were frosted and shining in the cold morning sunlight, but Markus didn't see them as he ran. All he could see was the face of that feathered man, bleeding like a stain through the wall behind Hilpfer. How had it done that?

How had it done that?

He should have picked up Karolus's notes, he knew it. Karolus would have written everything there – everything he'd intended, everything he'd done – only Markus had left them lying on the floor of that room. They would have to wait. He had to find the priest – this had cost three lives already; he had to stop it before it cost any more.

In the long stone wall, in the shadow of the Marienkirche, stood an iron gate, and behind that gate, an oak door with a shuttered slit and a single iron ring. It was a door only ever opened from the inside. It was the door to the convent of the Marienkirche. The place where Henriquez had said he would be.

Drawn, and breathless from running, Markus banged the heavy iron ring against the door.

But no one came.

He hammered on the door again, and this time the little shutter flicked open, but only onto another grille – there was no face to be seen, no glimpse to be had inside.

'Yes?' said a woman's voice softly.

He pushed his mouth close to the grille. 'Is there a priest here – a Father Henriquez? I have to speak with him.'

There was a moment's pause. 'There is no one of that name here,' said the voice.

The shutter began to close, but Markus jammed his fingers into the gap, his voice even more desperate now. 'He told me that I could find him here. I *must* speak with him!'

There was another pause, then the voice said, 'You will wait.'

The shutter closed.

Markus stepped back, pacing impatiently and looking up at the high wall as though searching for another way in. He'd been about to beat at the door again when he heard the bolts being slid back and the heavy latch lifting inside. It was opened just wide enough for him to step through, then closed again behind him.

He found himself in a narrow passage of whitewashed stone. On the wall a crucifix was set over a trestle table and a bowl of water, but there was nothing else.

He turned and looked at the nun who'd opened the door. Her face was framed by the stiff, spotless white cloth of a wimple.

'You will come with me,' she said.

He followed her as she led him down the flagstoned passage. It ran along one side of a cloister, but he couldn't see into the centre; it was hidden by a pierced screen, the daylight coming through it in pinpricks, like little stars. At the end of the passage was another door that led into a plain, unfurnished room.

A tall, severe-faced woman was standing there. 'You will leave us,' she said to the nun who'd brought Markus, and the nun bowed her head and withdrew, closing the door behind her. All the while, the tall woman looked at Markus without kindness. Only when the door was quite shut did she speak.

'I am Sister Ignatia,' she said. 'Mother Superior of this convent. This is a closed order, and we do not welcome visitors. I am told you wish to speak with Father Henriquez . . . ?'

'I have to see him,' said Markus urgently.

'Then, if you will tell me what it is you have to communicate with him, I will see that your message reaches him.'

'No, I have to speak with him now,' said Markus desperately. 'Is he not here? He said he would be here.'

Sister Ignatia looked at him icily, and Markus realized that whatever Henriquez's business was here, it wasn't something that she wanted or was going to help with any more than she had to.

And he was right.

'I have already explained, sir. We are a closed order. If you will give me the substance of your message, I will see that it reaches Father Henriquez.'

But Markus hadn't time for that. He had to find Henriquez now. There was a door behind Sister Ignatia, the one she must have come through – it had to lead into the convent itself. It had to lead to Henriquez, if he was there.

The moment he glanced at that door, Sister Ignatia realized what he meant to do. She took a step towards it. 'You have no business here, sir!' she said firmly. 'You must leave!'

But Markus paid no attention. He pushed past her and, pulling open the door, stepped out into the cloister, shouting the priest's name as loudly as he could. 'Henriquez! Henriquez!'

He saw the shocked faces of the nuns in the cloister as they turned and stared, then fled before him like hens as he crossed the yard, shouting Henriquez's name for all he was worth. Then, somewhere, someone began noisily ringing a little bell in alarm – but that wasn't going to stop him.

'Henriquez!'

He had to find the priest.

Klaus sat with his knees to his chin. He was trying to make himself as small as he could – as if by doing that, Ramos and Henriquez might forget that he was even there. But there was little chance of that. The end of the cord that tied his hands had been knotted through a loop in the wall. There was nowhere he could go. He sat looking out into the room; it was an almost incomprehensible place to him now, because he could feel sticks and leaves beneath his fingers as though through cracks in the hard cold of the stone floor. The heavy warmth of the forest was all about him. He could see pale faces watching him from between dark trees. They were watching Ramos as well, watching everything he did.

In the candlelight, muttering prayers that Klaus couldn't understand, Ramos had marked shapes and patterns on the stone of the floor, carefully filling them with paint and dust which he mixed with water from the jug on the table. Klaus hadn't understood what he was doing until the room grew lighter with the coming day, and then he saw that the floor had been covered with patterns of winged men and feathered snakes – the men with hooked beaks, claws, and rows of sharp biting teeth. When Ramos had finished them, he painted eyes on the walls; last of all, in a space he'd left in the middle of the floor, he drew the figure of a kneeling man, hands stretched out as though in prayer. Then, reverently, he laid next to it a shallow silver bowl and a long silver knife.

Henriquez had taken no part in any of it; he'd stood silently by, watching. But when Ramos laid the knife down on the floor, he finally spoke.

'You are sure it will come?' he said. 'You promised me it would come.'

'He has already been woken,' said Ramos. 'He has already been called. His soul has moved between the worlds.'

'How can you know?'

Ramos looked at the priest with contempt. 'I see what you cannot see.'

With another blade, thin as grass, he slit his own hand across its palm and, walking slowly around the room, let his blood drip onto the drawings on the floor.

'You must make the boy ready then,' said Henriquez.

Ramos looked at him darkly. 'Do not tell me what I must do, *Priest*.' He almost spat the word. 'I will keep my promise. Keep yours.'

'It was not me who stole it from your people,' said Henriquez quickly. 'It was me who found it again for you. Remember that. I've kept my promise. Now keep yours.' He leaned towards Ramos almost beseechingly. 'Prove to me that there is a god.'

Ramos turned away from him. Taking pinches of paint and dust, he mixed them with his blood in the palm of his hand and, squatting down in front of Klaus, looked into his face. Klaus tried to turn his head away, but Henriquez caught hold of him and held him still. Ramos's eyes glittered like black glass. With the quill of an iridescent blue feather and the pad of his thumb, he began to mark Klaus's face with blood and paint. Then he pulled open Klaus's shirt and drew on his chest – feathers and eyes, like the patterns that covered his own hands.

Whispering prayers to the dead, Ramos fetched another bag and placed it on the painted cold stones beside him. He touched his forehead to the floor in front of it, like a supplication, then undid the strings and opened it. It was filled with flowers and feathers – faded and dry, as though they'd been kept for thousands of years. As he tipped them onto the stones, they filled the room with a scent as sweet and sickly as death. Then he loosened the cord that bound Klaus to the wall and, holding onto him, wound the flowers about Klaus's arms and pushed the feathers into the scrub of his hair.

In the half-seen other world about him the pale children leaned forward and Klaus felt a breath through the leaves like the coming of a wind. The little flick of light in his eye burned brighter and sharper, like a walking man.

'Please,' he whimpered, looking at Ramos, then at Henriquez. 'You said I could go.'

Henriquez bent close to him and looked into his face, into his eyes, and at the paint and dust, at the feathers and flowers. 'And you shall go,' he said, almost in a whisper.

Then the expression on his face changed, and he suddenly turned to look at the door as though he'd heard something that Klaus hadn't. Ramos turned as well; they both did.

Then Klaus heard it too.

It was the little bell.

It had sounded so often through the night, but now it was being rung noisily over and over again . . . and there was something else.

Someone, somewhere, was shouting Henriquez's name.

Without a word, the priest straightened. He crossed the room and opened the door; stepped out into the hard daylight of the cloister.

Markus was standing in the middle of the court-yard, breathless and pale. The pigeons his shouts had put to flight were circling in the cold blue sky around the spires of the Marienkirche – he could hear the clap of their wings. The cloister had emptied around him and every door had been shut.

Every door except one.

On the far side of it he saw Henriquez emerge from beneath a tracery of arches. The priest stopped and stared at him, because Markus wasn't the man he'd expected to see.

Markus started towards him. 'It's alive!' he shouted. 'Karolus is dead.'

Henriquez didn't move. 'I told you to warn him,' he said.

Markus's face was drawn and colourless. 'Don't lecture me, Priest!' he shouted. 'Just tell me what has to be done.'

But Henriquez still didn't move. 'You don't even begin to understand, do you?' he said coldly. 'Little assistant man, you don't even know what it is.' He shook his head dismissively. 'I do not need you.' He turned his back on Markus and began to walk away under the arches, but Markus shouted after him.

'Wait!'

Henriquez turned and looked at him again.

'Tell me what has to be done,' said Markus. 'Tell me what I have to do!'

The priest smiled, but there was no kindness in it. 'You pay its price,' he said, looking at him with eyes as colourless as water. He put his hand to the door behind him and pushed it open.

Markus came after him: Henriquez was his only hope; he couldn't let him go now. But the moment Markus stepped through that door into the small room, he saw the painted floor, the walls, the bowl and the long knife, the barrel-chested man with raven-black hair – and the terrified boy cowering against the wall.

It was like Menz again – the cup and the bowl.

'What in God's name are you doing?' he said.

Henriquez looked at him like a serpent. 'Paying its price,' he answered.

He glanced at Ramos, and without a word, Ramos walked slowly behind Markus and closed the door.

'This was the bargain his people made with the dead all those centuries ago,' said Henriquez, his eyes following Ramos as, out of Markus's sight, he stooped and picked up the long knife. 'Years longer than we can even comprehend – this is how they paid their messenger. The mine doctor knew it, but he was a fool.'

Now, suddenly, Markus understood what those two words scrawled by Karolus had meant; what the search for the boy had been about all the time. Two lives – one to summon it from that other place, and one to send it back. The boy was the price.

'Yes,' said Henriquez, as though he had seen Markus's thought. 'It is a messenger between the dead and the living – do you not see, do you not understand what it can tell us? Do not ask me to believe that you don't want to know what waits for you beyond the grave; to know where life goes. Is there even such a thing as God?'

That was what Karolus had wanted; had maybe even tried. Markus saw it all now. 'You want to speak with it,' he said dumbly.

'Yes!' said Henriquez. 'I will send it back to whatever world it has left, you have my word. But not until I have spoken with it. Not until I know whether there is a God.'

'You cannot mean this,' said Markus, his eyes on the boy, painted and garlanded like an offering. 'It would be cold-blooded murder.'

'No,' said Henriquez. 'A bargain sealed in blood, Herr Assistant. You cannot break it. It will hunt the boy down, and every life it takes until it finds him will be on your head. How many are you prepared for that to be? Ten? A dozen?'

He shook his head again. 'There is no choice. This is the price they agreed to pay to have that soul carry their prayers, to appease their gods – one child chosen by a curse. Spare him, and you condemn how many others? No, Herr Scientist. Think instead of what we will learn. That is a far greater thing.'

Markus looked at the boy, pale and shaking. His face might have been the child mask on Karolus's wall, only it was living and afraid, daubed in blood and paint.

'Please, help me,' cried Klaus.

This was madness. It was murder. Even if Henriquez was right, this was a price that Markus wasn't prepared to pay.

'I will not let you do this,' he said. He started towards Klaus, his hand held out towards him. 'Come here, boy!' he said. 'You're coming with me.'

But before he could reach Klaus, Ramos stepped between them. He pushed Markus back with a flourish of his hand that Markus didn't understand, but it felt like a punch, and then he saw that Ramos had a knife in his hand. Markus put his fingers slowly to his heart: his coat was wet with blood. His legs began to buckle beneath him as though they had no strength in them any more. Henriquez caught hold of him, lowered him gently to the ground and looked into his face.

'It is the price that has to be paid,' the priest said coldly. 'I will let no one stop me.'

He closed Markus's eyes, then turned and looked at Klaus. 'Come here, boy,' he said, reaching out towards him. 'I will not hurt you.'

Klaus backed away from him.

All about him the air was filling with noise, like the wailing of a wind. Light was streaming into the room above the dead man like sun through the branches of trees; there were figures moving in it, and on the stones of the floor the pattern of winged men and feathered snakes was coiling and twisting, with a life of its own. Henriquez didn't even seem to see it, but Ramos did. He stood looking at Klaus, the long knife in his hand. Without taking his eyes from him, he bent down and picked up the silver bowl.

'No!' cried Klaus.

He could feel the hard wall behind him – and then suddenly it wasn't a wall any more, it was the trunk of a tree. He could feel the twigs and leaves against his head as he backed against it. Henriquez grew faint like a ghost in front of him – his voice thin and far away, sounding like a reed above the noise of the wind. He saw Ramos walking towards him as though through a mist, the knife in his hand, but the room was melting around him, the forest flooding into its place, until all that was left was one last shimmering square of light that was the walls of the room and the arm of Ramos reaching out of it towards him.

But Ramos's fingers closed on thin air, and Klaus turned and ran.

Chapter Twenty-two

Klaus ran blindly, the undergrowth whipping against his legs and face. The air was suddenly hot and heavy, his skin damp with sweat, his shirt sticking to his back. Sunlight poured through the trees. He heard the screeching of birds and the zip of insects. But all around him the forest was full of running people; they were crashing through the undergrowth, whooping and shouting like madmen: barrow boys and urchin girls, fine gentlemen and ladies – rich and poor, young and old – their faces pale and dead, their skin stretched thin as parchment over their bones, feathers pushed into their hair, flowers circling their arms. Their clothes were ragged and torn. Some carried sharpened sticks, and stone clubs and axes. For a moment he was swept up amongst them, running blindly with them as they jumped over rocks and tree roots. Through the trees ahead, he could see a man running away. They were chasing him, hunting him down like dogs. Then the man fell, and with a cry they were on him, tearing at him with their hands and teeth, hacking at him with the axes and sticks as he lay on the ground – until, with another whoop, they were gone again, running and jumping, their hands and faces wet with blood.

Klaus threw himself against a tree, his heart racing, the little flick of light hard and sharp in his eye. Through the dappled sunlight he saw the man weakly moving, as though he was trying to stand. He reached his hand out towards Klaus, but Klaus turned and ran. He didn't know where he was or where he was going. He fell amongst a thicket of branches and leaves, his eyes wide with fear and confusion as he looked about him. He had no idea how he'd got here. He could still hear shouts and calls – they were everywhere; he caught flickers of movement amongst the trees as people ran through them, but there was no sign of Ramos, no sign of Henriquez, no sign even of the room. Only thick, humid forest. It fell away behind him onto a low plain. Down there, the unbroken green of the canopy spread out like a cushion. Bright, hyacinth-coloured birds glided in long loops of flight over the treetops. And in the distance, thin plumes of greasy smoke rose through the trees like a haze. There was nothing else – no buildings, no roads or bridges, only forest. It went on for ever.

But there were people: they were standing in little groups in the shade of the trees. Their clothes all faded and torn, their bodies bone-thin and pale. As he looked, others came through the forest and joined them, like so many moths drawn to a lamp. None of them spoke. They just stood still, as though they were watching something that Klaus couldn't see.

He crept through the undergrowth towards them: he wanted to know where he was, what they were doing, but they paid no attention to him even when he was close enough to touch. They were all looking at a shimmering lightness in the air in front of them. It hung there like a painted tissue, its edge blurring into the trees. It held a room – Klaus could see the walls and curtains, the drapes of a bed, but he could see the forest as well – as though he were looking through a windowpane into a house and the trees and forest were the reflections on the glass outside. There were people moving inside the room, real people – he heard the sounds they made, thin and far away: the clink of a glass being filled, the scrape of a chair on a floor. He wanted to shout to them, wave at them, but all around him were the pale, thin people, and he was frightened. So he stood very still and watched.

On the bed lay an old man, his eyes wide and staring; he was looking out into the forest as though he alone could see the faces peering down at him. He struggled feebly to lift his hand and push them away. A woman came and sat by the bed. She took his hand and held onto it, but she couldn't see the faces pressed all about her in the small space of the room.

As Klaus stood there, the watchers in the forest came closer still, until their faces were right against the drapes of the bed, against the pillow, their lips parted, their eyes fixed intently on the old man, on the rasping heave of his breath. Then, like a whisper, there was a movement amongst them, and from their hands they began unwinding little threads of barbed silk, like spider's webs. These caught like thorns in the sheets and bedclothes, in the old man's nightshirt and skin. He tried to push them away too, but the woman held onto his hand, and the threads wound about him as the watchers pulled them taut – until, as light as a feather, they pulled him in amongst them. He fell out of the shimmering room and onto the forest floor like a fish into a boat, and all at once they were on him like animals, biting and tearing at him with their teeth. In one twisting movement he was up and running into the forest on his pale, bone-thin legs, his night-shirt awry; screaming and shouting, they were after him, sticks and axes in their hands.

They disappeared into the trees in one yelling mob, their echoing shouts and the crashing of branches growing fainter.

Just for a moment more the room hung in the air in front of Klaus like a window, but as he watched, it faded. The woman leaned forward over the body that lay empty and motionless in the bed. She began to cry. The few watchers that hadn't chased after the man stood there, their lips silently half forming words as they watched the woman cry; then even they seemed to lose interest, and turned their faces away. Hollow-eyed and gaunt, they began to wander listlessly into the dappled sunlit undergrowth like moths in search of another lamp. Finally, only Klaus was left. He let out a cry, clawing at the empty air as the room faded into nothingness and was gone.

He heard voices laughing at him from amongst the trees. He could see them in the leaves – pale-faced children.

'Get out of it!' he shouted, and he picked up a stone and threw it, but they only laughed more. So he found a stick and ran at them, swinging and beating at the branches, but there was no one there, just the humid damp air.

As he stood there amongst the trees, a fat man stumbled towards him out of the deeper shade, whimpering and crying. The sleeves of his coat were torn, his fist was stuffed into his mouth, his eyes wild and confused as he looked about him. Blood was oozing from his nose, and the fat folds of his face were sweating and pale.

And Klaus stared dumbly at him.

Then, with no other thought than that of recognition, he ran towards him. 'Kusselmann! Kusselmann!'

And then stopped.

Because he knew that it couldn't be Kusselmann because Kusselmann was dead.

His fist still pressed to his mouth, the fat man turned and stared at Klaus.

'Kusselmann?' Klaus whispered.

It was Kusselmann. He was alive.

But Kusselmann didn't answer. He began to back away from Klaus, whimpering and trembling like a beaten dog.

In a wave of confusion, Klaus held out his hand towards him. 'It's all right,' he said. 'It's me.'

Just for a moment he saw a flicker of recognition in Kusselmann's face; then, far off amongst the trees, he heard an echoing whoop and a shout, and the sound of sticks breaking underfoot. Kusselmann heard it too. He lifted his head quickly, eyes wild, then turned and ran stumbling back into the thick, humid forest.

'No!' shouted Klaus. 'Kusselmann! Wait!' He plunged into the trees after him, but the forest was so thick and dense, he couldn't see him. He stood lost and alone in the damp, humid shade, the air around him full of the sounds of insects and birds. 'Kusselmann!'

He heard the laughter again, saw the faces in the leaves, their mouths smeared with chocolate. Then, one by one, the voices and the birds began to fall silent. There was a breath of a wind through the trees, like the coming of a storm. Klaus felt it warm against his face. It set the leaves rustling. He turned and looked back into the silence of the forest behind him.

Far off in that deep dappled shade he saw something coming towards him, shimmering an iridescent blue where the sunlight fell onto it.

Instinctively he began to back away, and then to run.

Chapter Twenty-three

Liesel opened her eyes.

It was morning.

Something had woken her. Somewhere, someone was banging on a door and shouting: 'Herr Brennen! Herr Brennen!'

She lifted her head.

She was lying on a little truckle bed, but she didn't know where she was. She looked around at the strange room. It wasn't Frau Drecht's house.

There was an odd taste in her mouth, and her head felt wrong and heavy.

The last thing she could remember was the bridge – being cold and watching for Klaus. Then,

302

like pictures in a dream, it all came back to her – the man, and the fire, and the voices.

Henriquez's voice.

The convent.

She sat bolt upright, as though cold water had been poured over her.

If that's where Henriquez was, then that's where Klaus was.

She swung her legs onto the floor. The room swam giddily. She screwed her eyes shut, and opened them again.

She had to find Klaus.

Her boots were on the floor by the bed. She pulled them on and tied the laces, and as she did, she heard footsteps coming quickly downstairs outside the room. They didn't stop.

There was a small window by the bed; she pressed her face to the cold glass and peered down into the street. Two men passed quickly just beneath her, one of them still pulling his coat on. She recognized him.

Then the door behind her opened.

Frau Hofker was still wringing her hands and shaking her head as she came into the room, but she stopped when she saw that Liesel was awake. She pushed the door closed behind her, but it didn't quite catch.

Liesel looked at her suspiciously, and edged away. 'I got to find Klaus,' she said.

Frau Hofker didn't move. 'That's as maybe, my girl,' she said, 'whoever he might be – but you're not going nowhere till Herr Brennen gets back.'

Liesel scowled at her.

'You needn't have no worries about him, girlie. He's the one what done that,' said Frau Hofker, pointing at Liesel's bandaged arm. 'But you got to wait here till he comes back, 'cos he wants to talk to you about something. You understand?'

Oh, yes. Liesel understood all right.

There was only one thing that anyone would want to talk to her about, and that was Kusselmann's diamond. She looked at the gauze on her arm. People never do anything without a reason; they don't give you something for nothing.

'I ain't soddin' got it,' she said, edging further around the wall away from Frau Hofker. 'I got to find Klaus.'

Frau Hofker put her head on one side. What on earth was she to do with a Bergenstrasse rat like this until Herr Brennen got back? ''Spect you're hungry, ain't you?' she said.

Liesel didn't answer. She was as hungry as could be – her stomach was growling with it – but she just looked at Frau Hofker darkly.

Still watching Liesel, Frau Hofker took down a stone jug from a shelf and poured some milk into a bowl. Then, breaking open a dark loaf of bread, she put the bowl and the bread onto the little table that stood in the middle of the room. 'You come and drink this,' she said.

Liesel looked at the bowl and the bread, and then at the door that wasn't quite latched shut.

Before Frau Hofker could stop her, lithe as an alley cat, Liesel was through the gap. Frau Hofker shouted after her, but that was all she did. She wasn't going to chase a Bergenstrasse girl, not even for Herr Brennen.

Liesel ran down the steps out into the street; she didn't know for the moment where she was, but she knew exactly where she was going.

When she reached Marienkirche Platz, the alley by the convent was already full of ragged children waiting for the clock on the spire to strike the hour and the basket of bread to be lowered down from the Beggar Boys' window. She'd stood there often enough with her Klaus; now she was going to stand there for another.

The nuns never waited to watch what happened to their charity – everyone knew that: they'd lower the rope and only come back later to haul it in when the basket was empty. You could even scramble up the wall using the hanging rope and peer in through the Beggar Boys' window if you wanted – see right along into the cloister if you hooked your elbows over the ledge; they'd all done that at one time or another, just for a dare. But no one ever climbed right in – not unless they wanted the window to be shut up for a week, and that would mean no bread for anyone.

But that was what Liesel meant to do.

Exactly on the hour, the painted plasterwork horsemen below the Marienkirche clock began to turn, and as the big bell chimed, the Beggar Boys' window opened and the basket was lowered down.

She waited a moment for the nuns to be gone; then, pushing her way through the children fighting over the bread, she scrambled up the wall and got her elbows onto the window ledge. Heart in her mouth, she hung there for a moment, looking in along one side of the cloister, and then the other way towards a narrow flight of stairs at the end. The nuns who'd lowered the basket were already walking back across the cloister yard. There were other nuns there too, but they were all looking away.

If she was going to do it at all, she had to do it now.

She pulled herself up onto the ledge, and as she did so, she caught one glimpse of startled faces turning up towards her from below, calling at her to come back down. But she took no notice of them. She dropped down onto the hard flagstones of the cloister and ran towards the little flight of stairs at the end.

Then two things happened at once: someone started shouting at her and a bell began to ring. She took the stairs two at a time, and it was only then that she realized that it wasn't her they were shouting at. Heart racing, she stopped halfway up, and listened.

They were shouting for Henriquez. They were shouting for the priest.

Craning her head, she peered out from under the lintel of the stairs and across the cloister yard. A man was striding across it, shouting the priest's name – it was the same man she'd seen earlier, the man from the Anatomy. The nuns all turned and fled before him.

Quickly she climbed to the top of the stairs. There was a passage, open on one side. It looked down onto the cloister below. She stood half behind a pillar watching the scene unfold, but then, out of the corner of her eye, she saw something move. Instinctively she turned and looked.

Almost at the end of the passage, in the shadows at the bottom of the wall, sat the little black monkey. It had caught a sparrow and was playing with it – flicking it between its paws – and the sparrow was fluttering in little broken-winged circles on the ground, like a singed moth. Then the monkey picked it up and began pulling feathers off it, and as it did so, it looked round and saw her. For a moment it stared at her with those yellow eyes; then, with the sparrow gripped tightly in its fist, it turned tail and ran.

They were here. Henriquez was here.

She couldn't afford to lose sight of it. The monkey was already disappearing round the corner. She took to her heels after it, but at the end of the passage there were two more passages, and they were both empty. She hesitated between them; eyes on the ground, she ran a short way down one, stopped, and retraced her steps, still looking down. There was a tiny grey feather on the stones. Then another. It had gone this way. She picked up her skirts and ran again, down the flight of steps at the end of the passage and round the corner – and there was the monkey.

It had stopped by a closed door and was pawing at the bottom of it. When it saw her, it put the sparrow in its teeth, turned and leaped straight up the wall, over the gutter and onto the lead of the roof.

Liesel swore. There was no way she could follow it up there.

Only maybe she didn't have to.

The monkey sat watching her from the gutter, as though waiting for her to go. She turned and looked at the door – that was where it had been going. As she glanced back along the passage, the little bell stopped ringing. Someone was bound to see her soon, she knew it. She leaned forward and put her ear to the door. She could hear voices inside, but not what they were saying.

Then she heard a cry.

Klaus's voice.

She stepped back. There was no window, just a

narrow slit along the very top of the wall – enough to let light in – but it was too high for her to reach. As she looked at it, the door handle began to move. She darted back through the tracery of arches that ran along the edge of the cloister, but there was hardly anywhere to hide before the door jerked open.

For a moment Ramos stood in the doorway – a silver bowl in one hand, a long knife in the other; a wind blew past him out into the cloister, twisting and lifting the winter brown leaves and grit of the yard. As he stood there, it dissipated and was gone. He turned his head, his gaze scouring the cloister and the dark passages and stairs on the other side. Henriquez rushed to the door behind him. Liesel could have touched them both, they were so close. She held her breath.

'Can you see him?' said Henriquez.

The words were in a language that meant nothing to her.

Ramos stared out into the cold air. 'It is not his time yet,' he said. 'He is only just on the other side. He will find a way back.'

'But can you still see him?' asked Henriquez.

Ramos turned and looked at him with contempt. 'I see what you cannot, *Priest*.' He spat the word.

Henriquez looked around as though trying to see what it was that Ramos could see. But there were only stone walls and arches.

Ramos gave a sharp whistle. From the roof above him the little black monkey leaped down, holding what was left of the sparrow tightly in its fist. As it landed, it turned its head, and Liesel saw it look right at her through the tracery around the stone arch and pillar. But Ramos didn't see it. He swung the monkey up onto his shoulder and, balancing it there, began to walk slowly along the cloister away from her. He was closing his mind to everything, following something that even his eyes could barely see – shapes and shadows in the air about him, as faint and dark as the reflections of a forest in a pane of glass.

Henriquez watched for a moment, pulling the little cloth from his pocket and cleaning the lenses of his wire-rimmed spectacles. Then, putting them back on, he followed Ramos.

Liesel crept round the arch as she watched them walk down the cloister and into a passage on the other side. Behind her, the door of the room was still open. She looked quickly back at the receding figures of Ramos and Henriquez, then, before her

311

courage could fail her, slipped from behind the pillar and into the room.

It was dark after the brightness of the cloister, heavy and silent. The walls and floor were daubed with patterns and paint – feathered eyes and beaked men – and in the silence, it felt as though they were watching her.

She stepped forward uneasily. 'Klaus!' she called.

She was certain it had been his voice that she'd heard, but there was no answer, and she felt an empty crawling fill her stomach as she took another step forward – because Ramos had been holding a knife. Then her breath stopped in her chest. The man was lying there on the floor beside the table, his face turned towards her, his eyes closed.

It had been his cry she'd heard, not Klaus's.

There was blood on the floor all around him, wet and shining in the light from the doorway.

Liesel edged around him. 'Klaus!'

But the room was empty; there was no one there – she could see it all.

She looked down at the man again, only this time she saw something else; something glinting in the light from the open doorway – bright and hard like a little shard of malice.

312

It lay there on the floor only feet away from the man, wound in a thread of his blood.

Kusselmann's diamond.

She stared at it.

She only had to pick it up – there was no one to see her do it, no one to tell her not to. No one would ever even know she had it. Frau Drecht wasn't going to let her go even if she did give it back to her – she'd been stupid to think that she ever would.

So why not take it? No one would ever know.

Liesel glanced quickly at the door, then back at the diamond. It lay there, glittering darkly.

Almost as though she expected the man to catch hold of her wrist and stop her, she reached out hesitantly and picked it up.

It was hard and cold, like ice, and now there was blood on her fingers. She shuddered at the touch of it and wiped her hand clean on her blouse. Then, looking at the door all the time, she untied a little pocket in her skirt and dropped the diamond into it, then knotted the cord again as tightly as she could.

Standing up, she edged back past the man and around the wall to the door, and peered out into the passage. Which way had she come?

And where was Klaus?

She stood for a moment, biting at her lip, looking both ways. It had been the monkey she'd been watching as she ran, and now she couldn't say which way she'd come.

But the cloister was empty; she couldn't see Henriquez or Ramos anywhere.

Looking nervously about her, she started along the passage and down the flight of steps at the end; then she stopped because it didn't look right at all. She took a couple of steps more, and stopped again.

It was the wrong way. She was lost.

But as she stood there, not knowing what to do, somebody reached out of the stone alcove behind her, and grabbed hold of her, pulling her back and down. She gave a cry, kicked and struggled, tried to squirm round to get her hands and nails at their face, but whoever it was, they were lithe as a snake. They rolled her over, and pinned her down, catching hold of her fists . . .

And all at once she stopped fighting.

Because, as if it had come out of nowhere, the face looking down at her was Klaus's.

Chapter Twenty-four

His nose was stitched and crusted with blood, his face painted with feathers and eyes; his eyelids too – even when he blinked it looked as though they were open – and there were serpents and patterns drawn all over his skin. His mouth was smeared with chocolate.

She stared dumbly up at him. 'What they done to you?' she said. She'd been going to say that it was all right, that she'd got it – she'd got the diamond. But the words dried to nothing in her mouth.

Klaus grabbed hold of her wrists and pressed his face close to hers, as though trying to see her through a mist. 'It's all forest,' he whispered. 'They're all dead.'

She was lying beneath him. He wasn't even sure that she was real at all. She'd just appeared in a shimmer of air amongst the roots and the trees – just like that room had done. The air was still blurred and moving all about her. He could see flagstones and the walls again, could feel them, touch her. But through the shimmering air, as though through an open window, he could hear voices whistling and calling – could see the shape of a man coming towards him through the trees. He pulled Liesel to her feet, his face filling with panic. 'We've got to run!' Gripping her wrist so tightly that it hurt, he began to pull her along.

'This isn't the way!' she said. 'We've got to get to the Beggar Boys. That's how I got in.' She shook him free and would have run back the way they'd come, but he grabbed at her again, shaking his head.

'No! Not that way! It's all forest.'

There was such a terror in his voice. He dragged her stumbling down the passage and up a flight of steps at the end. It was the wrong way – she knew it – but Klaus wouldn't listen and she couldn't stop him. He was running blindly, turning and looking behind him as he pulled her along. At the top of the steps the passage turned, and there was a dark little spiral stair in the wall in front of them.

Klaus pulled her into it, and for a moment he felt their breath stuffed in around them. He hadn't a clue what he was doing; he was just running. He dragged her to the top of the stairs, and then they were in the bright daylight of the roof.

Below them was the square of the cloister, and towering over them the twin spires of the Marienkirche with their gargoyled niches and lichen-weathered walls.

Breathless, he stopped and stared at the world around him. Up here he could see the stone roofline of the town, and Liesel's face against it – but there was the forest as well. It was spread across a thousand shimmering windows like a moving picture all around him as far as he could see, and somehow he was standing on flagstones above it, looking down at a dark river running through it. There was a wind against his skin, warm and cold all at the same time.

He caught hold of Liesel and stared into her face. 'Can't you see it? Can't you see the trees?' he said.

He had such wild eyes, his face all painted and

smeared. It scared her so. She backed away from him, but as she did so, she looked over the parapet into the cloister, and saw the foreshortened figures of Ramos and Henriquez as they passed through an arch right beneath her.

She looked about frantically. There was no way back down to the Beggar Boys' window now, not that way, and there was nowhere else to go except across the narrow wooden slats that ran over the lead of the convent roof.

A line of statues and gargoyled waterspouts stood along the wall where the roof of the convent joined the Marienkirche. All Liesel could think of was finding a place to hide amongst them. Klaus was still staring at her. Catching hold of his arm, she pulled him across the slats towards the wall of the huge church. The wood and the lead were slippery and green, and they hadn't gone more than a dozen steps when, from below them, the little black monkey climbed over the parapet of the roof. Klaus froze. It crouched for a moment, looking straight at him, then turned tail and dropped like quicksilver back into the cloister. They could hear it screeching and jabbering as it went.

'Come on!' cried Liesel.

Worming her way between the gargoyles and statues, she tried to find a place to hide. But there was something even better. There in the wall behind the worn statues of the saints was a small door – a workman's opening onto the roof.

It was only latched shut. Liesel pushed Klaus through it and closed it behind her.

Inside, everything was silent. There was a draught of cold, damp air but not a crack of light. Yet Klaus could see through an opening in the darkness a sun-lit forest far beneath his feet. It was so bright, it was as if he'd suddenly stepped into thin air. He grabbed wildly at Liesel. She'd turned towards him as though from the black square of an unlit window at night, and he caught hold of her and gasped, because the forest was gone, and suddenly he felt the cold bricks and stones of the Marienkirche and the cramped darkness all about him.

'It's all right,' she said. 'I've got you!'

He held onto her.

He could dimly see the dirty unfinished mortar of bricks and stonework, and the planks of a floor, and stairs that ran up and up inside the wall.

There was nowhere for them to go but up.

As they climbed the rough wooden staircase, it

shifted and moved, and Klaus could feel the dark pull of the drop beneath him. Sometimes there was a little slit in the wall – narrow as a hand – that let in a crack of light, and then sometimes he could see out between the worn statues and over the roofs of the town and sometimes out across the tops of the trees. Finally, there was a door. Liesel pushed it open.

Like a great deep well in front of them lay the quiet vault of air and the gilded boss stones of the very ceiling of the Marienkirche. The chequered tiles of the nave were like dots far below them. As they looked out across that huge empty space, the carillon clock set amongst the painted saints and angels in the opposite wall struck the quarter-hour. They could see the little moving wires and the hammers on the bells – they were almost level with them.

They were in a narrow little gallery high above the floor of the church, the people like toy men and women below them. Benches and workmen's tools were laid out along the side of the wall, and at the end of the gallery was a gate and a turn of stairs leading down into a lower gallery that ran behind a long row of arches the whole length of the nave. It was dusty and damp. At the end of this gallery was a staircase – tight and dark, barely wider than their shoulders. As they turned giddily down it, Liesel felt the walls pressing in against her, heard the rasp of their breath and the scuff of their shoes on the stone steps. At the bottom was a worn oak door. Lifting the latch, they stepped out onto the tiles of the nave, where the candles were lit and the murmuring business of the church was going on quietly around them.

They made their way towards the great door of the Marienkirche and out into the cold daylight of the square.

No one followed, no one called after them, and a kind of elation filled Liesel as they went down the steps and across the pigeon-filled square. It felt almost as if it was her Klaus that she'd saved – as if she'd put all the past to rights at last. What was his face going to be like when she showed him the diamond? She turned towards him and would have laughed out loud, but when she did she saw that it wasn't her Klaus; it was someone who only looked like him, and she didn't know where they were going, or what they were going to do now, and people on the street turned and stared at them as they passed – because he looked like a wild boy, a painted tumbler from a travelling show.

Klaus held onto her arm as though he would never let her go. He couldn't always see her or the street at all. Sometimes she was no more than a shadow leading him between shimmering windows in the air that opened onto forest paths or across narrow streams that were filled with the empty faces of dead people, their hair winding about them like weeds in the water. And then those windows would disappear, and the world was hard and real again, and he could see her properly against the dark brick walls of an alley. Then the next moment it would all dissolve in front of his eyes and he would see them both together – the leaves and branches of trees through tears in the bricks and stones, see streets that were pierced with torrents of black water tumbling over rocks.

But wherever she went, there was a shimmer of air around Liesel like a window, and through it, faint and far away, Klaus could hear the echo of whistles and calls, and he knew that something was following him through the trees, coming closer all the time.

At a pump on a street corner Liesel tried to wash

Klaus clean of the paint and the smeared chocolate, but the bright colours – the reds, and the yellows and the greens – had stained his skin, and for all the ice-cold water, and for all that she could do in those few snatched moments, the patterns that Ramos had drawn there were etched like ghosts into his face.

She had to find somewhere safe for them; somewhere she knew. 'There's a place down by the river,' she said as she dried Klaus's face with her hands. 'It's warm there. It's where me and Klaus—' She stopped. 'Where me and my brother used to go. And I've got something to show you. You wait and see.'

But he didn't answer her; he hardly spoke at all, and when he did, it was to try and tell her what he could see in the forest – and it scared her so because he was saying things that simply weren't there, like a madman, and she just wanted to leave him then, but she couldn't – not like that – because it would be wrong. It would be like leaving her Klaus all over again.

So Liesel let him hang onto her as she went down through the town towards the street markets by the river and the place she'd once known, and he could have cried as he clung onto her because he just couldn't make her understand what he could see. All the time he kept glancing back, waiting for that little flick of light in the corner of his eye to become a feathered man emerging from the dappled shade of the forest.

But as she drew nearer to the river, reached the last rows of little market streets, Liesel began to notice something. She began to notice the looks on the faces of the ragged children in the alleyways and the doorways of the tenement yards, and once she'd noticed them, the more she began to see them – until finally she came to a stop and looked about her.

'This ain't right,' she said to Klaus – and then, to the children on the steps of a doorway, 'What you staring at?'

But they didn't answer. They turned and slipped away.

Still holding onto Klaus, Liesel walked a dozen more steps, and then some voice in her head told her to turn round. On the other side of the street, keeping pace with her and watching her, were Frau Drecht and Spitzel.

Liesel might not have been quite where Spitzel had said she'd be, and that had been a worrying few moments for him with Frau Drecht, but it hadn't taken him long to find her again, not when he'd known where to start, and there'd been Frau Drecht to make people tell.

'You can be running along now, Spitzel,' said Frau Drecht. 'I won't be needing you any more.'

Liesel drew Klaus nearer to her, and began to back away. In the street behind her, barrow boys were calling their wares, and there was a row of buildings, a gate with iron railings and a narrow little alley – and there was Mutzi too. They hadn't seen him. He stepped out from the railings, fastened his hand around the back of Liesel's neck, swept her and Klaus together, and carried them kicking and struggling into the dark of the little alley, then dropped them. They scrambled to their feet and ran, but there was nowhere for them to run to. The alley was no more than a long narrow blind between two buildings and there was no way through it at the end. It just stopped in a pool of filth beneath a high stone wall.

Silhouetted against the daylight of the street behind them, they could see Frau Drecht and the huge shape of Mutzi coming down the dark alley towards them.

'I was too kind to you, wasn't I, little Liesel?'

called Frau Drecht. 'Took you in, looked after you, and this is all the thanks I get, is it?'

Liesel knew just what was coming next. But maybe there was still a way she could stop it. 'I've got it, gnädige Frau!' she said quickly. She fumbled at the pocket of her skirt and, tearing the cloth open, pulled out the diamond.

Klaus stared at it. Even in the dark of the alley it glinted like a star in her hand; he saw the forest leap hard and bright out of the shimmering air all around her. 'No!' he shouted. He tried to pull the diamond out of her hand, but she pushed him away.

'I was keeping it for you, gnädige Frau.'

'Course you was, Liesel. But I bet you've been telling everyone where you found it, haven't you, lovey – on that floor in Kusselmann's shop – and we can't be having people believing lies like that, can we now?'

'I wouldn't tell on you, gnädige Frau,' Liesel said. She hooked her arm through Klaus's and tried to pull him towards her. 'And he wouldn't either.'

'But I'm not prepared to take that chance, am I, Liesel?' said Frau Drecht and, glancing at Mutzi, she started purposefully towards Liesel.

Mutzi glanced quickly back up the alley towards

the street: he knew what she meant. He could hear the cries of the barrow boys muffled against the alley walls, but there was no one coming; there was no one to see.

Desperate now, Liesel pulled back her hand. 'I'll throw it, Frau!' she said. 'I will.'

But Frau Drecht didn't even stop. 'You wouldn't want to do a thing like that, little Liesel,' she said. ''Cos it will only make it worse for you in the end. You know that.'

'You let us go or I will!' said Liesel, backing away still further.

Frau Drecht smiled and shook her head – the little black ringlets dancing against her pink powdered cheek. 'And what you going to do then?' she whispered.

Only she never found out, because Klaus was staring wide-eyed at something that none of the others could see – the little diamond shard of light in his eye resolving into the shape of a figure coming towards him out of the thick forest, the birds and the voices falling silent all around it as it walked towards him. He could hear the rustle of feathers and quills as it moved, taste a taint in the air like rotting meat.

In the wall of the alley behind Frau Drecht, two feather-lidded eyes flicked open.

Klaus could see it all like a shimmer in the air. He tried to pull himself free of Liesel, but she didn't realize what he was doing; her eyes were fixed on Frau Drecht, and she held onto him as he struggled and pulled against her hand. But then she saw it too – a figure dressed in blue feathers stepping like a dark shadow out of the wall. Her eyes widened in disbelief even as Frau Drecht grabbed her by the hair and hit her.

'Take my diamond, would you?' spat Frau Drecht.

Klaus blundered away in panic through the filthy puddle at the end of the alley as Frau Drecht hit Liesel again. But even as Frau Drecht jerked her from the ground to close her eyes once and for all, Liesel stared past her at something else; and Frau Drecht turned – hand paused mid-air – to see what could possibly mean more to Liesel than dying.

A man covered in darkly shimmering feathers was standing against the wall of the alley.

Mutzi turned and looked as well. He thought it was some street tumbler, all feathers and bells, come down the alley for a piss. Well, he'd picked the wrong time for that.

'Get out of here!' he growled and, stepping across the alley, grabbed the feathered man by the throat and shoved him back against the wall – only suddenly the man wasn't there any more, and Mutzi's knuckles came up against the hard brick and plaster. He heard his mother cry out, and he stepped back, trying to see where the man had gone. A fist of razor-clawed nails came out of the wall in front of him in one raking cut across his fat stomach. With a groan Mutzi staggered back, clutching at himself, his eyes wide with the shock of it, the word 'knife' flashing through his head. He could feel the muscles giving way beneath his fingers. He looked down at his hand, it was wet with blood, but he couldn't see the man anywhere, only hear a rustling in the air all about him. He looked around wildly. He could see everything, every bit of the dark alley – his mother and the girl staring open-mouthed, the boy scrabbling at the wall, trying to get away – but he couldn't see the man with the knife; he couldn't see him anywhere.

And out of nowhere something hit him again, only this time Mutzi was quicker: he caught hold of the arm and, twisting it beneath him, leaned all his weight down onto it. With a growl of triumph, he felt it break, and suddenly there was the man beneath him. He'd fought men who'd had knives before and he'd always won – he'd taken the knife off them, and when he'd finished using it, they'd wished they had never been born. And that's what he was going to do now.

Lifting the feathered man as though he were a doll, Mutzi drove him back into the wall and hit him as hard as he'd ever hit anyone before. He felt the crack of the dried face breaking like a shell under his fist, and he jammed his elbow across the man's throat to choke the last of the life out of him.

But there was no life there for Mutzi to choke. It had been taken away centuries before.

It was only as he leaned all his weight into his arm and glared murderously into the broken face that he realized that it was a face of dried and hollow skin; that the ends of the feathers were like needles driven into a empty space, the eyes deeper than any grave. His whole body shuddered, and he gasped.

He looked down – almost as if in surprise at the hand of curved claws driven like a knife through his chest, and the deep dark stain of the blood filling the thick felt cloth of his coat. He felt his knees beginning to buckle under him. He grabbed wildly at the man, trying to hold himself up, but the man only watched, head tipped slightly to the side, and Mutzi felt the cold rotting breath on his face as, with a twist of its hand through his heart, the feathered man sent Mutzi's blackened soul into the bright, unforgiving light of another world.

Frau Drecht still held Liesel by the hair, but as Mutzi slipped to the ground, she let go and, with a scream of fury, threw herself at the feathered man. She was caught by the neck like a puppet, and for a moment she hung there in the air, gagging and kicking, until the man closed his hand of curved nails through her throat.

Only Liesel didn't see that happen because, as she dropped to her knees, the world about her was already filling with dappled shadows and light that poured into the darkness of the alley around her and Klaus – until there was no alley any more.

There was only forest, and the pale, bone-thin faces of the dead.

Chapter Twenty-five

Suddenly the world made no sense at all.

All about her, a bedlam rush of ragged people shrieked and whooped through the deep undergrowth. She could see Klaus struggling between them as they plunged past, leaping and jumping like madmen – flowers and feathers in their hair, sticks and axes in their hands. He caught hold of her and pulled her down into the thick ferns and leaves. She was blind with confusion.

There was blood on her dress – Frau Drecht's blood.

'It just come out of the wall,' she whimpered, clutching at his arm. She was looking wildly about her. 'Where's Mutzi? Where's Frau Drecht?'

But Klaus was looking into the darker shadows of the forest where the sun fell in bright-edged shafts between the trees. The feathered man wasn't there. All he could see was an outline like a flick of light in his eye.

Liesel turned and looked at him. 'Where are we?' she whimpered.

He held onto her. 'It's where the dead go,' he said.

She shook her head, not even able to frame the word 'no'.

'It's where Kusselmann is,' he said. 'It's true. I've seen him – he's dead, isn't he?'

He caught hold of her wrist and opened her fingers. The diamond lay like a shard of glass in the palm of her hand. 'Where did you get it?' He looked up into her face. 'That's what it's all about,' he said. 'You've got to get rid of it!'

It was all madness. *His* madness. She pushed him away. 'Get off me!'

Faint and distant, she could hear clocks striking, the murmur of people in a street. 'It's the town,' she said.

She leaped to her feet, but all she could see was ragged people wandering aimlessly through the thick, humid undergrowth of a forest. She stared dumbly at it. 'What is this?' she murmured.

'It's where the dead come,' Klaus said again. 'Only we're not dead.' He caught hold of her arm. 'It was coming for me – but it killed Mutzi and Frau Drecht.'

Liesel was struggling to understand. She looked down at the diamond in her hand. It gleamed maliciously in the dappled light. 'Is this what it wants?'

Klaus shook his head. 'No,' he said. 'But—'

'Then I'm not throwing it away,' she said sharply. 'Not now. It's ours, don't you see?' She stuffed it into her pocket – defying him to take it away from her – pulling the little string tight where the cloth had ripped.

Then she looked around. She could still hear the sounds of a town, but they were almost gone. 'Someone will find us,' she said.

He shook his head again. 'No one will find us. There is no one.'

She looked at him uncertainly, then at the dense green forest. 'What do we do?'

There was movement in the trees above them, the cold laughter of the pale children, but Klaus couldn't see them. He leaned closer to Liesel. 'There's places . . .' he whispered. 'Maybe ways back – I've seen them, but . . .' He hesitated.

'But what?'

'We have to watch someone die.' He looked up at her. 'We have to watch them die, and then . . .'

He didn't finish what he was going to say. The colour had drained from her face. She was looking at the blood on her dress.

'But you don't have to look,' he said. 'I'll do it for you. It will be all right.'

Klaus held out his hand and, with one last glance up into the branches, led her into the dappled sunlight. And as he did so, there was a movement and rustling behind him, and the sound of laughter as the pale children followed.

All about them Liesel saw ragged people wandering like sleepwalkers through the trees – thin women with starved children clutching about their skirts. Old men and soldiers, their clothes soiled and torn.

'Come on – we've got to follow them,' Klaus said and, glancing into the trees behind them, hurried her on.

But the ragged people scared her so – they were

so pale and thin, their faces so haunted and empty. It was as though they didn't even see each other. 'Why don't they look at us?' she whispered.

'Because we're not dying,' he said.

Amongst the trees she could see the outlines of buildings and wide pavements, and at first she thought it was just the play of shadows and light, but then she realized that they *were* buildings – but only ruins. Stone blocks carved with faces and figures, the walls fallen and hung with creepers and moss. They were desolate and empty. 'There is no one, is there?' she said.

Then, very softly, with a sound like dry rice falling on the leaves all about them, it began to rain.

Through the trees ahead of them they saw people standing like a crowd before a fairground booth.

Klaus stopped.

'What are they doing?' whispered Liesel.

He looked at her uneasily. 'Watching someone die,' he said.

He pulled her forward and, holding her hand, pushed his way through the crowd. It parted and closed around them. Liesel felt the brush of threadbare clothes and the touch of cold skin, and as she looked around, she saw patterns flickering across the pale faces, their lips parted in anticipation. They were staring at something she couldn't yet see, and in their hands they held threads of silk.

It was only when they pushed their way to the front that she saw what it was.

Like a moving picture, a shimmer of air hung before them. It was a building – she could see into the rooms, the staircases and passages, and they were full of flames and choking smoke. At the top of the stairs, a man was carrying a small girl in his arms; a woman was trying to help him – but their clothes and hair were already on fire.

Liesel stood watching the whole awful scene unfold before her – she could feel the heat of the fire against her face, hear the crackle over the softly falling rain, far away, as if through thick glass, and there was nothing she could do.

In a shower of sparks and flames the stairs gave way in front of the man, and he had to turn back, but there was nowhere to turn to. The girl lifted her face one last time and looked straight into Liesel's eyes, and as she did so, Liesel knew that the girl could see her; could see all the watching faces.

She was so close, she could have touched her, but there was nothing she could do. She couldn't bear to see what had to happen next, but though she tried to turn away, the pale people pushed her towards the room, and she saw the man and the girl fall onto the burning floorboards, and the flames cover them.

There was a shudder like a breath through the watching people, and they leaned forward and, casting out their threads of barbed silk, drew in the girl, and the man and the woman, and fell on them like wolves.

But as they did so, Klaus pulled Liesel into the flames.

For a moment they were standing in the burning room, coughing and choking as the fire roared about them. The smoke and heat was almost blinding. Liesel felt the floorboards cracking beneath her feet, saw the curtains and the bed all ablaze, but there was nowhere to go – no door, no stairs – and the flames beat them back into the falling rain. They fell in a tumble onto the damp earth, their clothes and hair burned and smoking. Through the crowd of people Liesel could see the man struggling to his feet, but they pulled him down again; she couldn't see the girl anywhere – the mob were hacking with sticks and branches at something trying to crawl away from them on the ground. Then they picked it up and ran with it, whooping and leaping into the wet green forest.

She staggered to her feet and caught hold of Klaus. He tried to pull her away, but she shook him off; all she could see was that last awful look on the girl's face before the flames swallowed her – and the mob hacking at the thing on the ground.

'She just died!' she whimpered. 'I couldn't help her. I couldn't stop them.' Just like her Klaus had died . . .

Her eyes widened and she stared out into the rain and the wet leaves and ferns, because suddenly she realized what that meant. 'Klaus is here . . .' she said in a whisper.

She turned towards this Klaus. 'My brother. I can find him, get him back.' She would have started to run, but he caught hold of her.

'You can't,' he shouted.

She pushed him away. 'Why not?'

'Because he's dead – he'll be like them.'

She shook her head. 'No! You're a liar! He's not like them!'

Without another word she turned and ran into the thick undergrowth, shouting his name, and the leaves and ferns closed behind her. It was like

Kusselmann all over again. Panic rising in him, Klaus plunged after her, but all he could see was a curtain of trees; all he could hear was the mocking laughter of children all around him. 'Liesel, come back! Liesel!'

He blundered on, thin branches whipping into his face. The rain was falling in torrents now. He caught a glimpse of her between the creepers that hung about the stones of a fallen wall and floundered after her. 'Liesel!'

Breathless, he grabbed at the back of her dress and they fell in a tangle amongst the wet leaves. She rolled over, kicking and punching at him.

'Let go of me! I'm going to find him!'

He held her down, the rain soaking them both to the skin. 'He won't be the same! You can't have him back.'

How could she have thought he was like her Klaus? How could she have wanted him when she could have the real one back?

She bit him and pushed him off. They tumbled over each other in the mud and leaves. He pressed his hand hard over her mouth and held it there, and she thought he was going to kill her. She clawed at it, struggling for breath, and then suddenly realized that he wasn't trying to hurt her at all; he was trying to keep her quiet.

Not more than a dozen yards away, standing among the creepers and fallen blocks of stone, was Ramos.

Liesel stopped struggling and Klaus took his hand away.

Ramos was standing perfectly still, his eyes closed as if he were sleeping. Flowers were tied about the tops of his arms, green and gold feathers pushed through his black hair. There were serpents, feathers and eyes painted in dazzling colours all over his bare skin – and all the eyes were closed.

Sitting motionless on his shoulder, as though waiting for him to wake, was the little black monkey.

They crept into the cover of long curving leaves, but Ramos hadn't seen them.

He stood there without moving, his chin to his chest. Then, with a slow exhalation of breath, he lifted his face and opened his eyes, and every one of the painted eyes opened as well. Like a man waking from a sleep in the dark, he turned and peered around at the rain-filled forest and the pale ragged people wandering between the trees. The monkey leaped off his shoulder onto the creepers, and disappeared into the lush green foliage above him.

They watched, breathless, as Ramos lifted and opened his arms in prayer, then, bending down, he plucked a fern. He held it for a moment in his hand, then drew it sharply like the blade of a knife across the skin of his palm. Opening his hand, he let the blood drip from his fingers onto the forest floor.

And as he did so, Klaus felt a pain like the needle-sharp quill of a feather being drawn across his face. He put his hand to his cheek and his fingers came away smeared with paint and blood.

Liesel turned and stared at him, her eyes widening.

Like pictures moving in his skin, the patterns that she had washed away beneath the pump were etching themselves again across Klaus's face – blurring and running in the rain. A stain was soaking through the wet cloth of his shirt – a pattern of feathers and eyes, and behind him – faint and thin as shadows in the air – she could see the ghost of flagstones and a painted floor: the convent floor.

And motionless on it, like a man asleep, sat Ramos – a shallow silver bowl and a long thin knife laid out on the stones in front of him.

Across a distance immeasurable in miles, Ramos

the priest was summoning the chosen child back.

In the forest of the dead, with the monkey shrieking and barking in the branches above it, Ramos's spirit shade turned and began to walk through the thick undergrowth and pouring rain towards Klaus. A thousand shadow worlds seemed to open in the air about it, shimmering and mixing like oil and water – streets and forests, towns and oceans – Klaus could see them all.

In the middle of them he could see the spires of the Marienkirche, streets and buildings – and a ship like a toy against the town wharf, its sails unfurled, its ropes cast loose. Suddenly he knew what he had to do.

As the dead lifted their faces in anticipation and turned like moths towards the swirling windows of light, Klaus caught hold of Liesel and, pulling her with him, leaped into the shimmering air.

For one whirling moment he had a sensation of falling. He could see Ramos reaching down towards him – the flickering shadows of the forest – and then there was nothing but silence and darkness.

In the cold quiet of the convent, Ramos breathed deeply and opened his eyes.

But not before he had seen where Klaus had fallen.

Chapter Twenty-six

Klaus lay very still.

He wasn't in the forest any more.

A thin light leaked from a square grating, like a hatchway, somewhere above him, and gradually he made out barrels, and bales of cloth, and sacks and crates tightly roped and stacked in the darkness all around him. The air was wet and cold, thick with the heavy vapour of spirits and tar.

He could hear footsteps and voices muffled through thick planks. Hear the slow creaking movement of timbers and ropes.

Pulling himself up to the grating, he looked out onto the deck of a ship – the masts and rigging towering above him. Through it he could see the warehouses of the town wharf, and beyond them the tall spires of the Marienkirche.

Glancing back, he saw the pale circle of Liesel's face turned uncertainly up towards him.

He climbed down into the darkness. 'We're on a ship,' he said breathlessly. 'It's the town – we're back in the town.'

She stared confusedly at him and at the darkness all around her; then, pushing past him, she would have scrambled up towards the grating and the light, but he caught hold of her, his mind racing.

'No! If they see us now, they'll put us ashore. But if we let it sail . . .' He didn't have to finish the words.

She stood looking from him to the light of the grating above her.

He was right. If they were put ashore now, Henriquez would find them, she knew it. Sooner or later, he'd find them both. And then he'd find the diamond in her pocket, and when he did, he'd close up her eyes for good – because that's what he'd done to that man from the Anatomy, only this time there would be no bringing her back. It would be for ever, and she knew what that would mean.

She shuddered, and Klaus let go of her.

'We'll only have to hide until the ship's far

enough out that they can't put back a boat,' he said. 'Then we can come out, and we'll just have to take our chances. What can they do?'

He looked around at the dark of the hold, at the barrels and the bales of cloth. No one would find them in there.

But as he looked at the shadows and the dark, each time he blinked he could still see a little flick of light, bright and sharp – like the shape of a feathered man.

The ropes had already been cast off. Klaus and Liesel settled themselves in the cold, damp dark and waited. They felt the movement of the ship as it was rowed out from the wharf into the middle of the channel. Klaus had watched it happen from beneath the bridge more than a hundred times. They felt it swing beneath them as its prow turned on the tide, and began its way down the river towards the open sea.

Then the light through the grating began to fade as the day closed, and then there was nothing but dark.

Klaus fell asleep with his head on Liesel's shoulder and she was too tired to move him. But she couldn't sleep; she felt more than heard through the wood of the ship the rippling wash of water behind her head.

She undid the little tie in her pocket, and felt for the diamond. Even in the blackness of the hold she could see it. And, her eyes filling with tears, she wept for her Klaus.

Finally she slept too, her stomach growling and empty.

But at some point in the night she was woken by a sound – something dragging past the timbers near her head – and heard voices, but they were low and unhurried, and there was no alarm in them, and she didn't hear the words they spoke. After what might have been a minute or an hour, she couldn't have said which, there came another bump and the voices fell quiet. Footsteps passed across the deck above her, and she sat for a while listening but there was nothing else to hear – just the sounds of the ship and the slipping of the water past the timbers behind her head. Finally, in the creaking quiet and pitch darkness, she fell asleep again. Only this time it was a sleep troubled by a dream in which she held a diamond in her hand, and the face of Frau Drecht appeared above her like a stain through a wall that was the timbers of a ship, while all around her, in a velvet whispering darkness, the pale faces of the dead gathered like moths at a window.

She woke with a start.

The air was cold and damp, thick with the smell of spirits and tar – it was making her head ring. She felt giddy and sick. But there was light falling through the square of grating.

The motion of the ship had changed – she could tell at once. There was a heave and thump to it. The sound of the water along the side was different too; it was louder, alive. An empty bottle was rolling backwards and forwards in the shadows, the ropes swinging and moving.

Klaus was still asleep, curled up on a pile of sacking beside her. She couldn't stir him.

She stood up stiffly, had to steady herself in that cramped place.

Pushing between the stacks of cargo, she found herself in a narrow passage between bales of cloth. At the end of it a pale grey daylight fell through an open hatchway onto a ladder beneath. She could smell cold wet air, and the sharp salt of the sea. Groping her way towards the dim light, she climbed the narrow ladder and looked around.

Above her, the sails were pressed drum tight and

there was a low leaden sky over a steel-blue ocean, the waves white-capped on the plunging swell. Maybe three or four miles distant was a long, low ribbon of land. She could see the line of waves breaking on the shore. It was all so vivid after the darkness of the hold, she had to shield her eyes, blinking against the brightness of it.

Some of the men working on the deck turned and looked towards her, but Liesel didn't care if she was seen now. Holding onto the ropes of the rigging as the ship plunged and pitched, she walked unsteadily towards the bow. But as she drew nearer, she saw that there was a man already standing there – tall and thin, a long black coat wrapped around him. He was looking out to sea.

And like a blow, she realized what that noise she'd heard in the night had been – the sound of a boat coming alongside, of the men it had carried climbing aboard.

Because the man standing at the bow of the ship was Father Henriquez.

As though aware of her gaze, he turned round and looked at her with those pale, colourless eyes. 'Where is the boy?' he said.

She turned and fled back across the rolling deck

towards the hatchway. One of the men tried to catch hold of her, but she ducked past him.

'Leave her!' shouted Henriquez. 'I want the boy!'

She half dropped, half fell down the ladder into the tar-thick air below. 'Klaus!'

An orb of light was moving between the piles of cargo. Someone was already there, searching with a lantern.

She shouted another warning, pushing her way between the barrels and bales of cloths to where she'd left him, but Klaus wasn't there any more. She heard a scuffle and a cry from somewhere in the darkness of the hold. 'Klaus!'

Liquid as a cat, the little black monkey leaped from the shadows above her, bared its dirty yellow teeth and hissed at her, and out of the darkness behind it stepped Ramos. He had one arm hooked around Klaus's neck, his hand pressed tightly across Klaus's mouth, and he was holding a lantern. The flame guttered and flared wickedly in the vapour-filled air.

'Go back,' he said. 'I do not come for you.'

As he stepped forward, as though from the very timbers of the ship itself, the air began to fill with a sound like the rustling of quills. Klaus was kicking and struggling, but suddenly he stopped, his eyes widening. Like a flower unfolding in the darkness all around him he could see the forest – green and bright, a breeze moving the tops of the trees. Faces stared at him from amongst the leaves, and out of the dappled shadows a man was walking towards him, shimmering where the shafts of sunlight fell across him.

Ramos's face filled with a wild joy, and he turned towards Liesel. 'I have called Him and He comes!' he breathed.

Only he wasn't looking at her. He was looking at Henriquez, who'd stolen through the rustling darkness after her, a lantern in his hand. The priest grabbed at her, but she ducked away from him, and the lantern fell from his grasp – the glass breaking with a crack on the hard planks of the deck. A wash of burning oil spilled from it in a yellow-blue tongue of flame. It ran between the barrels and the tarred sacks and, with a thump, they burst into flames, the fire curling like a sheet up and across the roof of the hold, burning everything it touched. Liesel's skirt and hair caught like a torch. She beat at them with her bare hands. The monkey leaped screeching from the flames and vanished into the leaves of the forest. Klaus slipped from Ramos's grasp. Ramos made one wild grab at him, but Klaus disappeared like a rat between the piles of cargo. Bales and barrels were bursting into fire all around them.

'The boy!' Henriquez shouted. 'Get the boy!'

Ramos turned and plunged back into the fire after Klaus.

There were shouts from the deck above as flames leaped up through the grating, and a bell began ringing furiously. Liesel, her hands shielding her face, was trying to see Klaus, but she couldn't see him anywhere. All she could see was a wall of fire. It was like the burning room all over again – the girl, the woman and the man. She was screaming Klaus's name, but the fire had swallowed him.

From behind her, men pushed past with buckets of water, throwing them uselessly into the roaring flames. And as they did, the flames parted, and for just a moment she saw Henriquez standing in the middle of them, the forest trees behind him, his clothes all ablaze and threads of silk tangled around him. His arms were held wide before a man who shimmered like a blue fire. Then the flames closed around them both and she heard Henriquez scream.

352

One of the men pulled her away. He tore off his coat and smothered her with it, beating out the flames, then half lifted, half carried her up to the deck as the panic of the fire ran through the ship.

Of all things men fear at sea, it's fire they fear the most. Ask them what it is to be caught on a burning ship of wood and tar, and they'll tell you that once it's alight there is no saving it. You can pour a whole ocean onto it and you won't put it out. It will burn like a coffin on a pyre.

The moment those flames leaped through the hatches and caught the lower sails of the ship, there was no saving her. She wallowed drunkenly in the heaving swell, smoke billowing from the hold and blowing in swirls, thick and black with tar, about the deck. In just a few awful minutes the fire was above deck too, and there was nothing the men could do: the blocks and ropes of the rigging were burning and falling about them, and they had no choice but to swim or burn. Anything that could float was thrown over the side, and the one boat was lowered away, barely full.

Liesel stood helpless in the middle of it all, looking up into the rigging and at the blazing deckhouse. Her face stained and distraught, she ran

353

back towards the burning hold as though Klaus might still appear, but the man who'd carried her up from below caught hold of her again and dragged her to the side of the ship.

'Can you swim?' he shouted.

When she didn't answer him, he picked her up and, with both arms around her, climbed onto the gunwale. Taking one last look along the line of the burning ship, he jumped with her into the sea.

The water was bone-numbingly cold. They came up coughing and gagging. The sailor pulled her to him, caught hold of a floating piece of wood and hung onto it, his arm hooked around her, as he looked for the longboat. It was already twenty yards from them. 'Here!' he shouted. 'Here!'

They saw him waving in the water, and turned towards him. He struck out for the boat, and the men pulled them both in.

Shivering and choking, Liesel fell into the bottom and, turning round, looked back up at the burning ship, at the wooden rail and the leaping orange flames.

Somewhere in that awful forest, the dead had already wound him in. They were leaping after him even now, chasing him through the trees, and there was nothing she could do to bring him back.

It had all happened again.

She sat staring dumbly at the burning ship as the men leaned on their oars and pulled the boat away.

But there was still another man in the water. She felt the boat tip as they reached down and pulled him out of the sea. Struggling, he caught hold of the wooden gunwale just above her head, and she saw that his hand was patterned with feathers and eyes.

They pulled him into the boat.

And they pulled in the boy he was holding.

They were both burned and blackened.

She clambered to her knees, and pulled Klaus out of their hands, dragging him along the boards, away from Ramos. But Ramos did nothing. He swept his wet black hair out of his eyes and looked darkly at her; his bare chest and arms were painted with feathers and serpents and eyes, and every one of the eyes was open.

The men looked at him and passed each other uneasy glances as Klaus lay coughing and retching in the bottom of the boat. But Liesel didn't care; she was only looking at Klaus. She pressed her face against his, her wet hair falling over him. 'You're alive!' she cried. 'You're alive.'

She looked up at the sailors for them to share in her joy, but they weren't looking at her; they were still looking at Ramos.

There was a taint like rotten meat in the air, and a sound that was growing louder. They could feel it through the bare wood of the boat. One by one they let go of their oars and looked at each other with uncertain faces. It was in the very wood itself.

Klaus opened his eyes.

The man was coming towards him through the forest – he could feel a movement in the air about him like a wind, warm on his face, he could see Ramos at the edges of the two worlds where the forest became the sea; saw him lifting his arms and crying out in words that the men in the boat couldn't begin to understand as the feathered man rose out of the boat amongst them. There were shouts and cries of confusion, the boat rocking and tipping.

Klaus tried to scramble away, to run into the trees, but there were no stones or roots beneath him; there was only a cold, icy sea. His arms flailing wildly, he plunged into it. Liesel made one grab at him, and tumbled after him. As she broke the surface, she heard the crack of a pistol shot above her, saw through a welter of water the flash of it and the white smoke, the men beating desperately with their oars at the feathered man. Ramos and a sailor were locked together, fighting with a knife. But Klaus was floundering in the water, the cold pulling him down. Only strokes away was a wooden grating thrown from the ship. They both caught hold of it and held on, gasping and choking, and only then turned their heads and looked back towards the longboat.

It had tipped right over. There were smears of blood along the white painted sides, the hull stark against the grey-blue of the water. The plunging swell was already carrying it away from them. There was no one moving in the water.

'Where is it?' gasped Liesel.

She hauled herself up onto the grating, then reached back for Klaus, and as she did so, the pocket of her skirt caught against the wood and tore. Something glinted in the light as it dropped through the grating and into the sea. 'No!' she cried.

She tried to catch it, but she was too late. She saw it for one last moment, sparkling as it sank beneath the ice-cold water, and then it was gone.

Klaus lay gasping across the grating. Then he lifted himself onto his elbow. 'Look!' he whispered, and he pointed at something that Liesel hadn't yet seen.

It was Ramos floating face down in the sea with a sailor's knife through him.

Liesel turned to look at Klaus, but as she did so, the words dried on her lips. Frowning, she reached out and touched her fingers to his burned and blackened face.

There were no patterns or paint on it any more. The deep, fathomless sea had washed it clean.

They watched as, moment by moment, the deep swell carried the body of Ramos further away from them. And then they couldn't see him or the long-boat any more in the rise and fall of the sea.

Liesel closed her eyes. She was so cold. She pulled herself nearer to Klaus, put her arms around him, and when she opened her eyes again, she saw in the distance the long ribbon of land and, against that, like hope, square white sails already turning towards the smoke of the burning ship.

Epilogue

Many things are washed ashore, often far from where they started.

After a hard winter and fierce storms, any number of them can be found caught among the rocks and pools. And fishermen's children idling amongst the stones will find them; will stop and look in appalled fascination, call to each other to come and look at the rotten pelt of a seal as the surge of the tide pours it from pool to pool.

Sometimes they will find a boat, the paint all peeled and the wood bleached bare.

Sometimes they will find a body, some drowned soul. And, breathless, they will run to fetch their fathers; stern-faced and grim, the men will carry it on a boat board to a place above the tide and cover it so that the gulls can't reach it any more.

And so it was, a season of storms later, that the children stood above a pool and stared down at the flaccid thing caught amongst the rocks below them – its feathers dark and salt-stained, its skin leached white as any drowned man's fingers.

And they didn't know what it was.

They lifted it with a stick, and it hung sodden over the wood. And one of them said it was a merman because you could see its arms and legs, and where its eyes had been. And then they let the stick fall because it scared them, and they ran back over the rocks, calling to their friends to come and see what they'd found.

They'd found a dead merman amongst the stones.

But it wasn't the skin of a merman.

And as they ran away across the cold wet sand, they never saw its two feather-lidded eyes flick open.

Acknowledgements

There are three particular people I would very much like to thank for the parts they played in the making of this story. Netta Brooks, who, in clearing out the lumber from her house, gave my daughter Alice a life-sized feather and chicken-wire sculpture of a kneeling man and so unwittingly sowed the seeds of the idea. David Fickling, who helped me see that there was always more that could be done, and our friend Erin Rhoades, who came to stay with us and was another sailor in the sieve just when we most needed the extra crew. Thank you all.

Also by Jeremy de Quidt

The Toymaker

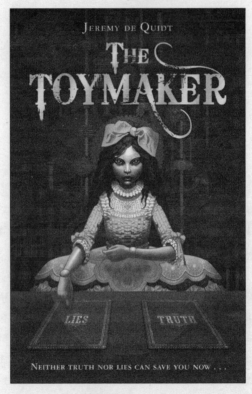

'This is an edge of the seat thriller which will stay
in the mind long after the book finishes'
Irish Examiner